BEYOND ROMANCE: BOOK ONE

BEYOND

LIGHT & DARKNESS

A ROMANTIC SUSPENSE WITH A MEDICAL TWIST

D PICHARDO-JOHANSSON

BEYOND LIGHT AND DARKNESS
A Romantic Suspense with a Medical Twist
© 2020 by Diely Pichardo-Johansson.
All rights reserved.

ISBN: 978-1-951400-04-0

Cover Design by Roland Hulme, ginger@hiddengemsbooks.com

Developmental Editing by Savannah Jezowski
www.dragonpress.com/author-services

Copy Editing by Krista R Burdine, iamgrammaresque.com

Proofreading by Marla Esposito ,www.proofingstyle.com

Formatting by Champagne Book Design
champagnebookdesign.com

ACKNOWLEDGMENT

Special thanks to the Federal Bureau of Intelligence (FBI) Office of Public Affairs, for their extensive answers to my questions during this process.

DEDICATION

To my friends Donna Johnston and Ilene Davis, who've been my loyal readers from the beginning and keep encouraging me with their (lovingly biased) positive feedback.

PROLOGUE

THEY DID IT. THEY FOUND A WAY TO KILL ME. EVEN IN HERE.

In her hot, stuffy cell at the Brevard County jail, Rachel Hayes interrupted her writing to take her own pulse at the wrist. She felt so dizzy she expected to find it racing, but, surprisingly, it beat slower than ever.

Way too slow.

Somewhere in the distance, another inmate's groan of despair echoed down the colorless corridors. A premonition invaded her fractured thoughts. *I'm going to die. Very soon.*

She'd never been afraid of dying. For someone who believes in instant reincarnation, death is nothing but a mild inconvenience—the annoyance of having to start all over again. And she'd prepared for weeks for the eventuality. Still, that didn't make the moment any less daunting. Her plan to work out a deal with the FBI to reduce her sentence, her hope to emerge as a new spiritual leader after this, all drifted away.

It was too late, and she knew it; the death sentence had already entered her body. Her blurry eyes strained to focus on the pile of paper she'd been writing on. She needed to send the FBI a message, but it had to be concealed—the other masters had eyes and ears everywhere and would find a way to destroy the evidence.

Frantically, she returned to the beginning of the document and wrote at the bottom of the filled pages.

"1." She flipped a handful of pages. "3." She passed some more. "60."

Everything in her narrow cell seemed to undulate—her cot, the shelf where her writings rested, the metal commode next to her chair. At moments, her hazy mind betrayed her and she stopped, pen in hand, unable to remember what came next; but she pushed through. In the high-security cell she now called home she had no roommates or neighbors to entrust with this message.

A wave of nausea hit her and she realized her time was limited. She dragged herself to finish. "51."

"Guard! Guard! I need to give you something!" She needed to hand off the pages and hope he'd get them to the right people.

Shaking, she rose from her chair and stumbled to the bars. As she did, the sheaf of papers fell from her hands. Her eyes glimpsed the pages flying away and scattering across the floor before darkness overcame her.

CHAPTER 1

Richard Fields' black SUV screeched to a halt in Holloway Hospital's parking lot and he barely slammed it into Park before leaping out. As he strode the distance to the hospital, he loosened his tie, then tugged at his white shirt collar to unfasten the top button. *Whoever invented business suits deserves to be skinned alive.* What kind of idiot would wear something like this in August in Fort Sunshine, Florida?

After navigating the eternal construction zone around the entrance, he flashed his FBI badge at security, ignored the impossibly slow elevators and headed for the stairs. He couldn't believe this bomb had been dropped in his lap precisely today. He was still catching up with work after three weeks of mandatory leave—standard procedure after the rescue operation where he'd been stabbed and also shot two people.

Well, shot *one* person—but as far as the official FBI record was concerned, it had been two.

He climbed the stairs to the fourth floor. His left leg burned from the healing stab wound, but he kept on climbing. He'd learned since childhood that the best way to diminish pain was to ignore it.

When he arrived at the ICU, he found his friend and boss, Assistant Special Agent in Charge Samuel Elliott, waiting for him at the double doors.

"Please tell me she's alive," Richard begged.

Samuel exhaled through pursed lips. "Hayes is still alive. Not that it will do us any good; she's in a coma."

An unprintable string of cusswords escaped Richard's mouth as Samuel guided him through the double doors into one of the glass-encased ICU rooms.

In the narrow bed, a blond woman lay unconscious, tied to IV drips. A breathing tube in her mouth connected her to a ventilator.

"What happened?" Richard asked.

"The doctors still don't know. She collapsed in jail with low blood pressure and a slow pulse. They thought she might've had a heart attack, but it doesn't seem the case. Overnight, she spiked a high fever and they say she's now in septic shock."

Richard tugged at his torture of a blue-striped tie. "This 'health crisis' is too much coincidence."

Samuel bowed his head and they didn't have to say more. It seemed extremely suspicious that Rachel Hayes ended up in the hospital right after she'd agreed to cooperate with the FBI in the multiple-murder case involving the "Lords of the Universe," or "LOTU," the so-called spiritual group she had founded.

Richard studied the comatose woman, something unfamiliar tugging at his heart. Was it compassion? It couldn't be. He reserved his compassion for people who deserved it and she belonged to a group of cold-blooded murderers. The Lords of the Universe were the most fearsome type of criminal: those who feel zero remorse about killing, because they're convinced they do it for a greater good.

"If this was the LOTU's attempt to eliminate her as a witness, they must've done something different this time." Richard mused, recalling the details about the murders they knew about so far—politicians in four different states. "Their previous victims died instantly, yet she made it to the hospital alive."

Samuel gestured for him to follow and they strolled out of the ICU. "We're investigating the jail personnel and screening Hayes for every possible poison. But now that we can't count on her testimony, we have to speed up striking a deal with our other potential informants, 'X, Y, and Z.'" As the double doors closed, he glanced over his shoulder, making sure they were alone. "All we need is for *one* of them to confirm that Dr. Joshua Levenstein was a member of the LOTU. If I've learned anything in twenty years at the FBI, it's to listen to my gut. And my gut is screaming that Levenstein is hiding something big."

"I agree." Richard pressed the call button and, in an exceptional event, an empty elevator arrived promptly.

As they entered, Samuel commented with a snicker, "You look *sexy* in that suit, man."

Richard's eyes shot daggers at Samuel. "You owe me big. As the Assistant SAC, *you* should be the one running that ridiculous press conference this afternoon, not me. The damn O'Hara case has become a circus here in town."

The recent leak to the press about the LOTU's first confirmed crime—the murder-faked-accident of Congressman Michael O'Hara two years back—had become a morbid fascination for the local residents. For the first time in history, this small beach town where nothing ever happened had made national news.

Samuel nodded as the elevator door closed. "That's why that press conference is so important. If people are hungry for answers, we'd better control the flow of information."

Richard groaned. "That's what the SAC claims, but you're both using me as a distraction. You're letting the mob satisfy their curiosity about me."

Samuel's apologetic expression confirmed Richard's suspicion. "You kind of *are* this town's biggest celebrity right now."

"You mean a damn reality-TV celebrity," he grouched. "All because of that gutter-press witch, Blair Sanders."

"Press leak or not, you're the most appropriate person to handle this conference. You solved the O'Hara case practically single-handedly. And you *are* the FBI's ultimate expert on the LOTU case." Samuel tried to keep a straight face, but soon his features twisted and a snort escaped him. He slapped his own knee and exploded in a whole-hearted guffaw.

Richard glared but couldn't blame him. Who would've thought Richard Fields—the most problematic agent Fort Sunshine ever had—would become the Bureau's expert on anything? The FBI was flying in agents from New York, Alaska, and Nebraska—the other states where political murders had occurred—to have Richard brief them in person about the case progress.

The sound of an incoming text dinged, bringing Richard back. He flushed in excitement, wondering if it came from Joy. He'd been so busy catching up at work he hadn't had a moment to answer her last messages on his burner cell, yet he'd done nothing but obsess about the moment he'd see her again.

But the sound had come not from the burner, but from his official phone. It was a text from his son asking for money—the main reason fourteen-year-old Ray would call or text. Only God knew what his ex-wife had done this month with his child support.

Damn timing. Richard's credit card was about to max out; he'd barely be able to afford groceries until his next paycheck. But that boy was everything to him, and if he had to go hungry for Ray, he would.

The elevator door opened and Samuel giggled his way to the lobby. "Come on. I told Keith I'd ride back with you to the office."

Stepping from the freezing indoor AC to the outdoor furnace was always a shock. As they walked to the parking lot, the construction workers loitering outside whispered and pointed at Richard in recognition and he felt like punching something—or someone. Fame was the worst possible thing that could happen to an undercover agent.

"Damn Sanders!" he grumbled while searching for the keys in his suit pockets. "Because of her, I'm going to end my days sitting at a desk doing bureaucratic work. My undercover and field days are over."

Samuel tapped his dark forehead. "Speak of the devil! My secretary mentioned she has two new messages for you from Blair Sanders—"

"Tell her to burn them!" Richard snapped. "And to tell Sanders I hope she catches bubonic plague and dies slowly and painfully."

"—asking for a face-to-face interview with you."

As they approached the black Lincoln Navigator, Richard cussed inwardly. "Like Sanders doesn't know that if I find myself in the same room with her, I'll strangle her."

Samuel scoffed. "You'd never hurt a woman and you know it. But today you may meet her in person. Isn't she attending the press conference, like every other newsperson in Central Florida?"

"I doubt it. She may call herself a member of the press, but she's nothing more than a sensationalist reporter."

As he climbed into the car, Richard tried to calm himself down. His personal inconvenience was the least important problem of all. As tabloid-worthy as Sander's viral news video had been, it had probably alerted the other LOTU members that the FBI was behind them. By the time the FBI intervened it was too late. Her video and article had gotten hundreds of thousands of clicks and reposts.

"So, you have your statement ready for the press, right?" Samuel asked.

Richard rubbed his eyes with the heels of his hands. "I will reassure the citizens of Fort Sunshine that Congressman O'Hara's car accident was due to sabotage from a personal enemy." He turned on the engine. "By God, I will dissuade them from believing the 'false rumors' that O'Hara's death was part of a multi-state political plot, or connected in any way to the death of Senator Flowers in New York."

Samuel patted his back. "Good. Let's see how much damage control you can do."

Richard couldn't share the main reason why this press conference unsettled him. Dr. Joy Clayton, aka O'Hara's widow, would be there—the woman who had occupied every cell of his brain for months. He hadn't seen her in three long days, and his body and soul painfully hungered for her.

At the red light to leave the hospital's premises, he glanced at the building's reflection in the rearview mirror. Could Joy be there right now, visiting a patient? What an agony it would be to see her at the press conference today and be unable to touch her, or even acknowledge what was going on between them—at risk of losing his job.

Most stupid thing an FBI agent can do to screw his career: Falling in love with his suspect.

~

Holding hands with her sister, Joy Clayton crossed the short distance from the parking lot to the Town Hall building, where the press conference was about to begin. With each step, her heart ran faster. The humid summer heat did nothing to warm up her hands, turned to ice by anxiety.

Calm down. It's only a three-line statement.

Joy dreaded interviews and cross-examinations; they brought flashbacks from the times when Michael would wake her up at 2:00 a.m. to interrogate her, in bouts of paranoid jealousy. She'd done nothing but answer questions since the night his car was recovered from the bottom of the Indian River two years back.

What a day this has been! That afternoon, caught in a family emergency, the nanny had dropped Joy's three boys at her private office at the CeMeSH—the Center for Mental and Spiritual Healing. It was difficult to focus on work while a six-year-old and a pair of two-and-a-half-year-old twins launched themselves on wheeled stools through hallways and jumped on every sofa in the waiting area. The patients loved it, but the kids wore out the whole staff before Joy's emergency sitter came to get them—and all that was *after* Joy spent the morning doing procedures at the Fort Sunshine Hospice House. Joy's unusual blend of specialties—internal medicine, psychiatry, and pain management—made her a rarity in town and kept her in high demand.

"*When are you going to stop trying to save the world at the expense of neglecting your children?*" Michael's scolding words still echoed in her mind, flooding her with guilt. She could still see his disappointed glare as he clicked his tongue and shook his head in disapproval.

The moment they entered the building, flashes blinded Joy. She squinted and recoiled as an avalanche of reporters shoved microphones and cameras on her face, all asking questions at once.

"Dr. Clayton! What do you have to say about the recent capture of your late husband's murderers?"

"Is it true that Congressman O'Hara was a victim of a plot to de-stabilize the country politically?"

"Mrs. O'Hara! Is it true there was an attempt against you as a potential witness?"

The noise grew louder as the two women wedged themselves through the chorus of yelling reporters.

"Holy moly!" Joy's sister, Hope, held on tightly to her arm to avoid getting separated. "This place is more crowded than Universal CityWalk on bar-hopping night."

Swimming in people. That's how it felt to Joy as they crossed the mob of journalists and curious citizens filling the town hall. Nothing made sense to Joy; she wasn't newsworthy. She was nothing but a rattled, shaken woman, still trying to put her life together two years after her husband's death. A woman still trying to figure out what was real and what was not, after he'd convinced her for years that *she* was the one who was crazy and in need of help.

Thank God for Dr. Venkat Patel, who appeared out of nowhere, elbowing his way through the crowd and reaching for Joy's arm. Joy felt like the baton in a relay race as Hope released her and stayed behind while Patel dragged her to the podium. As they advanced, he repeated to the reporters in his polished British accent, "Dr. Clayton will provide a statement for all of you. She will *not* give interviews or take questions."

Joy was thankful for Patel, her psychiatrist colleague. If it hadn't been for his help, both of her work places would've collapsed in the past few weeks from her lack of focus.

Trembling, Joy stood in front of the microphones while the flashes sparked all around her.

Remembering the words of her mentor Dr. Carl Andrews, she scanned the people in the room and tried to imagine their challenges, their hunger for love, and their struggles. Love for them budded in her soul and her fear diminished, allowing her to utter her FBI-cleared statement.

"My prayers go to the suffering members of the O'Hara family, especially Michael's mother, who still grieves his death two years later. I've forgiven his murderers. I thank the law enforcers who made their capture possible."

She stepped down from the podium, ignoring the rumbling of the reporters asking for more. Patel blocked them from her, silencing them all with his resounding voice. "Listen, all of you. Dr. Clayton is affected by PTSD and cannot be disturbed."

Even if she'd agreed to that statement, Joy cringed to hear "PTSD," the abbreviation for Post Traumatic Stress Disorder. Over the years, she'd treated many severe cases in her medicine-psychiatry practice; she felt like a wimp for receiving that label for something as small as her experience.

PTSD? Come on. She hadn't gone to war and seen a friend blown up in front of her. She hadn't been *physically* abused. She'd only endured seven years with a psychologically unstable husband; two years of coping with his sudden demise, which turned out to be murder; and a recent rescue from a brush with death.

Oh, wait.

Saying it like that, it does sound serious.

Now a notch more relaxed, Joy's playful imagination flew, as she watched Patel ward off the reporters. She pictured him as a jungle explorer, wearing a safari outfit instead of his business suit, cracking a whip and waving a torch to keep the wild animals away. All without breaking a sweat on his flawless chocolate skin or messing up a lustrous lock of his jet-black hair.

Her sister, Hope, rejoined her and squeezed her arm softly, bringing her back from her distraction. "Great job, sweetie. Now breathe; you're starting to turn purple."

Joy exhaled.

They found their way to the first row of chairs. Only Joy had an assigned seat there, but until the FBI members arrived and the conference started officially, Hope could keep her company. On the way there, Joy spotted her therapist, Dr. Allison Connors, sitting in the back row, and waved at her.

"I can't wait to meet Agent Fields today." Hope fanned herself with a smirk while taking a seat. "Is he as steaming hot as he looks in pictures?"

Joy blushed. "Uh. Well... I don't... Hot?"

"Oh sweetie! You're so pathologically distracted you wouldn't have noticed if he were ten feet tall and neon green." Hope tittered and poked her sister's side. "But don't worry. I'm happily taken now and won't embarrass you by flirting with him, like I used to with your high school classmates." She tucked Joy's long brunette hair behind her ears and straightened her teal work dress. Her dark brown eyes, so similar to Joy's, softened. "All I want is a chance to thank him for saving my sister's life."

Saving my life. The words sounded surreal to Joy. She was barely processing that the LOTU group had tried to eliminate her. Heck, she was barely processing who Richard really was.

"Now seriously, that Agent Fields deserves a medal," Hope continued. "To think that he almost got himself killed to rescue practically a stranger."

Joy felt guilty for keeping Hope in the dark. But Richard had been clear that if anyone learned what was going on between them, his career would be in danger.

Biggest sign that your relationship is hopeless: Your man insists on keeping it a secret.

Speaking of which.

Joy didn't have to turn around to know that *he* had entered the Town Hall; she could feel the change in the energy of the room. Her body stiffened and her chest fluttered as her eyes traveled to the entrance.

Yes! Agent Richard Fields stood at the door—more handsome than ever in his dark business suit showcasing his wide shoulders and impressive stature. The three long days not seeing him had blurred in her mind how powerful his presence was. Richard Fields didn't enter a room—he possessed it.

As if he'd felt her gaze on him, he turned toward her and his hazel eyes met hers across the large hall, making her heart leap. Slowly, holding eye contact, he walked toward her.

Her pulse racing and her hands trembling, Joy prayed she could hide her feelings from everyone in the room.

CHAPTER 2

As Richard approached, Joy felt her chest pound and waves of warm blood wash over her cheeks. She invoked her neutral psychiatrist's face, but she was afraid every reporter could read her like a book. Read her desire, her guilt, her confusion.

How had she ended up here? Before Michael's death she'd had a sad, but predictable existence. And even after, she'd never done anything exciting. Who was that woman jumping off the back of trucks, running for her life through woods, and making out in ambulances with a drop-dead gorgeous FBI agent?

Photo flashes sparked around them as he arrived at her chair. She rose and remained still. What was the social convention for greeting the agent who'd saved your life? A simple handshake didn't seem adequate. Yet a hug seemed too much, especially for the man who'd lied to you for months, undercover, trying to prove you were a murderer. And both options felt insufficient for the man who taught you a new way to heaven barely days ago.

The skin contact for the brief handshake threatened to make her legs give out.

"Good afternoon, Agent Fields." Preventing her voice from quivering took all she had.

"Dr. Clayton." His head bow in response exuded appropriateness. No emotion. No avoidance of eye contact, yet no prolongation of it either. She would've preferred coldness—at least a hint that he struggled to conceal feelings. But no. His greeting was nothing but indifference.

Hope rushed to shake his hand and introduce herself, but someone signaled Richard to the podium and the greeting was cut short by a polite excuse.

He walked away from them without turning back. A heavy vacuum settled in Joy's chest as fear hit her.

Is he done with me?

Barely hearing Hope's mumbles of admiration as she left for a back row, Joy retook her seat and watched Richard begin his press statement.

"Good afternoon, ladies and gentlemen, members of the press. We're here today on behalf of the Federal Bureau of Investigation to put to rest the false rumors regarding the death of Congressman Michael O'Hara."

The previously noisy room fell silent as the audience hung onto Richard's every word; but she was unable to follow his speech, her mind in turmoil.

Allison, her therapist, had warned her, men are all about the chase, and get bored quickly after it's over. *So that's why I haven't heard much from him in the past three days. He already had me, and now he's done with me.*

She'd known from the beginning she took a risk with him, so she'd better accept with dignity that she was history.

～

Most attendants left before the end of the long press conference. Not satisfied, the reporters had surrounded Richard at the podium and peppered him with questions. Every time a journalist pronounced the name "O'Hara," memories of Michael's scolding voice sharpened Joy's blues.

"Do you really think anyone but me would ever want you?" Michael's voice snickered in her mind. *"You're a mother of three, past your prime."*

Feeling the need for air, Joy rose from her chair and headed to the door. Before she could get far, Patel intercepted her.

He greeted her as usual, with a kiss on each cheek. His black eyes radiated worry as he held her hand. "How are you managing, my dear?" Interestingly, when Patel was relaxed, he lost his British accent and sounded purely American. Rumor was that when he got angry or flustered, he showed a hint of an Indian accent—but Joy had never seen him lose his temper.

"I'm okay. Thank you so much for picking up the slack at work in the past weeks. Hopefully, things will get better when Dr. Harris joins us on Monday." She wished Patel could join her practice more than just temporarily, but he was on his way to bigger and better projects.

"It's the least I could do. You've gone through a lot lately."

Joy felt guilty around Patel. Arguing Joy needed time to recover from the recent events, he'd taken most of the workload at the CeMeSH private office—he'd even taken over the fundraisers trying to keep afloat the always struggling, nonprofit Hospice House.

He cautiously placed his hand on her shoulder. "Have you been getting all the help you need?"

She gave a single nod.

A known hugger, he embraced her for a moment and tapped her back. "You know I'm here if you need anything."

If he only knew that, for the past three weeks, she hadn't really been in therapy all the times she left work early—or home those days she called in sick. Her eyes gravitated to Richard at the podium, focused on the reporters without looking at her. *Well, apparently that's about to change.*

"Hands where I can see them, Patel." A grating voice interrupted the hug.

Joy felt a pang of distress at the sight of Dr. Josh Levenstein, followed by his ever-present bodyguard. The town's busiest oncologist, Levenstein was the main source of referrals for her Hospice House and she felt obligated to be polite with him—especially since he'd been an acquaintance of Michael. But his inappropriate teasing and occasional flirting had always made her feel uncomfortable.

An unusual flash of anger crossed Patel's eyes. Joy wasn't surprised; Josh could make a Buddhist monk lose his temper. "Good afternoon, Levenstein," said Patel with a forced smile. Short as he was, he had to raise his head to look at the lanky man. "How's our common patient Ms. Schmidt doing?"

Levenstein kept his expression blank. "Don't know and don't care who that is. I don't memorize patient's names unless they're behind in their bills." Before Joy had processed his words, he moved in her direction. His thin lips curved as his brown eyes slid slowly up and down her body, making her uneasy. "Hey, Pollyanna. Looking good, as usual."

Pollyanna. Mocking nickname number two hundred fourteen. At least that sounded better than "the babysitter of corpses"—the name he'd given Joy referring to her work at the Hospice House—or "the chanting hippie," referring to her body-mind-spirit practice at the CeMeSH.

Joy sighed. "Hello Josh."

Dyed black hair, dark circles under his eyes, and a hawk nose gave Josh a harsh appearance. But when a smile lifted his features, filling up his hollow cheeks, he was almost pleasant to look at. "Did you get my last referral? Mr. What's-his-face with the lung cancer."

Patel placed a protective hand on Joy's back and shot Levenstein a glower that seemed to say, *Leave her alone.*

Levenstein ignored him, a hint of playful defiance in his eyes.

Joy summoned compassion by imagining Levenstein as a six-year-old boy. A little kid on a playground who pushes the girl he likes and pulls her hair, preferring negative attention to no attention at all.

"You know, Josh," she said gently. "People think you refer those curable, uninsured patients to hospice because you're greedy and don't want to treat them. But I suspect you do it because you know *I* will find a way to get them treated. Deep inside, you do want to help them."

He snorted. "Nonsense."

"You don't fool me," she continued. "I've heard older patients mention how a decade ago you were the most compassionate doctor they'd had."

Blinking rapidly, the man took a step back, as if trying to gather himself.

"Oh, my poor Joy." He clicked his tongue. "You see the world through rose-colored glasses, and can find good in the worst dirt of society—the proof being that you married that scum, Michael O'Hara."

The comment felt like a punch in the stomach. Especially since Levenstein had supposedly been Michael's friend.

"This is the biggest circus in town, isn't it?" Levenstein jerked his head in the direction of the reporters circling the podium. "You should find a way to use this attention for something productive." He pointed at Patel. "A way to promote yourself as the Deepak Chopra wannabe you are"—he then waggled his fingers at Joy. "Or as publicity for your tree-hugger practice." He seemed to appraise Joy's curves, highlighted by her form-fitting teal dress. "Sometimes I wish *I* were a tree." He flashed her one last smirk and walked away, followed by his bodyguard.

Joy breathed through the frustration that man always provoked. She searched her mind for information about him that would generate empathy.

He really loves his dog.

For a moment, that was all she could come up with.

"Ugh! That man's so irritating!" There it was, a hint of Indian accent in Patel's voice.

As she processed Levenstein's last words, an idea brimmed in Joy. Maybe he was onto something. "Hey, Venkat?" She turned to Patel. As an up-and-coming celebrity holistic doctor, Venkat Patel was an expert on self-promotion. "Can you think of a way of using this press attention to help fundraise for the Hospice House?"

"That's a great idea!" He pondered for a moment, then grimaced. "But would you really want to load yourself with that? You have enough on your plate. Your priorities should be resting and healing."

"Are you kidding?" Joy chuckled. "The Hospice House has been my project for years. I feel terrible that I've been neglecting to fundraise for it lately. And this might help distract me and get me back on my feet." *Especially if Richard is done with me.* Her soul ached at the thought.

"Okay, let's see." He rubbed his clean-shaven jaw. "Hospice work and grief therapy go hand in hand. How about we launch an awareness campaign about grief, where you share some of your own grieving process after your husband died?" He shot her a cautious, sheepish look. "Perfect bait to attract press."

Joy cringed internally. She hated playing the role of the young widow, devastated by the death of her beloved husband.

If people only knew how many times she had fantasized about becoming a widow—a shameful regret she still carried around.

"Let's grab lunch Friday and toss some ideas around." Patel held her wrist. "By then, I may have a proposal for you."

An incoming text got Joy's attention. She checked her phone and realized it was a message from Richard's burner cell.

"If that man touches you one more time, I'm going to rip his head off."

Her heart somersaulted with joy.

She glanced at the podium where Richard stood surrounded by reporters. His face remained immutable, and he answered questions without losing track.

Wait. How did he do that?

She mumbled an excuse to Patel and paced away. Quivering in excitement, she teasingly texted, *"I'm sorry. Who's this?"*

She kept her eyes on Richard.

There it was. His gaze flicked down to read her reply and his right hand, behind the lectern, moved subtly. The only hint that he'd been distracted was his request for the reporter to repeat the question.

And then the text message popped on her screen.

"Forgot my name? You'll be screaming it tomorrow when I get my hands on you."

Her brain stumbled, rolled down her spine, dragged her heart on the way and landed in her pelvis.

Maybe he's not done with me yet!

By then, the next text reached her phone.

"Tomorrow. My house. Same time?"

She needed to say no. This was crazy. Last weekend had been a mistake and she had to return to reality.

Against her will, her shaking fingers flew across the screen keyboard.

"I'll be there."

CHAPTER 3

AFTER A LONG MORNING OF BRIEFINGS IN THE FBI conference room, Richard welcomed conceding the podium to his invited speaker—especially someone as critical to the LOTU case as Dr. Carl Andrews.

As Richard sagged in his chair, letting Dr. Andrews take over, the worries he'd drowned beneath work since yesterday's press conference resurfaced. Seeing those two doctors flirt with Joy revived the fear that someone could snatch her away any minute. He'd always known it was a matter of time until she realized she could do better than him.

A piece of Bronx white-trash like me has no business with an exquisite lady like Dr. Joy Clayton.

What grandiose delusion possessed him when he pursued her? The woman was an angel of mercy. And he? He was a selfish bastard who'd lived his life only for his own pleasure—unapologetically so.

Not to mention the "small detail" that getting involved with Joy could cost him his career. For how much longer could he hide their relationship from the FBI? And was it worth confessing, when he had no guarantee she planned to stay in his life for long?

He pushed away the painful thoughts and forced himself to focus on the ongoing lecture. Dr. Carl Andrews, a former suspect, had been cooperating with the FBI for months. As the founder of the Co-Creators, the New Age Thought society from which the Lords of the Universe group branched out, he was the closest thing they had to an insight into the LOTU and their dangerous minds.

Carl's next projected slide showed the emblem of the LOTU: a golden medallion engraved with Greek and Sanskrit characters. "After studying the few known LOTU members, including the group founder, Rachel Hayes, the FBI's behavior analysts and I have drafted a psychological profile of their typical member."

Is Carl aging in reverse? Richard asked himself, staring at him. Tall, and athletic, with that full head of silver hair and youthful face, Carl Andrews resembled a mature movie star more than a spiritual master with a day job as a psychologist.

"On the surface, the LOTU members are exemplary citizens. They tend to be overachievers and have strong ethical convictions—often very narrow-minded." Carl directed his laser pointer at the next slide. "Yet, their rigid self-control and perfectionism are a pendulum that alternates with secret acting out and blatant antisocial behavior. Let's take as an example their best-known member—and first confirmed victim—the late Congressman Michael O'Hara."

The picture of an attractive blond man with a politician's toothy grin filled the screen and Richard made an effort to mask his contempt. When he'd been assigned to investigate O'Hara's murder months back, Richard never imagined how loathsome the man truly was.

"Everyone knew Congressman O'Hara as the pride of Fort Sunshine." Carl rolled up the sleeves of the tailored navy sports coat he wore without a tie. "An honor graduate from Emory University, the youngest state senator in history, and predicted to someday become the first Florida-native President; he was famous for his charm, his strong family values and his devotion to religion."

Yet he practiced racism and bigotry and tortured his wife psychologically for years.

"Yet, he fit criteria for both narcissistic and borderline personality disorders," Carl continued. "We have accounts of violent mood swings, manipulative behavior, and 'splitting'—or fluctuating between idealizing someone and demonizing them."

Carl paced in front of the audience. "My theory is that the LOTU share a trait of 'internalized shame.' Raised by hyper-critical parents, they have a large amount of unresolved anger and project their own self-hate and self-rejection onto others."

Pointing at the text on the next slide, Carl continued, "The LOTU's agenda contains two main items: ascending to positions of political power to spread their beliefs, and eliminating everything that's 'morally wrong' in this country. Unfortunately, what is 'morally wrong' means something different for each one of them—no wonder they've attacked each other in the past." He lowered the pointer and paused, as if to reinforce the importance of his next words. "Beware of that, because they believe in endless reincarnation, they have no remorse about killing. And their strong convictions allow them to justify all forms of crime."

Samuel raised his hand. "And don't forget. They also share the delusion that they're of divine origin and that their minds harvest unlimited powers."

"But that's not a delusion, that's true," Carl deadpanned. At the baffled expressions in the audience, he added, "Their mistake is believing that divine lineage and unlimited power are a privilege of a selected few, when in fact it's true of every human being—you all included."

Richard stifled a snicker at Samuel's wary look and stood up. "To that I would add that they're also affluent and highly educated, judging by the sophisticated weapons we've recovered from them. For example, the micro-stun gun watch once used to immobilize me. But their most puzzling weapon is the device used to terminate O'Hara and the other politicians. It's terrifying to know we're dealing with a group that can kill someone and leave them with a clean autopsy."

Richard paced around the room, taking over. "So, we're investigating medical providers and electrical engineers in the four states where political victims were identified: Florida, Alaska, Nebraska, and especially New York, the main center of the investigation. Add to our list New Age authors who write about goal achieving through 'Law of attraction,' since we have an account from Hayes that their ultimate goal was spreading those principles." He removed his suffocating tie and turned to Carl. "Anything else?"

Carl considered it. "The LOTU members are likely to snap out of their rigid self-control and turn less subtle and more violent as they see themselves corralled. They're poisoned by righteousness, and would do anything to eliminate 'evil' on the planet."

Carl showered the audience with his serene blue-gray gaze. "I hope you understand the karmic mistake that comes with that type of hate. We are *all* a mixture of light and darkness, and no one is totally good or evil, so there's no point in attacking another group."

By now, Richard was used to Carl's style of teaching, but he could see the confusion grow on the blank faces of the agents in the audience. Hiding his amusement, he cleared his throat. "Let's give Dr. Andrews a round of applause and call it a day."

The applause was winding down as Richard walked Carl out of the conference room. With a spark of mischief in his eyes, Carl asked, "Did I overdo it? Too much love and peace talk for your gun-loving friends?"

Richard patted Andrews' back with a wry grin. "You're an acquired taste, Carl."

The older man laughed as they made their way to Samuel's office.

Samuel's non-glamorous office was a reminder that the FBI was, in essence, just another government institution. Only two flags and the FBI emblem against the dark paneling on the walls decorated it. A brown veneer desk, black vinyl office chairs and generic shelves displaying pictures of Samuel's wife and adult children summarized all the furnishings.

While waiting for Samuel to arrive, Richard and Carl chatted.

"I miss your visits. I got used to them during your leave," Carl said.

"I know," Richard groaned, sprawled on the chair. "I haven't had a minute off since I came back."

"I hope you can come over this week. After that, I'll be in and out of town and hard to reach. I've never been so busy."

The same press breach Richard resented sourly had boosted Carl's demand as life coach and professional speaker to unexpected levels. Blair Sanders' sensationalistic article had portrayed him as a Yoda-like figure using his wisdom and "psychic powers" to guide the FBI.

"I'm worried about you, Carl," Richard said. "After what happened to Hayes we should reinforce your security."

Carl dismissed him with a wave. "Didn't Rachel say I was untouchable?"

Richard didn't answer. Hayes had been clear that the LOTU founders still saw Carl as the "Master of Masters" and "The Universe's Chosen One"—even if he'd refused to join them in their political power-seeking plans. But Richard couldn't guarantee newer members felt the same. And no precautions were enough for him to protect Carl.

Richard could've never imagined that Carl, one of his assignments during the O'Hara case, would end up shoving him into a life-transforming experience. With his background in psychology and his gift of intuition, Carl had taken him on a fascinating and terrifying trip of self-discovery. And with the patience of a sculptor chiseling away marble powder from a block, he'd opened Richard's skeptical mind to the possibility of an immaterial world. Carl had practically—and literally—performed miracles on Richard. But the two men had silently agreed to never mention it.

Unwilling to show his concern, Richard joked, "Well, who cares if they kill you?" He twirled a finger. "You probably have an express ticket to heaven, or Nirvana or whatever, anyway."

Carl's pursed lips and small nod hinted that he'd read the worry behind Richard's joke.

Samuel joined them in the office and greeted Dr. Andrews with a stiff handshake. Behind his politeness, Samuel was still uncomfortable around Carl and his "esoteric theories."

"Were you able to recognize anyone from the photos we gave you?" Samuel asked while taking a seat behind the desk.

Carl retrieved a yellow envelope from a briefcase and handed it to Richard. "None of the pictures ring a bell. I wish I could be of more help identifying the LOTU leaders; but for me, most of them were only blurry faces in a huge crowd I lectured to." He reclined in his seat, lacing his fingers. "Any hope of narrowing your long list of suspects?"

"I'm meeting with some potential informants and their lawyers this afternoon." Richard opened the envelope and extracted the pictures of three men and a woman, setting them on the table. "Barbara Young, a dermatologist who's related to Michael O'Hara. Lucius Zimmerman, a real estate investor. And Rhodes Xenos, a family practice physician—we call them 'X, Y and Z' for short. They claim they attended 'a few LOTU meetings' but deny any involvement with the LOTU murders. They want to work some cooperation deal with us."

"Our biggest urgency is for them to identify Dr. Joshua Levenstein as a LOTU leader." Samuel pointed at Levenstein's picture on the table.

"We know from a good source that he attended the LOTU meetings with O'Hara and may've had some personal grudges against him," Richard filled in. "Unfortunately, he has taken the Fifth Amendment and refuses to talk to us."

"But we have another clue now; that's the reason why I wanted to talk to you two." Samuel retrieved a folder from a drawer and handed it to Richard.

Richard opened the folder, finding both of its pockets stuffed with paper. The pages were filled with script handwriting. "What is this?"

"It's Hayes' journal—or some attempt to write a book. Reportedly, she called for the jail guard, saying she needed to give him something. When he arrived at her cell, he found her unconscious, still clutching some of these pages."

Richard browsed the sheets, recognizing some of the philosophical terms Carl had used while training him. "Why would she want to hand this to him?"

"The guard said she sounded frantic and we can only assume it's something important. All our cryptanalysts could infer so far is that this text is about the LOTU spiritual theories and that it seems to be out of order—the pages were blown away by the hallway fans at the jail. We hoped you two could translate it for us."

After studying another page, Richard handed it to Carl. "These must be advanced lessons; I have no idea what this jargon means."

Carl extracted reading glasses from his jacket pocket, slid them on and took a long look. "And it may be my aging brain, but I can hardly read this handwriting." He handed the folder back to Richard.

Samuel addressed Carl. "The FBI deeply appreciates your work training Richard on the Co-Creators' principles as the closest thing we have to the LOTU's theories. But with the need to decipher these pages, we need to speed up the process. Would you be willing to intensify Richard's training?"

Removing his glasses, Carl winced in apology. "It's always a pleasure to work with Agent Fields, but I'm not sure he's ready yet to go deep into my teachings."

Richard slanted Carl a killer look. "Dr. Andrews is very protective of his principles. For weeks he's tortured me with painful exercises—"

"It's called *meditation*," Carl corrected.

"—and refuses to move me to more advanced classes until I 'open up to receive the messages from the Universe.'" Richard released an exasperated sigh. "He treats me like his special-needs student."

Carl shrugged, returning the reading glasses to his pocket.

"Opening up would be less of a problem if you learned to *be* instead of just doing."

Richard rolled his eyes, "Carl, unlike you, not all of us levitate and walk on water before breakfast."

With a fake gasp, Carl tilted his head. "You *don't?*" A smirk bent his lips.

Richard looked up at the ceiling. "The bottom line is, at the pace we're going, we'll never finish."

"The SAC is willing to assign you protected time for this training," Samuel explained.

"Still, I was just telling Agent Fields I'll be traveling quite a bit over the next few months." Carl looked at Richard. "Videochat?"

Richard frowned. "No. We can't risk information leaking if our calls are intercepted."

"Then I'll need to ask one of my advanced followers to help when I'm not around." Carl considered it. "Do you remember Laura Bonas?"

You have to be freaking kidding me. Of course, Richard remembered the odd woman he'd interviewed during the O'Hara case. He had serious doubts about her sanity. "Nope. That won't work either."

Samuel intervened. "We'll make it work somehow. It's critical for this case that Richard becomes an expert on these theories so we can learn to think like the LOTU. The Bureau is counting on his expertise to take over the case of Senator Flowers' murder in New York." He patted Richard's shoulder with a chuckle. "I'm going to miss him when the New York field office steals him from us."

Damned if you do, damned if you don't. Becoming indispensable for this case was Richard's best hope not to get fired when he confessed his involvement with Joy. But the more invaluable he became for the investigation, the more likely they'd transfer him to New York and away from her—the woman he was obsessed with.

And that was only the beginning of his worries.

Second Most Stupid Thing an FBI agent can do to screw his career: Lying under oath about having killed someone.

CHAPTER 4

Pacing back and forth in his living room, Richard checked the clock on his phone for the hundredth time. At 9:10 p.m., Joy was ten minutes late—very unusual for her.

A part of him knew he was overreacting, but he was still afraid she'd stop showing up one day. Joy Clayton was like a handful of Jell-O in his palm, threatening to leak between his fingers the moment he tried to close his fist.

Taking a deep breath, he imagined himself collecting his out-of-control feelings inside a bottle and shoving a cork in it. Carl teaching him to feel again was good at the time, but he had to gather himself and let his intellect take charge again.

The sound of the key turning in the back door announced that she'd arrived, and the imaginary bottle fell down from his brain-shelf, crashed on the floor and popped open.

The sight of the brunette beauty in her classy, curve-hugging work dress—today amethyst—stunned him with desire and awe. She'd barely closed the door behind her, when he launched himself over her, crowding her against the wall and clasping her arms. He made eye contact for a second, before his mouth fell over hers, devouring her luscious lips with frantic kisses.

Without trying to fight him she kissed him back, mirroring his passion yet neutralizing his desperation with sweetness. Her small hands ran through his hair and his back and his body relaxed, surrendering to her gentleness.

He was in heaven; a heaven that could be taken away from him any second.

So, he was in hell.

Pulling back her head, she freed herself from his lips. Despite her breathlessness, her voice was playful. "Good evening to you, too! I'm also happy to see you!"

He didn't feel like joking, or even talking today. He resumed his attack, deepening his kisses and letting his hands mold to the curves of her body, while slowly moving her toward the bedroom.

Giggling, she jerked her lips free. "Oh, boy! Someone's in a hurry tonight. I miss those days when we used to have *conversations*. Didn't you say once that you were fascinated with my mind and my soul?"

Walking her backward in his arms, like in a slow dance, he smirked. "That was before I sampled your body." He kissed her again.

He was bluffing. He loved that mind and that soul more than he could've ever conceived possible. But new relationships had always been awkward for him. They seemed like a poker game where both people involved hid their cards from each other—never admitting how much they care until the other admits it first.

And he'd once made the mistake of telling her he loved her—the day he confessed who he was—and she'd never yet said it back.

Entering the bedroom, she freed her lips again and surveyed him. "Sweetie, are you okay? You seem… upset."

"You're imagining things."

His mouth searched for the sensitive spot on her collarbone and her weak moaning announced he'd found it. Other men might have more to offer her, but he, Richard, had the key—and the combination—to her body.

As he guided her to sit on the bed, she stopped his hands and spoke in a faint voice. "Richard, sooner or later you'll have to learn to talk about what's bothering you."

He growled in impatience. "You know I hate it when you go shrink on me."

He resumed kissing her neck, but she gently held his face, keeping him away, and pierced him with her dark eyes. "Honestly, sweetie, what's going on?"

He both loved and hated that this woman could read through his bullshit—often when he hadn't realized it was there.

Scowling, he asked, "Why is Dr. Patel making 'proposals' to you and taking you out to lunch?"

She recoiled in surprise and released his face, but her voice was calm. "We're planning a fundraiser for the Hospice House. We're brainstorming over lunch next week." With a small grunt, she flinched. "How do you know who he is and what we were talking about? Please don't tell me you have me bugged—*again*."

"Don't be ridiculous. You're not bugged—*anymore*." He looked away before admitting, "I used my facial recognition software to research him and read your lips as you talked."

She squeezed her eyes shut. "You know it creeps me out when you go all FBI agent on me!"

He wrapped his arms around her waist, his voice turning husky. "Do you have any idea how hard I've worked on getting you over your phobia of men, just to risk another man collecting the fruit of my hard work?"

"Come on! I didn't have a phobia of men!" She winked. "Only straight ones."

She might be kidding, but he wasn't. In the recent weeks, sensing that she'd been traumatized by Michael O'Hara, he'd poured himself into the mission of showing her how delightful physical intimacy could be.

Damn if he'd done all the work of healing her for someone else.

"The bastard, Levenstein, doesn't scare me," he said, holding her face. "I know he's after you, but I also know you're an expert on dodging him. But that Dr. Patel? Who does he think he is, touching you and getting so close to you? And why did you let him?"

Too late he realized he'd raised his voice. Terror filled her features. She slumped her shoulders and shrank, her petite body quivering with each shallow breath. He knew that posture by now; she was slipping into a PTSD flashback.

Michael O'Hara's ghost had entered the room.

He released her face in a rush. "I'm sorry; I didn't mean to scare you."

"I'm okay," she replied, trembling.

She wasn't, but would never admit distress. Joy was so relentlessly cheerful he kept forgetting she'd survived years of living with a psycho.

She rose from the bed and paced away from him, and he wanted to slap himself. What had he done? Even on her best days, she reminded him of a dog who'd been kicked as a puppy and now ran from the hand feeding her.

"Joy, you're not okay. I'm not blind, I can see you shaking."

"I'm not shaking, I'm shivering." She hugged herself, "Why do you keep your AC set so low? This house is a freezer!"

She opened the glass sliding door and exited the bedroom. He followed her as she stepped onto the porch, and then to the overgrown, fenced backyard. The outside was much warmer than the inside, but a merciful cool breeze blew. The moon was almost full, and the chorus of crickets and an occasional owl filled the air.

Still shivering, she kept bracing herself, facing away from him. He extended his hand to touch her hair, but then changed his mind and lowered it. "You have to give me some guidance. When you have flashbacks like this, should I give you space? Should I hold you?"

She forced a chuckle. "You can never go wrong with holding me."

He made her spin around and wrapped her in his arms. Her hands felt like ice, and she was covered in goose bumps. Her fluttering heart drummed against his chest. "Joy, you know I'm a dog who barks and doesn't bite. I'd never hurt you."

"I know." Her arms around him, she poked his back. "You shot me that glare as if you wanted to kill me. But I think if you *really* wanted me dead, you wouldn't have worked so hard to rescue me last month."

He laughed. Releasing her, he searched for her eyes with a playful grimace. "Angel, if I wanted to see you dead, I'd just stop watching you when you cross the street."

Giggling at the reference to her pathological distraction, she tried to push him away, but he tugged her back into his arms.

A comfortable silence grew between them, as he held her tighter, letting the heat of his chest warm her up.

Then, in a soft voice, he said, "Sometimes I'm afraid you're pretending to do better than you are. I heard you talk in your sleep once, mention how the blood splashed your face when I shot that man."

She remained silent for a moment. "It's true. Ever since that night the LOTU tried to kill us, repressed memories from the years with Michael are coming back. A part of me sensed he never would've really hurt me—or the kids. But still, a corner of my brain always worried that he might."

Joy had only spoken once about those years married to Michael O'Hara—about his violent mood swings, his unpredictable temper explosions, and his relentless gaslighting. But Richard knew he'd never have the whole story about how deeply O'Hara had damaged her.

Tonight they only had a few hours while her neighbor watched her sleeping kids, but he'd prepared his backyard to make it special. He'd laid a blanket on the grass, next to the fire pit, for an improvised outdoor dinner—a change from constantly hiding in his house. He guided her by the hand to lie next to him on the blanket.

Lacing his fingers with hers, he asked, "Are the flashbacks happening often?"

"Not really," she replied, her eyes lost in the stars. "Last week I awoke in the middle of the night and felt you next to me. Half asleep, my brain thought I was back in bed with *him* and I panicked.

I had to go through Carl's nine hundred meditation exercises to stop myself from running away."

She turned her head toward him and smiled weakly, as if trying to pass it off as a joke, but he didn't find it funny. He couldn't stand the thought that she might mix him up with O'Hara.

Rolling onto his side, he pressed his rough fingers against her silky cheek. "And days like today, when I go all mean, and jealous and paranoid on you are not helping. I'm sorry."

His skin tingled as her soft hand trailed across his forearm. "Don't apologize for being you. If I learned anything from my nightmare with Michael, it's that there's no point in trying to change people." She propped herself on an elbow to face him. "And I don't want you to change. Your paranoia makes you a great agent. And your harshness and cynical touch are part of the unconscious pull that draws me to you—because your qualities and flaws complement mine."

Leave it to Joy to twist even the worst experience into a life lesson. "Still. I should know better by now than to be harsh with you."

Silence fell, only broken by the crickets.

Having an idea, he sat up on the blanket and did the time-out sign, touching his fingers to his other palm. "Brain-stretch break."

She relaxed immediately and her face lit up.

"Brain-stretch" had become a code between them when he was investigating her undercover. It was their cue to set work aside for a minute and launch into stimulating chat. From debating ethical dilemmas to brainstorming about the big questions of life, he'd known he was in trouble the day he woke up excited about going to work for the pleasure of talking to her—his suspect.

"I'm listening." She straightened on the blanket.

"Do you remember that time we got locked in a debate about positive and negative reinforcement to get rid of an unwanted behavior?"

She nodded. "You loved the idea of aversion therapy and I still maintain that rewards are better than punishment."

"How about we create a system that combines both to help me shed the bad habit of raising my voice? Aversion therapy for me that is also a reward for you. In that way, if I ever do anything that triggers your bad memories—interrogating you, getting sarcastic, getting too jealous—you get something positive out of it."

She studied him with interest. "Like what?"

He got up from the ground and offered his hand to help her rise. "I voluntarily agree that every time I slip, I'll have to do one thing that you enjoy and I don't like. Ballroom dancing, for example! I'll have to take a fifteen-minute dancing lesson from you."

She laughed. "You're a fake! I know you're starting to like that."

You got me. He pressed his lips to hide his humor.

As he walked her back to the porch, she pondered his offer. "Shouldn't I also pay a penalty when I do something that annoys you? For example, when I psychoanalyze you?"

She was too fair to agree to a deal that wasn't two-sided. "Sure. Why not?"

"Then, assuming I agreed," she asked, "what would my punishment be if I didn't keep my end of the deal?"

He answered without hesitation, "Striptease."

Stopping in her tracks, she gaped at him. "What?"

"I've been dying to see you dance for me ever since that Hospice House party, when you told me about your dance lessons growing up." He playfully nudged her with his shoulder. "I'm even doing *you* a favor stretching you out of your comfort zone. You're too squeaky-clean and need to embrace your inner bad girl."

The sound of her silvery laughter was music to his ears. He opened the sliding door and guided her back into the bedroom.

Once inside, sudden melancholy filled her expression as she tugged him to a halt. "Richard..." She stopped.

His eyes searched hers. "Yes, angel?"

Her attention flicked away, then returned to him. "Have you heard anything about your transfer to New York?"

Every muscle of his body tensed. "We'll worry about that tomorrow."

Sighing, she shook her head. "You told me the same thing the other—"

Instead of answering, he extinguished her words with his mouth.

She pulled back, breathless. "Sweetie! You can't keep avoiding—"

He kissed her again, slowly and deeply. He poured everything he had into the kiss; his desire; his wordless declaration of love; his fear of losing her—anything that could stop them from thinking about what the future might hold for them.

When her hands rose to his back and head to bring him closer and deepen the kiss, he knew she'd surrendered.

A loud noise coming from beyond the bedroom door startled them both. His stomach clenching, Richard realized he'd forgotten to lock the door when they moved from the living room to the bedroom.

"Did anybody follow you?" he breathed into her hair.

Her dark eyes latched on his, filled with terror. "No. I took all the usual precautions."

His senses heightened and instinct took over. "Stay here." He reached for his gun on the nightstand, finding comfort in the familiar feel of the grip against his palm. As Joy backed against the wall, he moved to crack open the bedroom door.

CHAPTER 5

H IS PULSE RACING, RICHARD TIPTOED ACROSS THE HALLWAY
and into the family room. Another clashing sound emanated
from the kitchen. Holding his gun up, he peered in.

His son Ray shoved a plate of frozen nuggets into the microwave
and slammed the door.

Relieved, Richard stashed his gun in a drawer of the nearby end
table before approaching. "Ray! You scared me." He spoke loudly so
Joy could hear him and keep hiding.

The boy gave his father a quick, sideways hug. "Sorry, Dad, I
didn't mean to. Mom forgot to feed me again and there was nothing
in her fridge."

Of course. Richard silently cursed his luck. Had Sandy spent this
month's child support on new clothes again or did she have a night
on the town?

"Ray, didn't I give you cash last week and ask you to save it for
buying food in an emergency?"

Ray deadpanned, "But I needed a new leash and wax for my
surfboard."

Resigned, Richard held his forehead. Arguing with the boy logically was a lost cause.

Before Richard answered, Ray yelled, "Hi, Joy! I know you're
here; I saw your car in the garage."

Damn it. Richard still hadn't forgiven himself for the reckless-
ness that led to Ray meeting Joy and her kids when he was working
undercover.

With a tense smile, Joy appeared in the kitchen. "Hi, Ray! How are you? My Arthur asks about you all the time." She searched for something on the floor. "Well…" She cleared her throat. "I have to go."

"I'll walk you out." Richard approached her.

"No, no. It's okay." She picked up her purse and keys from where she'd dropped them when Richard received her at the door and gave him a quick kiss on the cheek. "Enjoy your time together. And you enjoy your dinner, sweetie." She waved at Ray.

As she headed to the back exit in the laundry room, her gaze met Richard's. He sent her an apology with his eyes, and hers communicated understanding. She gave one last weak wave goodbye before disappearing through the door to the garage.

While getting the chicken nuggets from the microwave and setting them on the breakfast bar, Ray cleared his throat and jerked his head in the direction where Joy had left. "I see you're making progress." With a smirk, he wagged his eyebrows.

Richard sent Ray a warning glare. "As much as I enjoy your visits on days you're supposed to be with your mom, I would appreciate a call ahead."

The same scowl that made suspects tremble had no effect on that teenage mini-me of Richard's. Ray forked the first nugget and waved it in the air to let it cool down. "I like an element of surprise."

Richard rolled his eyes to cover his amusement. He pulled out a barstool and sat next to his son at the kitchen counter.

"I like Joy," Ray continued between bites to his nuggets. "She seems nicer than the last one… what was her name? The psycho redhead who burned all your clothes when you broke up with her?"

"Hailey," Richard mumbled, uncomfortable.

"That's right." Ray swallowed another bite. "And the one before that, the blonde with the back brace and the drinking problem… was that Lisa?"

"No, that was Kate," Richard grumbled.

"Oh yes. Lisa was the one who broke all the dishes in your kitchen cabinets when you left her for Kate." He snickered. "Man, you've had a collection of drama queens."

And the worst of all was your mother. No wonder he'd sworn to never get married again.

Damn it, maybe Carl had a point when he said Richard gravitated to women who needed saving, in a never-ending attempt to rescue his own lost-cause mother. He still had no idea what had changed for him to break his pattern and fall for Joy.

He slanted Ray a look. "Is it safe to assume that, as usual, you got a friend to give you a ride here, but after dinner *I* have to drive you back?"

While munching on his chicken nuggets, Ray simpered. His hazel eyes, so similar to his father's, twinkled. "You're a smart man, Dad."

$\sim$

"I am sorry again, Angel. I promise tonight will be different."

At her office at the CeMeSH Friday, Joy glanced at Richard's third apology since their frustrated date two nights before. With her overnight bag in her car, she'd head to his house as soon as she finished work.

She wished she could call him on his burner cell—but with their constant fear of the FBI intercepting their calls, that was out of the question.

"It's okay, I'll see you tonight," she texted back. Then on impulse she added, *"I wish I could hear your voice."*

She set the phone down on her desk with a sigh. *What am I doing?* The thought of spending the night with Richard made her tremble in excitement, but this constant hiding and sneaking, the looking over her shoulder and checking her rearview mirror, made her stomach knot. Like she didn't have enough doubts about her readiness for a new relationship.

Her desk phone rang and assuming it was her secretary, she picked up. "Hello?"

"This is Guardian."

Joy's spirit soared at Richard's voice and the code name they'd agreed upon.

It was almost unheard of for him to call her; if he ever did, it was from a payphone or a random landline he trusted was untapped. Swallowing, she followed the usual procedure. "And this is Angel. Everything's clear here."

His voice softened. "I just called to say I'm dying to have an orange."

She blushed at the memory. The weekend they'd spent together during his leave, she'd mentioned the oranges growing in his back-yard were the most delicious she'd tasted in her life. He'd replied that *she* was the most delicious thing he'd tasted in his life. He'd licked the orange juice dripping down her chin and neck, kissed her sense-less, then taken her to the bedroom again. Ever since, talking about oranges in his texts was his secret code for lovemaking.

She could hear the humor in his voice, as if he knew the effect his words had on her. "See you tonight, angel." He disconnected the call.

Joy hung up the receiver and stared at the phone, mute for a moment. She was hopeless to escape that man's power over her.

She regained her focus just in time to catch a blond bullet, sprinting across her office. She picked up Edward, her two-and-a-half-year-old son, held him with one arm while he kicked and wig-gled and used the free one to scoop his brunette twin, Alex, from the playpen where he was supposed to be napping and never did.

It threw her whole day askew when the nanny dropped the kids at her work, but hopefully, this would be Donna's husband's last den-tal procedure. "Arthur, sweetie," Joy spoke to the husky six-year-old drawing at the front desk with markers. "Bring your backpacks and come with me."

"Do we *have* to go with Grandma?" The despair in the little boy's voice as he obeyed pierced her soul. Maureen O'Hara couldn't help tainting the interactions with her grandkids with unresolved grief about Michael's death.

"No! No Grandma! Auntie Fe's coming!" Alex protested, invoking his favorite babysitter. He seemed to believe that stating wishful thoughts as absolute truth made them magically happen. Joy amused herself thinking that her beloved mentor, Carl Andrews, would've said the boy was onto something.

Carl! She still had to return his call about his donation for the Hospice House.

"It's just for a little while, sweetie," she replied to the boy. "After that, Aunt Hope is picking you up for a sleepover."

"Yay! Auntie Hope!" Alex clapped and Edward bounced in Joy's arms, almost making her trip over her high heels on the way to the golden elevator.

Wearing a black dress and pearls, her gray hair tied up in a bun, Maureen O'Hara seemed to have aged two decades in the past two years. She scowled and reprimanded one of the three uniformed maids around her.

Joy flashed back to a high school party when Maureen had embarrassed Michael by scolding him in front of all his friends for missing his curfew. Whenever Joy had trouble forgiving him, she reminded herself of the hard childhood he'd endured under that woman's iron fist.

"Thank you so much for rescuing me, Maureen." Joy greeted her with a kiss on the cheek.

"If you'd agreed to move in with me, you'd never have to worry about childcare again."

Joy ignored the repetitive, uncomfortable invitation. "Hope will get them around six."

"Tell her to take her time." Maureen took blond Edward from Joy's arms—her favorite, because he most resembled Michael. Her face contorted in grief, regarding him, and her voice cracked. "These boys are the only joy I have left."

Little Edward squirmed in Grandma's grasp, as if uncomfortable with her sadness. Joy felt torn between her desire to help Maureen and her instinct to shelter her kids from the secondhand exposure to their grandmother's gloom.

Maureen snapped her fingers and the three maids sprang into action, taking one child each. Joy rushed to hug and kiss the boys goodbye.

The goodbye was always harder for Mom than for the kids. As Joy blew kisses and "I love yous" at the closing elevator doors, the guilt she always felt when she took time for herself clogged her throat.

"*You can be very selfish sometimes,*" Michael accused her in her head. She pushed him away. She wanted nothing to do with his voice tonight.

She returned to the clinic to meet her last pain management patient, there for a procedure. After this, she still had to complete her charts and a ton of paperwork.

Dr. Barbara Young exited the dressing room buttoning the jacket of her pink pantsuit. "You have divine hands, girl. My pinched nerve is already feeling better!" She slapped Joy's back, then massaged her own shoulder.

Young had always been overly affectionate with Joy, making her slightly uncomfortable. They'd never been close, but they'd known each other for over a decade since Barbara was Michael's older cousin.

"I'm glad the injection helped," Joy said. "Now don't go straight to the gym to wreck it up again."

Young's guilty grin showed Joy had guessed her intentions. The woman was a gym rat, and it clearly showed in her Barbie doll body, only paralleled by the flawless skin that went with her dermatology specialty.

Nobody knew for sure how old Barbara Young was. To the untrained eye she appeared to be in her thirties, but a closer look would show the telltale signs of cosmetic work. With silver hair and a face enhanced with fillers, she could've been any age between forty and sixty.

As Joy guided her to her office, Young fluffed her lustrous silver pixie. "Hey, sugar babe, today I noticed for the first time that most of your patients are women."

"I never intended it that way," Joy replied, working on the computer to print Young's post-procedure instructions. "But women are more interested than men in the mind-body-spirit services we offer here."

Young retrieved a mirror from her purse and retouched her makeup. "You and I should brainstorm some ideas to promote our practices together."

Joy nodded as she hit "Print" on the computer. "That sounds good. But I wouldn't have time for another project. Right now I'm trying to launch a new fundraiser for the Hospice House."

"What is it?"

"There's nothing definitive yet. Patel and I are exploring an awareness campaign about grief, to capitalize on some of the recent press attention." Even saying the words tied Joy's stomach in knots. She wasn't ready to talk about Michael. Yes, she'd endured horrible grief after his death. But there was something else Joy had never forgiven herself for feeling.

Relief.

Young's face lit up as she lifted it from peering into the mirror. "I would love to help you fundraise!"

"I haven't decided yet if I want to deal with the press." Joy sent Barbara a wordless message with her eyes. The rest of the O'Hara family was still in denial about Michael's mental illness and how hard Joy's marriage had been, but Joy wondered if, being a physician, she had noticed.

"Are you kidding, babe?" Young tittered. "I would *kill* to get some of that press attention!" Rising from the chair, she placed a hand on her narrow waist and popped a slender hip. "Honey, I am not trying to be generous and selfless here—that's *so* not me. If I'm offering to help you it's because I see a great opportunity to promote my practice. Give me a call when you get a chance."

Joy hesitated. Young and Patel had a point. Maybe the goal of keeping the Hospice House afloat was worth putting aside her reluctance to speak about Michael.

Young grabbed the instructions from the printer at the table next to the mahogany desk and fanned herself with them. "Maybe we can grab coffee and toss some ideas around. Are you free after work?"

"Sorry, today I'm in a hurry to get somewhere." Joy rose from her desk and indicated Young to follow her to the reception area.

As they stepped out to the waiting room, Young's eyes slid over the teddy bear lying on the floor. "Where are you going? Didn't Aunt Maureen just pick up your kids?"

Yes, and after that I'm sending them to a sleepover, so I can sneak out with my man. Joy felt like the worst mother on Earth.

She quickly searched her mind for a possible excuse, but it was hopeless. Joy was the worst liar in the world.

A lifesaving monotone voice interjected from the waiting room door. "Joy and I have plans."

It was Dr. Allison Connors, her therapist. Joy exhaled in relief at her intervention.

Recognizing the blond Amazon, Young lost her levity, apparently assuming Joy was heading to a therapy session. She shot Joy the pitying, tilted look Joy dreaded and then gave her a long, suffocating hug. "Hang in there, sugar babe. We'll catch up later. Now, try to have a nice evening." She gave Joy's arms one last squeeze before releasing the hug and sashaying away.

"If she only knew what a nice evening you're planning to have." Allison's ice-cold voice still made Joy blush.

Joy rushed to pick up her kids' toys from the empty waiting room. "Thanks for saving me explanations, Allison."

"You left a message that you needed to talk to me?" Since Allison's office was only one floor above Joy's, they often stopped by without calling—easier than navigating each other's secretaries.

"You offered to share with me your list of sponsors?" She'd asked Allison for the list of donors supporting the Women's Shelter, where she volunteered. Joy hoped to approach them when fundraising for the Hospice House.

Allison adjusted the lapels of her aqua skirt suit. "I was going to give it to you at last week's appointment."

Oh yes, that appointment I canceled to go see Richard. Joy stopped with a toy car in her hand and gave an apologetic grimace. "Sorry; I'll call your secretary to reschedule."

A hint of reprimand shone in Allison's cold blue stare, reminding Joy how unorthodox their client-therapist relationship was. Allison had once been kind of a friend she vented to—a colleague and former college classmate. Yet when Michael died suddenly, she ended up as Joy's therapist almost by default. It wasn't ideal, but Joy's choices were limited in the small town of Fort Sunshine, where most mental counselors were Joy's own clients.

Allison flicked a strand of golden hair off her porcelain-skinned forehead. "So, you're on your way to see *him*, right?" She'd easily guessed that Joy's recent love interest and the undercover FBI agent who'd rescued her were one and the same—the "Richard" who'd become Joy's platonic crush when he'd shadowed her at work.

Joy threw a nervous glance at the deserted front desk—the secretary must've taken a break. She signaled Allison to follow her into the privacy of her office.

Once in Joy's office, Allison crossed her arms and tapped her expensive high-heel strappy sandals on the laminate floor. Joy wasn't sure if her expressionless face was part of professional poise, or if she'd overdone it again with her Botox. "I celebrate that you're doing something crazy for the first time in your life and having an adventure," Allison said without intonation. "But be careful."

Sometimes Joy wished she'd had someone warmer and more nurturing as a therapist, but overall she was grateful for Allison. She'd been a tremendous help in the past two years, taking the edge off Joy's PTSD with hours of debriefing about the nightmare years with Michael.

"Be *very* careful," Allison repeated. "You might end up getting attached to that man."

"I'll be fine." Joy threw the armful of kids' toys in the playpen. It wouldn't help her case if she admitted it was too late for precautions; she was already hopelessly attached to Richard. "Like you said, he's just an adventure."

I'm the worst liar in the world.

Allison shook her head. "Don't underestimate the power of an intense bonding experience. You were nearly killed together. You're at very high risk of falling hard for him."

Joy walked toward her desk and busied herself going through the pile of mail on it, avoiding Allison's gaze.

Allison strolled closer and gently tipped up Joy's chin, making her look at her. Apprehension shone in her blue eyes. "My dear, you're very vulnerable, and it's easy to take advantage of you. Anyone willing to treat you half-well would seem like a god after Michael."

"You're preaching to the choir," Joy mumbled, looking up to the ceiling. Then she lowered her eyes again, feeling despair rise inside. "I know this will end soon. Richard is getting transferred to New York, and there's no way we'll be able to stay in touch if that happens." There was no need to add, *while hiding from the FBI.* If making their relationship work while living in the same town had been a challenge, trying to sustain it across the distance would be a lost cause.

Why am I prolonging the agony? I have to tell Richard that we can't see each other anymore.

Feeling hopeless, she returned her focus to the mail on her desk.

A manila envelope without a return address caught her sight and she opened it first. She couldn't help smiling when she realized it was a snail mail package from Richard.

It was an orange.

The unsigned letter in the envelope read, "I can't stop thinking about oranges now. You should be ashamed of yourself for being so absolutely divine."

The note made her giggle. Richard had learned to bypass her resistance to praise by mixing a compliment with a reprimand.

"Joy?" Allison cleared her throat.

She forced herself to return her attention to Allison. "Don't worry about me; I have no unrealistic expectations. All I want is a little break after the hard years I had; I'll deal with my broken heart later."

Joy noticed another envelope without sender's information. Wondering if it was another message from Richard she opened it, but instead she found a greeting card. The white roses on the front picture elicited a bad memory, as those were the flowers Michael had always sent her for special occasions.

A chill went down her spine when she read the message.

Michael is now an angel looking down on you. Everywhere you go, everything you do MICHAEL IS WATCHING YOU.

CHAPTER 6

CANDLELIGHT BARELY ILLUMINATED THE MEDITATION ROOM in Carl's house. Incense sticks and sage burned on a plate, saturating the air with their scent. Soft flute music mixed with the dripping sound of water from a tabletop fountain.

It was all so damn relaxing it was nerve-wracking.

Sitting cross-legged on a rug, Richard made an effort not to fidget. He felt naked without his gun, but apparently no weapons were allowed at "spiritual initiations." *What kind of brainwashing did Carl submit me to?* Six months ago he didn't even believe in the existence of the soul, and the only deity he'd acknowledged was the pleasures of the flesh.

Carl's "senior disciple," Laura Bonas, sat in front of him. Her dull brown hair, as messy as if she'd just walked out of a twister, distracted from what would've otherwise been a decent-looking, petite middle-aged woman. She'd always half-amused him, half-freaked him out.

"They've been lying to you all your life." Laura dropped the words with such gravitas that Richard jerked out of his musings.

Puzzled, he stared at her. "Who's been lying?"

"The consensus reality. The world has sold you the idea that first our eyes see, and then our brain interprets what we've seen."

He eyed her warily. "And that's a lie because…" He gestured for her to complete the sentence.

"Take that idea and reverse it completely." She leaned forward and fixed her glassy green eyes on his. "First, we think a thought, an idea; and then, *only then*, the eyes will see."

He sent Carl, sitting in full lotus position some distance from him, a silent cry for help. Carl half-smiled, as if enjoying Richard's disturbed expression.

Richard turned back to Laura and admitted, "I don't understand."

She undid her knotted legs, got on her hands and knees and crawled closer to him. As she placed her face right into his, he instinctively leaned away from her intense scrutiny. "It's simple," she announced in a solemn voice. "Everything you see is there because you, or someone else, or the consensus reality *expect* it to be there. You're convinced that you will see it—so you do. And everything that's in your life right now was created by you, by your expectations and thoughts."

"Whoa… hold on a minute." He made a *T* with his hands. "That makes no sense. You're in front of me right now; how can I have created you?"

She sat inches away from him and re-did her lotus position. "You attracted me into your life when you became ready to hear the messages I had for you. And you are the creator of me as you see me. No one else in the world sees and knows the exact same Laura that you see and know."

She froze for a good ten seconds, sitting as still as a statue, hardly blinking.

He was about to wave his hand in front of her face when she threw out her arms, startling him. "This is an illusion! Nothing is real!" she exclaimed. "Our senses are unreliable filters. You'll never know, as long as you live, if others around you see the same images you see. And do you know what? They don't. Two human beings could witness the exact same occurrence and see a different scene."

Richard wasn't sure that he understood, but he nodded anyway.

Her whole skin flushed and her voice rose. "Do you understand how serious and liberating that realization is? Everything you heard before is probably a lie! Labels, limitations, how-to instructions, what you can and cannot expect from life—even history books! It's a reflection of someone else's illusion but may have nothing to do with your own dream."

Even history books? That did it.

Richard unfolded his long limbs, sprang to his feet and glared at Carl, who was starting to shake with laughter. "You, come here. Right now!"

With one last cautious look in Laura's direction, he stormed out of the room.

Carl was roaring as they stepped out from the meditation room and the house onto the river-facing back porch. "You should've seen your face!"

Richard glowered at him. "Are you doing this on purpose to make me quit? You know that woman creeps me out!"

Carl used the collar of his white shirt to dry a tear from the corner of his eye. "Laura is one of my most advanced followers, and the best person I could think of to help you and the FBI when I'm not around." He half-shrugged. "Yes, she gets a little too passionate about the lessons, but you'll get used to her teaching style."

"No, I won't." Richard scowled. "Because I have no intention of having her a as tutor. And enough with initiations. At this pace we'll never make progress!"

"It doesn't matter how long it takes." Carl's expression turned dead serious. "You can't rush the process of Awakening."

Richard grunted in frustration. *This is the most high-maintenance spiritual master I've ever met.*

After months working with Carl, Richard knew the man couldn't be rushed. Ever since the LOTU founders had misinterpreted his teachings and deserted his group, he was determined to keep his guidance vague and let people "find their own answers." Richard suspected it was his way to filter out less-than-ideal followers by testing their patience again and again.

After walking a few steps, Richard dropped onto the nearby wooden bench and took in the majestic view of the Indian

River—which Carl already planned to trade for an ocean view, as his new luxury home was under construction. Months into their friend-ship, Richard still hadn't grown used to Carl's ridiculous wealth.

Richard's day had been exhausting and he couldn't wait to finish this last task and get ready to meet Joy. He'd been working without rest, trying to understand the jargon in Hayes' writings on his own. He also continued to search for evidence against Levenstein and worked on striking a deal with the lawyers of X, Y and Z—Xenos, Young, and Zimmerman—hoping to use them as potential witnesses against him.

"Carl, all I need is your help organizing these pages. Look at what I just found." Richard extracted the folder from his laptop carrier on the floor next to the bench. "Do you see those ink smudges and the sloppier handwriting in the small characters at the bottom of random pages?" He flipped some sheets. "It seems that Hayes wrote those in a hurry, maybe even the day she ended up in the hospital."

Frowning at the pages, Carl nodded. "Do you think she was try-ing to send you guys a message through those characters?"

Richard pulled out the blank page where he'd scribbled the full series of characters. *neSh13WoSpod32Suringsbrisin#19d60geDr951FtFL.*

"The pages are not numbered. All I need is your help to read through the document, figure out the order of the pages, and hope that those characters then make sense."

Carl laced his fingers. "And miss your chance to learn the real essence of the teachings?"

Richard heaved in exasperation. "Carl, you don't understand how frustrating this is for me! The Fort Sunshine agency is terribly under-staffed—even Samuel, the Assistant SAC, has to work in the field." He raked a hand through his hair. "When Sam said they'd give me 'protected time' to meet with you, that only meant I have to squeeze all my usual work into the other hours. I have no freaking time for a personal life anymore—"

"Oh! So that's what this crankiness is all about!" Carl tapped his own forehead. "No time to meet with Joy recently."

Without answering, Richard slouched on the bench. He'd tried to conceal from Carl what was going on with Joy, but it had been as useless as trying to resist when Carl dug in his brain, extracting childhood memories that needed to be healed.

"No wonder you're in a rotten mood." Smiling, Carl took a seat next to Richard. "Joy has mastered the art of infusing people with peaceful energy. She learned that from me; she was once my star student."

Carl had a point. Every time he'd met with Joy, she'd filled him with peace and bliss. And now, days after seeing her, he was running out and desperately needed a recharge.

He limited himself to shooting Carl a warning look. "For a spiritual master proud of abandoning the concerns of the flesh, you seem to enjoy my heart trouble too much."

"Richard, do you remember the first question you have to ask yourself when you're unhappy?" he asked.

Richard huffed in frustration before mumbling the answer he'd learned in previous sessions. "What do you *really* want?"

Carl nodded, "So, tell me, Richard, what do you want?"

Impatient, Richard groaned. "No, you're not doing this to me again. We already went through that step a dozen times during my leave."

"Just humor me."

"I already told you what I want!" he exclaimed. "Like every man, I want success and money. I want my son to be proud of his father." *I want to become the type of successful man Joy deserves by her side.*

Carl studied him intently. "And what exactly does the word success mean?"

"Career advancement. A salary raise."

"But isn't the fastest way to obtain that accepting your transfer to New York?"

Taken aback, Richard didn't answer. Carl was right. Moving on from his small resident agency to the New York Field office—the center of the LOTU investigation—was, in theory, the best thing that could happen to his career.

"That's exactly what impedes most people from finding success," Carl said. "When your goal is mutually exclusive with another dream or covenant you have, you'll find ways to fail."

Richard's wits betrayed him for a moment. Working for the FBI had once been his biggest dream. Now, that goal seemed incompatible with his latest dream of having Joy. And soon he might be forced to choose.

"Our conscious thoughts are only the tip of the iceberg," Carl continued. "Your mind is a labyrinth made of more rooms and hallways than you perceive. Your soul is, too."

He grumbled, "Carl, it's so frustrating when you talk in riddles."

Richard's phone buzzed with a text from Samuel. He'd let his last call go to voicemail earlier so he opened the message. It read, *"Urgent. Call me back. It's about X, Y, Z."* Excusing himself from Carl, he walked out of earshot to call.

Samuel answered on the first ring. "Richard. It's about our witness Zimmerman…" His grave tone immediately revealed something bad had happened.

"What's going on?" Richard asked, feeling adrenaline dump into his veins.

Without further preamble, Samuel answered, "He's dead."

~

Richard and Samuel had spent several hours gathering information separately, talking to the police, doctors, and hospital staff. Now they sat in Samuel's office, sharing their findings.

"This can't be a coincidence," Richard said for the tenth time that evening, needing to process it himself. "We were finally making progress with his lawyer—and now he's dead?"

"What did you find out from the hospital staff?" asked Samuel.

Richard retrieved his notes. "Zimmerman passed out at home and his wife called nine-one-one. At the hospital, the emergency room doctors found only a low blood sugar but decided to admit him overnight for observation."

"I found out that barely hours after he made it to his hospital room, a nurse aide came to take his vitals and he was dead," Samuel offered. "The nurse called the code-blue team, but they were unable to revive him. Nobody knows how long he'd been gone when they found him, but it couldn't have been long. There were no signs of struggle."

"Aren't patients in the hospital video-monitored?" Richard asked, trying to remember his last admission for job-related injuries.

"Not everywhere. Only in some areas, like the ICU."

"Let's review again what happened to Hayes. Any similarities?"

Samuel reached for some notes on his computer. "The ER triage records said that for two days, Hayes had complained of feeling tired and urinating too often. The jail doctor was checking her for a urinary infection, but they never got to start her on antibiotics. The next day she cried for help to one of the prison guards and then collapsed. The ER physician's diagnosis was a cardiac block: an extremely slow heart rate and low blood pressure."

"And she had no previous cardiac history," Richard mused.

"None. Zimmerman's death could still have been a heart attack or something; he had the common health issues of overweight middle-age: hypertension, cholesterol, and type-two diabetes. But Hayes? She was quite healthy for someone in their fifties," Samuel replied. Her drug screen at the ER was negative—Zimmerman's was too."

Richard tapped his fingers on the desk. "So, in conclusion, both Hayes and Zimmerman complained of feeling sick and ended up in the hospital."

"That's where the similarity ends. Zimmerman was dead within hours. Hayes has lingered for days, now dealing with sepsis. Our only hope to shed some light into this is waiting for his autopsy."

"But knowing the LOTU history, chances are the autopsy will be inconclusive."

"Yes. And there's also the possibility this is truly a coincidence."

A buzz from the intercom announced a call from the secretary. "I'm sorry, I should've left long ago. Do you still need me?" Only then did Richard realize how late it was.

"It's okay, you can leave," Samuel replied.

"Please remind Agent Fields of his phone messages. Blair Sanders left three more today."

Richard still had things to do to get ready for Joy's visit tonight. As Samuel disconnected the call, he said, "Sam, I need to go."

Samuel drummed a pen on his desk. "How can you walk away in the middle of brainstorming? We'll be done when we're done."

Richard released an impatient huff. "My brain is fried. Can we continue tomorrow?"

"What's your deal, Richard? You're distracted lately; it's like—" Samuel's frown broke abruptly and a light illuminated his face. "Oh, God! Please don't tell me you're still seeing *her*!"

Richard's lack of answer seemed to be enough confirmation. Samuel rose from his desk and walked to the office door to close it and engage the lock. "Fields, we need to talk."

Shit. If Samuel was addressing him by his last name, nothing good was about to happen.

CHAPTER 7

S AMUEL TRUDGED TOWARD RICHARD. "YOU ARE SO SCREWED and you know it." For someone usually even-tempered and benign, the glare Samuel sent in his direction chilled Richard's bones. "We have to speed up that transfer to New York."

Richard shuddered. "Sam, you can't force me to go to New York."

"*Force* you?" A guttural sound came out of Samuel's throat. A fine sweat pearled his dark forehead and his brown eyes bulged. "Are you freaking kidding me? You begged me for years to get you out of this dead town. And now that you *need* to get out of here before your career goes down the drain, now you've changed your mind about it?"

Jittery, Richard rose from his chair and paced away. "You're exaggerating. My career's not going down the drain."

Samuel spoke between his teeth. "You slept with your suspect."

Richard spun around to look Samuel in the eye. "Nothing happened between me and Dr. Clayton until after the case was solved."

Not because you didn't try, buddy.

Richard pushed the thought away. If Joy's resistance to letting him in had delayed things enough that he could now claim that, he'd use it.

"You know you're stretching the truth," Samuel alternated between whispering and raising his voice. "Something must've happened before the case was solved. You admitted to me you were involved with her."

Richard retraced his steps back to their first kiss months ago, in the dark Hospice House parking lot. "We had exonerated her from suspicion when I first went after her. I never imagined she'd be back in the spotlight after that."

Samuel looked up to the ceiling and threw his hands in the air. "She was the widow of the freaking victim! Of course, she'd always be under the spotlight."

Richard didn't answer.

Glowering at him, Samuel continued, "You'll need to face disciplinary action if this comes out. And it will; this is a small town where everyone knows everybody and the local pastime is gossip."

It was true. To make things worse, the tabloid reporters were circling him. He worried it was a matter of time until someone made up the "false news" of him being involved with the witness he'd rescued. If that led to the FBI questioning him about it, he'd be pushed against the wall.

"Then maybe I should come clean and be the one to confess." Those were the words haunting Richard for weeks—and now that they were out, he felt relieved.

Samuel shot him a baffled stare, then slowly shook his head. "You can't take that risk."

"You said it; I'm becoming indispensable to the case."

"Don't believe that being the man of the hour will stop the Bureau from firing you, my friend." With a scoff, Samuel snapped his fingers. "They'll replace you in a second."

"With whom?" Richard asked, defiant. "I'm the only agent they have who's trained by Dr. Andrews on the foundations of the LOTU principles. You know he's very protective of his teachings and won't agree to train just anyone."

Samuel gawked at him without answering and Richard continued, "That is my best hope. If I can become irreplaceable for the LOTU case, they'll be less likely to let me go. I just have to plan the best timing to confess the truth. Right after a big breakthrough on the case, but before it's solved, so the disciplinary action committee has to weigh that in."

Samuel folded his arms and tipped his head. "And do you understand the Pandora's box this can open? Can you swear in front of the disciplinary committee that you never disclosed any sensitive information to Clayton?"

Richard's jaw clenched. When he'd confessed to Joy who he really was, he might've revealed more than he should.

But there was more than Samuel knew. If confessing his involvement with Joy re-opened a thorough investigation of his behavior in the case, he was doomed. Richard had lied under oath in one of his depositions. He'd taken the blame for the LOTU leader's death, claiming self-defense, to protect the man who'd saved his life by pulling the trigger—and who was on parole.

"I care for you enough to pretend I don't know anything," Samuel said. "As long as no one asks you about Clayton you still haven't lied, but I strongly recommend that you take that transfer to New York. Get as far away from her as you can, man. It's her or your career."

As the two men locked gazes, despair devoured Richard's soul.

How could he explain to Samuel that it was too late? Joy Clayton had become the only reason he looked forward to another day. She sustained his hope in humanity.

It might be a matter of time until they had to say goodbye. But for as brief of a time as he could enjoy her, he had to. "Sorry, Samuel, I can't. Not yet."

Samuel's deep sigh spoke of quiet desperation and resignation. "Then, man, for goodness' sake, be discreet. And remember, if you're ever caught, don't bring me down with you. I know nothing."

Samuel plodded out of the office, leaving Richard alone.

~

When Joy received Richard's text that something had come up at work and he'd be delayed, she had the feeling that the night would be canceled again.

"Hang in there a little longer," his last text said. *"I have one more errand to run."*

While she waited to hear back from him, she rescued her boys from Grandma Maureen's house to spend some time with them before their sleepover.

"Thanks for letting Tom and me borrow the boys," Hope said in the laundry room, while they tossed last minute additions into the kids' overnight bag. "They really help our project at the hotel—and deflect attention from me."

Joy felt grateful for Hope's new boyfriend, Tom—a single father of three she'd met at her last consulting job, re-launching a hotel chain in Orlando. Thanks to Tom, Hope was settling back in Florida after years of living in San Diego. For eternally single Hope, bringing her nephews to work was more than help testing the kid-friendly activities at the hotel. They were her ticket to fly under the radar while getting to know her future stepchildren.

"Are you sure you guys can handle six kids?" Joy asked as she replaced Edward's stained pajama top. Alex and Arthur sat in front of the TV waiting for the moment to get in the car. "Should I go with you?"

"Of course not! You know Super Dad Tom can handle an army." Hope started the laundry with the dirty towels. "We'll have a great time testing the new pool toys, and we'll bring the boys home to you tomorrow before dinner."

Edward disappeared onto the porch to jump on his mini trampoline, while Alex darted into the laundry room to tug on Joy's skirt, reminding her to pack his blankie. Joy searched for it among the clothes still in the dryer.

"I can't believe you have a night for yourself and you're still here with the kids," Hope whispered as she helped her search for the blanket. "For goodness' sake, woman, go *socialize!*"

"I will," Joy replied, emptying the dryer. "My mentor, Dr. Andrews, wants to give me his donation for the Hospice House." She glanced at her phone on the washer. No new messages from Richard, supporting her suspicion that the night was a no-go. "I might call him and ask if we should meet tonight."

Maybe that's what she needed. Nothing helped ground Joy's thoughts better than a casual chat with Carl. Over more than a decade he'd evolved from being her psychology professor and mentor, to her informal counselor and spiritual guide.

"I don't mean *that* type of socialization." Hope found the blanket and extended it to Alex, who hugged it in delight and ran back to the family room. "It kills me to see you stuck in this dead town with zero night life. Haven't you considered leaving behind all the bad memories and moving to a bigger city? Even Orlando would be a step up from here! And we'd be even closer."

Joy worked on sorting socks. "You know I can't relocate, sweetie. Maureen would never let me move her grandkids away from her."

"She can't force you to stay here!" Hope scoffed.

Wrinkling her nose, Joy tilted her head from side to side. "She can be persuasive. Besides her expertise in emotional blackmail, she also controls Michael's family trust—which Michael and I were planning to use for the kids' college education." She folded the twin's tiny shirts. "Maureen has insinuated that if I move away from her, my kids will lose their inheritance. I wouldn't care about the money for myself, but I can't deprive my children of what's theirs."

Hope grunted. "What a witch! When will she finally move to her house in Connecticut and leave you alone?"

"She won't do it unless the kids and I go with her." Joy transferred the folded shirts into the clean laundry basket.

"Moving in with the ex-mother-in-law? Yikes!" Hope cringed. "I can't think of a worse mood killer than that."

The silence that followed, and Hope's nonchalant expression as she folded laundry, hinted to Joy what she was about to say. "You know, it has been two years since Michael died…"

No, please. Not tonight.

With forced humor, Hope moved a hand, vaguely pointing at Joy's body. "Girl, by now you must have cobwebs *you-know-where.*" She lowered her hands and her countenance sobered. "Joy, when are you going to start dating?"

Darn it. Joy felt terrible hiding secrets from her sister. "Please, let's not talk about this again. Let me decide when I'm ready."

The sincere worry on Hope's face worsened Joy's guilt. "Sweetie, I'm your biggest fan. If the police ever knocked on my door and announced, 'Your sister Joy just murdered someone.' I'd answer, 'Well, if she did, she must've had a good reason—and I'm on her side.'"

Joy giggled, feeling thankful for her beloved sister. All those headaches Hope's rebellious youth had caused her had been worth it.

"So, yes, I trust that you're a bright woman, and an awesome shrink who'll know how to treat your own grief—and yada yada," Hope added. "I just don't want you to take so long that you waste your best years."

"Waste what best years?" Michael's voice scorned inside Joy's head. *"Those were gone a long time ago."*

"I wished you could be as happy as I am right now. You deserve to find love." Hope flung a sock from her pile at her sister. "And I won't say 'again' because you and I know you never really cared for Michael."

"That's not true; I did love him," Joy countered, organizing the folded clothes in the basket by sizes.

Hope rolled her eyes. "Let's face it, Michael was just the high school sweetheart you happened to be dating when Dad died, and you clung to him as something familiar in your life. Gosh, you were only fifteen!"

Joy felt her throat tighten at the memory. After their mother's death from cancer when she was only nine and Hope was eight, their father had sunk into a deep depression until his fatal heart attack six years later. "You were even younger than me when Mom and Dad died."

"At least I had *you* as my support all those years." Hope's voice softened. "But you didn't have anyone to do the same for you."

Joy's own tears surprised her. She'd done so much inner work since then, she could've sworn she was done healing. She discreetly dried her eyes with the sleeve of her emerald work dress.

"The bottom line is," Hope continued, "you should've never married the very first guy you dated. And I bet you wouldn't have, if most of your relationship hadn't been long distance during college and medical school—" Hope tapped her own forehead. "And *platonic* until the wedding night! Gosh! I still can't believe that! My sister the puritan!"

And what a horrible wedding night. Joy finished packing the kids' bag, avoiding Hope's eyes.

Hope had a point. Besides dating Michael for a decade before marrying him, Joy hadn't really gotten to know him deeply until it was too late. As a psychiatrist, she had plenty of theories of why she clung to him against her best instincts—starting with a need to save him from his depression because she hadn't been able to save Dad.

"Don't you think you deserve to live the experience of falling in love—and falling into temptation?" Hope asked. "The butterflies in your stomach when waiting for a phone call, your heart beating faster when you meet your man after time apart…"

Joy zipped the bag to avoid looking at her sister. *Well, I've sampled all that—and it's nerve-wracking.* "Maybe someday, Hope. I guess I'm just waiting for the universe to send me a sign."

The alert of a message on her cell got Joy's attention. She rushed to check it, excited to see it was a text from Richard.

All her hopes deflated when she read it. *"I'm so sorry. I'm being delayed even more."*

∼

Richard's last errand to run before meeting Joy was leaving Ray settled at his mother's house, so he wouldn't interrupt them again. But the boy had been in an unusually good mood lately—a rare privilege Richard treasured in his sulky teenager—and dinner out had extended longer than planned.

When dropping Ray off, Richard parked his car in front of his ex's driveway, feeling torn. It killed him to know his son was at the mercy of a woman as unreliable as Sandy. But she'd never agree to change the custody arrangements and give up any of her child support money. During the divorce proceedings almost eight years back, he'd regretfully relinquished most of the timeshare because his work as a new undercover agent kept him away too often.

He twisted in the driver's seat to face the boy and wrap up the conversation they'd had in the car. "Ray, I hate asking you to keep secrets, but Joy and I aren't ready to make our relationship public and I need to ask for your discretion. Do you understand?"

Ray placed a hand on his chest and playfully raised the other one. "No worries, Dad. Living with Mom has taught me to mind my own business and not ask any questions when I see something weird."

If it was a joke Richard didn't find it funny.

They exited the car into the warm evening and strolled toward the flamingo pink house. Being the long days of the summer, the sun had still not set at 8:00 p.m.

His mood sobering up, Ray asked, "Dad, does Joy know that you and I are moving to New York?"

Tensing, Richard stopped clear of the stone path to the front porch. "We still don't know if that's happening."

He was lying to himself. Richard's attempts to stop his transfer were comparable to the efforts of an ant trying to stop a train.

Damn it. And thinking about it, accepting the transfer to New York would be the easiest path to get control over Ray. The only way Sandy would agree to let him take Ray fast and painlessly was if he took him permanently, out of the state, so she could regain her freedom as a single woman.

"You know, I wouldn't mind staying," Ray said with a shrug.

"I'm still not convinced that the perks of New York City make up for not being able to surf." He waved a hand. "Well, see ya, Dad."

"Not so fast." Before Ray could sneak away, Richard embraced him. The boy startled and scanned the area around—God forbid anyone saw him being affectionate with his father. He then stayed still and tense, not making any effort to return the hug.

The instant Richard's arms loosened their grip, Ray darted away. "Bye, Dad!"

Richard smiled, watching Ray skip and jump on the stone path to the house—obviously happier about the hug than he'd ever admit. The energy that boy had!

He'd started texting Joy that he was on his way, when a feminine voice behind him called his name. "Richard Fields!"

For a second, his mind couldn't place the tall, attractive redhead addressing him, but soon his photographic memory matched her to the pictures he'd seen of her before, unleashing a surge of rage inside him.

Blair Sanders.

She walked toward him offering a handshake. "Agent Fields?"

"Has it occurred to you that you may get in trouble for stalking an FBI agent?" he snapped, ignoring her extended hand.

Moving her knuckles to her narrow waist, she tilted her head. "If you had the courtesy to answer my messages I wouldn't have to."

He strode away, leaving her behind.

She rushed to catch up with him; her tight pencil skirt and high heels slowing her down. "All I am asking for is ten minutes. Ten minutes of your time for an interview and a business proposal."

He ignored her and kept going to his car. She stopped and exclaimed, "I know you didn't really shoot the LOTU leader! You lied to protect the man who did it to save you."

Richard froze with the car door handle in his fingers.

His heart pounding, he pivoted to gape at the woman.

She continued, "My source is the clerk from the convenience

61

store where you were stabbed. He was hiding under the register and recorded a video with his cell of what really happened—I have that cell." Now that he'd stopped, she took her time strolling toward him and lowered her voice. "Another man pulled the trigger while the LOTU leader was attacking you. You agreed to take the blame so the man who saved you wouldn't go to jail for violating parole—which means you must've lied to the FBI under oath."

Caught by surprise, he was left speechless. He wished he'd said something sooner. By not having denied it immediately, he'd confirmed her words.

It was probably too late now, but he tried to remedy his error, forcing a scoff. "Have you been drinking?"

She simpered. "Not yet, but I'd love a drink if you care to join me."

CHAPTER 8

"*T*HIS ISN'T GOING TO WORK. LET'S JUST FORGET ABOUT IT.*"

Richard assimilated Joy's latest text on his burner cell, with the nagging fear she was canceling more than their date that night.

"Hang on. This won't take long," he fired back a response as quickly as his thumbs could manage.

At the Irish Pub, decorated with posters of old-fashioned liquor and beer ads, Blair Sanders drank the last sip of her whiskey and gestured for the waiter to bring her another one. She then addressed Richard, "How about you? Nothing to drink?"

Richard answered her with a murderous look.

She straightened his shirt collar and he held himself still, fighting the temptation to swat her hand. "I have to say, you're the hottest date I've had in a long while, but not the most cheerful," she commented.

"I don't enjoy being coerced into interviews—or dates," he replied coldly.

"Relax, Richard." She touched his arm. "I have no desire to use what I know to see you lose your job—or in jail. Our country needs more men like you serving."

She moved her thumb in circles, caressing his arm through the long sleeve of his shirt. The glow of desire in her eyes didn't escape his attention. *Unbelievable.* Did she really have the nerve to ruin his undercover career, ambush him with veiled blackmail threats, and now flirt with him?

He freed his arm. "Ms. Sanders, I've had a long day. If you

have something to ask, do it fast. Your ten minutes already started running."

From her purse, she extracted a folding tripod, mounted her cell phone on it and positioned it to record him.

She tapped a video app in her phone and began, "Richard Fields: hero and legend. Tell us about your life."

His flat tone advertised his boredom. "You need to be more specific than that."

"I'll tell you what I know and you'll help me fill in the rest," she said. "Richard David Fields, thirty-eight, born and raised in the Bronx. Divorced. You joined the NYPD as a patrol policeman at the young age of twenty. Your hard work and ambition earned you a recommendation for a Homicide detective position in record time, and that was eventually your gate to apply for the FBI."

He restrained himself from showing admiration. "You've done your homework."

"So you attended a community college and later on finished a bachelor's degree in Criminal Justice from an online university."

He snorted. "Not the most impressive CV, I know. I was the most surprised when my FBI application was accepted."

"Could it have something to do with those off-the-chart high IQ scores of yours?"

Frowning, he crossed his arms and leaned away. "How do you know about my IQ scores?"

"You'd be shocked how much I know about you." She winked at him. "I wouldn't have guessed that. No offense, but you look too hot and tough to be such a smart guy."

He shot her a glacial glare. "When the school you attend growing up has more bullies than kids to pick on you learn to hide such things."

She tittered. "Where did you go after the FBI accepted you?"

"After the training in Quantico, I went to the Tampa Field Office for my two-year probationary assignment and then transferred to Fort Sunshine. The rest is history."

"And what you hoped would be a two-year assignment has dragged on forever, because the Tampa SAC hates you for having screwed his daughter."

He glowered at her in silence, amazed by how much she knew. That wasn't the whole story. After his penalty, and right before the O'Hara case, Richard had been stuck in the area while leading an undercover investigation with a drug dealing gang based in Cape Canaveral.

"Is it true that the witness you rescued was Michael O'Hara's widow, Dr. Joy Clayton?" Sanders blurted out.

He kept his expression impassive at her sudden change in subject. "Why are you asking me now, if you and your colleagues already published everywhere that she was?"

She turned off the recording. "Are you seeing someone right now?" The seduction in her voice was so far from subtle something didn't compute.

"If you are turning off the camera, I'll assume the interview is over and I'm free to go." He signaled for the waiter to bring the check, ignoring her offer to share it. He'd never felt comfortable letting a woman pay for a bill. That was one of the reasons why his credit cards were about to explode.

She caught his arm to prevent him from leaving, and he sighed in exasperation. "Sanders, what do you want from me?"

She drew spirals on his chest with her finger. "I'm still trying to figure that out. What would *you* like from me?"

He withdrew from her touch. The senior couple next to their table left the place and their waiter was gone. The few other customers in the pub were far enough away he felt safe speaking in a whisper. "I want your assurance that what you know will stay a secret. But I'm afraid that if you came to me it was because you're looking for something in exchange. Blair, who else knows about this?"

"No one." She shook her head. "The store clerk sold me the phone and moved back to Mexico, traumatized by what he'd witnessed. But don't get any ideas; a friend of mine has a copy of the video in a sealed envelope, with instructions to mail it to the FBI if anything happens to me."

Richard scoffed. "You've watched too many movies; I'm not planning to kill you. How much is it worth for you? The phone. Any copies you've made of the video. Your silence."

Easing back onto her seat, she made him wait for her answer. "It's not about money. I've been dying to reconnect with you for years."

Reconnect? Do I know her from before? Richard's photographic memory scanned his brain files further back, but couldn't find any memories of her before the press leak. Was she lying?

"And, also," she added. "I have a client who wants to hire you."

Richard shot her a mistrusting look. "A client? I thought you were a reporter."

She tilted her head. "No one can make a living as a freelance reporter anymore. I moonlight for a couple of private investigators. My client is the owner of a"—she made air quotes with her fingers—"*'private security firm.'* He's in need of someone like you to work as a private eye."

"Why didn't he approach me directly?"

"He's a former FBI agent; he can't actively recruit someone from the Bureau. Also, he was afraid you'd say no, and I assured him you and I had a past together and I had ways to convince you."

Richard kept digging in his memory, but still couldn't remember having met Sanders before. "What's in it for you?"

"A recruiter's fee. The pleasure of working with you from time to time…" She briefly touched his chest and the flash of desire shone again in her eyes. When he didn't answer, she continued, "This man pays well. I strongly recommend you listen to his offer. It includes a generous signing bonus—it would help with that credit card debt."

Richard's senses heightened. He didn't give her the pleasure of asking how she knew about his credit card debt.

Is this the answer to all my problems? Quit the FBI, instead of living in the fear of getting fired? He could confess his involvement with Joy and use that as his excuse for his resignation. With luck, since there was no disciplinary action to decide upon, they'd leave it there.

Except that Sanders would still know his secret. And something told him she wasn't going to let it go.

"Blair, your proposal sounds too good to be true. I have the feeling you're omitting something."

She played with the ice in her drink. "I guess I should add that my client is currently working for the O'Hara family."

Richard's jaw clenched. He'd die before he worked for that monster's family.

"Maureen O'Hara—O'Hara's mother—is appalled by the rumors that her son was involved with the LOTU," Sanders explained. "She's convinced that the FBI is using him as a scapegoat to cover up for someone else. She'll go to any distance and spare no money to prove that he was innocent."

Richard shot her an appalled once-over. *Except he wasn't.* "Allow me to remind you the FBI has never released any official information accusing O'Hara—you were the reason for the press leak."

She flicked a wrist. "What do I know? You guys at the FBI are obviously hiding something. This woman is determined to uncover the truth about her beloved son's death. Yes, this may be a dead-end. Yes, this may take years. But who am I to criticize what rich people pour their money into?"

Sanders had to be crazy if she thought he had any intention of considering that offer.

Smiling, she tapped her fingers on the table. "Think about it and give me an answer during our next date."

"And I assume I have no say in whether we get to have a next date or not," he asked, scowling.

She rose from her chair and leaned toward him. "You assume correctly." Before he could react, she kissed him on the cheek. Then, she scooped up her purse and sauntered out of the bar, swinging her hips and clicking her heels on the laminate floor.

He stayed at the table for a moment, still stunned, processing the meeting before heading out of the bar. As he shuffled to his car, overwhelm rose and peaked inside him; the pulsating ache in his right temple heralded one of his infamous migraines.

Dropping himself onto the driver's seat, he buried his face in his hands.

I'm doomed.

He'd researched Blair Sanders after her article. Her first push to fame in journalism had been sinking the career of a senator she was having an affair with. After that, she'd been involved in more than one scandal, usually related to her becoming obsessed with and stalking a public figure, then using what she discovered to ruin him.

And now it was his turn. Blair Sanders was obsessed with him— only God knew why. He had the feeling she wouldn't stop until she drove him crazy.

Yet another reason to run away from Fort Sunshine.

Only then did he notice Joy's last message on his phone. *"It's too late to try to meet now. Let's forget about it. Good night."*

The short lines felt like a painful blow on top of an injury, knocking down the last of his energy.

Who am I kidding? We're coming to an end sooner than later.

He needed to put distance between himself and Sanders, and hope that once he was out of the picture, she'd move her fixation to someone else.

He had no choice. He had to accept the transfer to New York.

CHAPTER 9

A FTER KEEPING HER AWAKE ALL NIGHT, JOY'S MIND STILL drummed the next morning as she drove to Carl's house. He'd invited her to come chat over breakfast, since he'd be leaving town later that day. The silent car ride helped her ruminate on her thoughts, and by the time she arrived at the luxurious riverside residence, she'd reached a conclusion. She couldn't live in this anxiety, hiding her relationship with Richard from the world. Furthermore, she couldn't keep allowing him to risk his job because of her. She had to be the one to take the plunge and request they stop seeing each other.

As she followed Carl's instructions for parking in his garage, unexpected tears ran down her cheeks. She stayed in her red Prius for a few moments, letting them flow, trying to recompose herself before facing her mentor. Then, she dried her eyes with the hem of the sleeveless turquoise blouse she wore with jeans and headed to the house entrance, pressing the wall switch on the way, to close the garage door.

"It's so good to see you again, dear!" The moment Carl greeted her with a hug, Joy's spirit felt transiently restored. He was the master who'd once taught her how to heal souls with loving touch. If Joy could've chosen her father, she would've chosen Carl Andrews.

Sitting at his back porch, facing the Indian River, they talked over a breakfast of almond-milk oatmeal with berries and nuts—Carl ate no animal products. As a big treat, he'd made coffee for her—Carl considered caffeine a mood-altering substance and abstained from it, except for green tea.

Joy still marveled at how two people as different as eccentric, New-Agey Carl and herself—raised in the most traditional Christian upbringing imaginable—could've ever connected that well. But over the years he'd encouraged her to leave and take from his teachings, while often agreeing to disagree. For example, she still preferred the word "God" over Carl's favorite word "The Universe." And it didn't matter how many fancy names Carl gave to the process of "connecting with the creating energy," Joy would always call it "praying."

Jumping from one subject to another, they'd arrived at the topic of saving the Hospice House. "My colleague Dr. Patel has great suggestions on how to use the media attention around me to attract sponsors," Joy said, adding Stevia to her coffee. Maybe if she poured all her time into this project, she'd distract herself from the pain of breaking up with Richard. "And Dr. Young, a local dermatologist related to Michael, has offered to help me too."

"It sounds good."

"But I'm torn about taking either of their offers. I wish I never had to discuss Michael again." Joy sipped her coffee and her thoughts flew to Richard, flooding her with bittersweet sadness. Richard made the best coffee in the world; just one more of the things she'd miss about him.

"My dear, you know the drill," Carl said. "What's the first question you have to ask yourself before starting any journey?"

On another, less melancholic day, she would've smiled at Carl's favorite question. She drew in a lungful. "What do you *really* want?"

"Yes. What do you—the real you—want? Do you feel passionate about either of the two options your colleagues are offering you?"

Joy stopped to think as Carl's decision-making algorithm came back to her. "Neither."

He shrugged. "The best compass to know if you've found your right path is passion."

Passion. Despair rose within her, clogging her throat. She'd never felt more passion in her life than she'd felt with Richard—yet she knew she had to leave him, for his own good.

But she couldn't talk to Carl about her romantic trouble. "Hasn't passion caused enough damage in the world?" she asked. "What happens when the same thing you're passionate about could potentially hurt someone you love?"

Carl reclined in his chair. "I hope you're not talking about hurting feelings. That has little to do with you, and everything to do with the other person's unresolved issues."

She denied with her head. "No, I mean hurting them for real."

"We're all one," Carl replied. "You can't try to hurt someone without hurting yourself—without sooner or later paying the karmic bill. That was the biggest point the LOTU forgot from my teachings." He stopped as if searching for the right words. "But passion is only harmful if you're following the passions of your ego. Not of your heart."

"My heart is not reliable lately; it seems to have turned selfish, focusing on its own happiness." Her lips trembled and the traitorous tears brimmed again in her eyes. *If I were truly selfless, I would've focused on my kids and ended this relationship long ago.*

His voice softened. "My dear, searching for happiness is not selfish; it's one of the main reasons we are here. If you think that someone else's happiness is more important than your own, you're missing the point. We are all cells in the body of The Universe. By making one person happy, you benefit the whole world. That includes making *yourself* happy."

Joy processed his words slowly.

Carl narrowed his eyes and leaned closer. "But, dear, I have the feeling we're no longer talking about the Hospice House."

Blushing, Joy shrank into her seat, wishing to disappear. "I'm sorry, Carl, but you're like a father to me. I can't ask you for romantic advice."

He suppressed his amusement. "Okay, then. Change of subject. Let's talk about why I asked you to come over." He picked up an envelope from the table and extended it to her. "My donation for the Hospice House."

She opened the envelope and gasped at the amount on the check. "Carl, this is too much! Are you sure about this?"

The corners of his mouth twitched up. "It's not as generous as it might seem."

"Yes, it is!" She lifted the check. "This can keep the Hospice House going for months."

"And that's my purpose. I wanted you to feel free from fundraising for a little while." He served himself more tea. "I calculated your hourly wages as a physician, estimated the amount of time you had to spend fundraising, and added that amount to my donation. For the next couple of months, I want to hire your services for a project that will also help you in your spiritual growth."

Joy leaned forward, attentive. It had been years since he'd last assigned her a spiritual exercise. "I'm listening."

"Do you remember those times I asked you to tutor other students on my principles?"

Her lips curved up, a warm feeling spreading in her chest. She'd once relished helping Carl train new followers, before kids and work—and Michael quitting Carl's group—forced her to stop.

"This is my request," Carl said. "I'd like you to donate a few hours of your week to help me tutor one of my new students. It's something I know you enjoy and also works for a greater cause."

The idea was so exciting she didn't even ask herself where she'd find time to squeeze it in. This had to be the answer to her prayers on finding how to get Richard off her mind. "I'd love to do that! Who's the new student?"

"Hello, Carl, anybody home?"

Joy stiffened at the familiar voice behind her. She rose from her chair and turned around to face Richard, confirming by his expression that he shared her surprise.

"Perfect timing!" Carl beamed. "Richard, I would like to introduce you to your new tutor."

CHAPTER 10

SAGGING INTO THE COUCH IN CARL'S LIVING ROOM, RICHARD felt as if his head spun around. When Carl texted him to come over that morning, he'd never expected him to offer Joy as Laura Bonas' replacement.

Richard had never met a more complicated—and sometimes sadistic—spiritual master than Carl Andrews. As if Carl didn't know that working with Joy without being able to touch her would be torture for Richard. This had to be some scheme to push them together—supported by the fact that Carl had just left them alone, claiming he had a plane to catch.

A text on his burner cell got Richard's attention. *"This is Pitbull."*

The man Richard had been protecting by blaming himself for the death of the LOTU leader had received his message. That man was the only person in the world more interested than him in silencing Blair Sanders about what she knew.

"This is Guardian. But I can't talk now," he replied. Then, he quickly texted the address of an abandoned building where they could meet. They had to plan a way to break into Sanders' house and recover the phone with the video.

"You okay?" Joy's voice brought him back. She seemed to have sensed his blue mood and his tension.

As he put the phone away, he nodded, without answering. He couldn't tell her about Blair Sanders and his secret. And he couldn't tell her about New York—not yet.

"Everything okay with Ray? It worried me when you texted me that something had come up with him."

Of course, Joy would pour compassion and nurturing over any recrimination about their canceled night. "He's fine. I'm sorry about last night," he said sincerely. "I took Ray to dinner, trying to make sure he wouldn't interrupt us later, and it took longer than I thought." At least that was true.

"That explains why you look so blue today." Understanding lit up her face. "It always brings you down to drop him off at his mom's."

It was not untrue, so he nodded. "I hate knowing she's not taking good care of him."

Unexpectedly, she rose from her seat and sat next to him on the sofa.

"You're a great father." She reached for his hand. "I love to see how attentive you are when you take care of him."

He melted into the delight of her touch and his body relaxed. "He's my weak spot. I'd do anything for him." *And now I have a second one: you. I'm not used to having so many weak spots.*

He tugged on her hand softly to bring her closer, but she released his fingers and moved away from him, back to the armchair.

"So, is Carl serious?" she asked, clasping the armrests and leaning away from him. "You really need help understanding his principles for the case? And if I did agree to help, can you guarantee my identity would be concealed?"

He nodded. "The FBI only knows that we'll be using help from one of Carl's followers who has requested to remain unidentified—it would be the same as an anonymous consultant. At the same time, we'd conceal from you the identity of the author of the document we need to interpret." He wondered why they were wasting time babbling about the case; he just wanted to take her in his arms and kiss her. But he could sense in her tense posture that the wall between them was thicker than ever.

And what was the point anyway? Now that he'd decided to accept the transfer to New York, trying to continue their relationship would prolong the agony. How could Carl even propose shoving them together into this?

Without moving from the couch, he reached for the folder with Hayes' writings he'd brought over and extended it to her.

She picked up the folder, browsed some pages and returned it to him across the coffee table. "I'm sorry, I can't decipher this handwriting."

"It took me a while too." *What are we doing? This is never going to work.* Feeling like every drop of energy had been drained from him, he picked a random page and read aloud, "Don't run away from the darkness. It will only make it stronger."

To his surprise, she recited the next lines word by word. "'Your mind is a labyrinth made of more rooms and hallways than you perceive. Your soul is, too.' That means that for every conscious thought you have and for every aspect of your personality you manifest, there is a shadow. An unconscious part of you, pulling you down. And you first have to confront what's hidden in the dark, before you can fully master the art of creating with your thoughts."

He gaped at her, unable to reply for a moment. Had she really explained in seconds what had taken him months of work with Carl to start grasping? He shuffled the pages and read another passage. "Your divine origin entitles you to power over nature."

She squinted in concentration. "I never heard Carl say anything like that."

Oh well, maybe the first one had been a fluke.

"But," she added, "that's something Michael used to say."

Richard's pulse sped up as the realization hit him. Joy not only had knowledge of Carl's theories, but she'd also been married to one of the LOTU leaders. She wasn't "the next best thing to Carl" to help him understand these principles.

She was *better* than Carl.

The rush of adrenaline that always overcame him when he found a new lead raced through him. He straightened in his seat. "Let me make some coffee and let's go over a few of these pages."

∼

An hour later, on her third cup of coffee and hyped up on caffeine, Joy had kicked off her heels and now curled up with her feet on her chair. She and Richard were reviewing Carl's unpublished book of principles, *Manufacturing Miracles: Nothing is Impossible*. Every new topic led to a detour, which deviated to another topic, in a non-stop flow of conversation—sometimes a dead-serious argument and heated debate, sometimes a hilarious joke.

Richard sprawled on the black leather couch with his long legs on the coffee table. That man didn't claim a seat—he ravished it. "I hate it when Carl talks in riddles and makes me doubt even the most obvious things." Lifting an eyebrow, he touched the table and spoke with fake gravity. "Are you *sure* there's a table here?" He narrowed his eyes and imitated Carl's precise enunciation. "Or is this a projection of your deepest thoughts and your childhood traumas?"

Joy laughed. She'd missed the relaxed chats she and Richard used to have—she almost didn't mind that back then he'd used a fake identity to coax information from her. "This chapter is not that difficult, if you suspend your disbelief for a moment and accept a few assumptions." She took another sip of almond milk latte—darn it, it was delicious. Richard did make the best coffee. "The first assumption is, we're not who we seem to be. We're eternal spirits taking a temporary trip to this world, riding in avatar bodies. Everything happening to us here is nothing but a dream. And if you know you're dreaming—if you become a lucid dreamer—you can make anything happen by evoking it with your thoughts."

He squinted, formulating his answer, and her heart skipped a beat. There he was—the man she'd fallen in love with. Her debate partner; her favorite person in the world to have a stimulating conversation with. "So our problem is that instead of thinking about what we want, we dwell on what we *don't* want—thus making it happen."

"Exactly!" She spread her fingers. "That also explains why some people seem to be stuck in a nightmare, eternally miserable, while someone right next to them, in the same circumstances, is happy. It's like all of us are living a small separate dream."

He swung his feet off the table and leaned forward. "That theory is too simplistic. It implies that all is relative and everything is in our minds. But there *are* forces in motion that are real, black and white, and affect us all in the world, like good and evil."

She shook her head. "Be very careful when defining 'good' and 'evil.' Remember the chapter we just read?" She searched for a page of Carl's book on the table. "'Every light has its shadow; and fighting it is senseless.' There, Carl means that no one in this world is fully good or fully evil. We're all a mixture of light and darkness."

"I've heard him say it, and I disagree." He slid to the end of the couch to be closer to her. "Of course, some people are purely evil. Remember Hitler?"

She looked heavenward. "Come on! Everybody turns to the same argument. Can we please leave Hitler out and call him an exception to the rule? Short of legendary dictators and rulers, can you honestly say you know anyone—alive today—who doesn't have at least a little bit of good in them?"

Richard nodded. "Yes, I do. Joshua Levenstein."

Tough one. She fidgeted with the shoulder strap of her empire-waist turquoise top while thinking of an answer. "I know he's hard to digest but trust me, he's not purely evil either. Did you know he's one of the biggest financial sponsors for the Hospice House?"

"Come on." He cracked up and she melted at the sight of his gorgeous laugh lines. His fingers reached for her wrist, sending an electric charge up her arm. "He obviously only does that to score points with you."

Her chest fluttering, she used the excuse of turning a page on the book to discreetly free her wrist. "Fine, if you don't want to give him credit for that, here's another one. Did you know he has a dog he adores? It's an old beagle called Brownie he's had for sixteen years and no one knows why it hasn't died yet."

Richard extended his hand to help straighten her strap and casually caressed her shoulder on the way. "That's easy, the dog sold his soul to the Devil—he did the day he accepted that master."

Goose bumps spread over her arms. She held in a nervous giggle and softly pushed his hand away. "Be serious. My point is…" She leaned back in her seat and slid her chair away, increasing the distance between them. "There's no such thing as good guys and bad guys. There are enlightened people and unenlightened people. And it's our mission in this transient trip through this life to help enlighten the unenlightened."

He moved to the chair closer to hers. "That contradicts everything I've based my career on. You seem to forget that my job is to bring justice against evil people."

She was used to their debates, but it was difficult to come up with an answer. His knee pressed against hers, throwing off her concentration. *Is he doing this on purpose?* "What if instead of seeing them as evil people, you saw them through the lens of compassion," she finally said. "Most criminals became outlaws because they were victims in the first place. Have you ever tried to imagine the criminal as someone who was abused in childhood?"

He frowned, as if reflecting. He then extended a finger and moved the hair away from her face, making her flush at his touch. "I also know plenty of people who were abused in childhood and turned out to be decent and honest. Once someone chooses the path of crime they shouldn't be cut any slack. They need to be locked up—or killed."

The debate about the death penalty was also an ongoing topic between them. She made an effort to focus on the conversation instead of the heat spreading through her body as his hand slid from her cheek to the side of her neck. "Don't let the illusion of separation get you," she argued. "We're all cells in the same body—with different roles, but meant to work together. If you try to cut your own arm, you'll suffer. It's the same with other human beings. If you try to hurt or kill others, you'll be hurting yourself."

His hand skimmed down her neck onto her collarbone, getting dangerously close to her chest and making her breath catch. She stood up abruptly and stepped away, trying to recompose herself.

"Wow, that was fun," he commented picking up the pages from the table and returning them to the folder.

"I know," she reluctantly agreed, hoping he was referring to their chat and not the way he'd flustered her. "I wouldn't mind doing that work every day."

His face lit up as he lifted it toward her. "Does this mean you accept the job as my tutor and anonymous consultant?"

She eyed him with caution, then looked away and busied herself picking up her purse and sunglasses from the marble kitchen counter. "Do you think that would be a good idea?"

He rose and held her arm to walk her to the garage. "It would be a great idea. You helped me understand more in this hour than I've gotten from Carl in months. And considering you're the person most interested in seeing this case closed, I think it's a win-win situation."

His casual tone would've fooled Joy in the past. But she knew better now. The man holding her arm—making her pulse race and her legs wobble with his touch—was a professional actor and an expert liar. The same one who'd practically hypnotized her to join him in bed for the first time "just to cuddle."

As they arrived at her car in the dark garage, he commented, "Well, I'll text you later to coordinate our first meeting." He leaned toward her and she took a step back, escaping his kiss.

Tell him, she urged herself. *Tell him that you've already decided you shouldn't see each other anymore.*

But he did have a point. The LOTU case had been a nightmare, and she wanted to see it solved more than anyone.

"Okay, Richard, I'll help you," she conceded. "But if we'll be working together, it's best that we keep a distance from each other."

She sent him a message with her eyes that she wasn't kidding.

"It makes all the sense to me." Despite his words, he took a step forward and wrapped her in his arms, burying his face in her hair.

Darn it, it felt wonderful. His strong arms around her, his firm, warm chest, his masculine smell… Joy felt as if every shred of her will were stripped away. Against her orders her arms rose to encircle his torso and she stayed still, savoring the embrace and enduring the agony all at once. Waves of desire washed over her with every shared breath.

"This feels so right, doesn't it?" she whispered as if talking to herself.

"I know." His low, raspy voice hinted he experienced a similar torture. He separated her from his chest just enough to look at her. She trembled under the bewitching power of that hazel gaze. "And do you know the best part? We're off the clock right now." Slowly, his face moved toward hers.

He kissed her. Right? She wasn't completely sure she hadn't been the one who moved the last inch to make their lips meet. He kissed her softly, gently and undemanding. But the tension of his muscles and the grip of his hand behind her head showed he made an effort to restrain himself. Her traitorous tongue deepened the kiss and she regretted it almost instantly. He sensed her abandon and his kiss escalated to fierce, his mouth devouring hers while his arms enfolded her, pressing her against his hard body.

She was breathless, dizzy, and wobbly when he broke the kiss.

He seemed unsteady too as he backed away, a hint of pride on his face. "Well, I'll let you go now. I can't wait to work with you, my anonymous consultant." With one last devilish smirk, he re-entered the house.

Joy's hands trembled when she pressed the button to open the garage door and her legs felt shaky when she walked to her car. Her fingers refused to respond for a while when she tried to turn on the engine and she needed to recompose herself for a few moments before she felt ready to drive.

Had she really agreed to work with Richard?

I am in deep trouble.

CHAPTER 11

"I REPEAT. MY CLIENT IS TAKING THE FIFTH AMENDMENT. HE can't be incriminated by choosing to remain silent." Levenstein's lawyer dried perspiration from his balding head with a handkerchief. No wonder he felt hot, the man wore a heavy wool business suit and, despite the sauna-like conditions outside, the AC in Levenstein's house was set to minimum power.

The unproductive meeting felt like déjà vu from their interviews with Young and Xenos an hour ago—or rather their lawyers, as they'd also refused to say a word. At least the earlier parties had met Richard and Samuel at the FBI office; Levenstein had insisted they come to him.

What a waste of time this day has been.

Sinking in the brown leather chair, Richard checked the antique clock on the home office wall. The babbling of the lawyer faded into background noise. He was counting the hours until his meeting with Joy tomorrow to translate Hayes' manuscripts. Every bit of willpower he'd gathered to step away from her had vanished after that encounter at Carl's house. The more pain his psyche felt about their uncertain future, the more her presence became his best anesthetic.

Beside relishing her challenging conversation, he looked forward to what could happen afterward. How much longer could she hold on to her "hands-off" rule? Just the hope of making her cave in curved his lips against his will.

Who was this pitiful guy, daydreaming about soft petite hands and sensual lips all day long?

"…And since you have no real charge to make an arrest, except rumors, we demand that you stop approaching my client unless and until you have something concrete against him."

Richard's brief flash of good mood evaporated quickly as the lawyer's voice brought him back from his musings and into the lavishly decorated home office where they sat. Next to his attorney, Levenstein seemed to suppress a smirk at the futility of the meeting. Richard felt like punching the smug off the doctor's face.

He inhaled deeply, calming his frustration as an idea brimmed. He suspected Levenstein's megalomania would be his perdition.

Reaching into his pocket, Richard extracted his FBI badge and set it on the ebony desk, then did the same with his concealed gun.

"I need to have a word with Josh, man to man. Alone."

The lawyer startled and Samuel shot Richard an inquiring glance. With his eyes fixed on Levenstein, Richard continued, "We both know we need to clear the air about some things before we can move on. Talk to me. Off the record. Doors closed. No badges, no cameras, no titles. Nothing we say to each other will be admissible in court."

The two men locked eyes, the cold silence broken by the lawyer's tense chortles. "With all respect, I'm going to need to interrupt this dramatic display of—"

"I'll do it," Levenstein cut him off.

Richard hid his amusement. He knew the challenge would be too much for the man to resist.

Color drained from the lawyer's cheeks. "Dr. Levenstein. You need to let me handle—"

The doctor lifted a hand and slowly turned to face the attorney with narrowed eyes. "I'm not an idiot like most of your clients. I can handle Mr. James Bond-complex here."

The lawyer's head vibrated as he shook it frantically. "It's my strong professional advice—"

Levenstein signaled him to stop again. "I've put up with enough of your bad breath and ugly face for one morning. Take a break and go check if your wife is cheating on you with the mailman again."

The attorney winced and Richard held his breath. It wasn't easy to make a dent in a thick-skinned lawyer, but Josh Levenstein had a gift for demoralizing people.

Recovering, the lawyer spread his fingers. "Then do as you please." Clearing his throat, he picked up his briefcase and left.

Richard suddenly understood the word "karma" in a new light. Levenstein was digging his own grave. Not even his lawyer cared for him enough to help him.

~

Joy's favorite part of living in Florida was that here she always felt young. Here, seventy-five was the new fifty, and your eighties could still make it to the countdown of the best years of your life. The Hospice House was testament to that.

As Joy arrived at the Hospice House that morning, she had to stop frequently to answer greetings and give hugs. Scattered around a central courtyard within the three-building complex, elderly residents and daycare attendants busied themselves with painting classes, beginner yoga stretches, or sharing breakfast at garden tables. Every patient greeted Joy with delight, as if she were a close friend they shared a secret connection with. Witnessing their cheerfulness, an outsider could've never guessed they had some form of terminal illness, from cancer to advanced age.

The outdoor speakers played ABBA's "Dancing Queen," one of her favorite songs, and Joy felt the sudden urge to dance.

Pushing the cart with the food trays, Malcolm, the oldest resident and her dance partner at all the patient parties, waved hello. On impulse she dropped her purse, extended her arm and bowed. Immediately understanding the invitation, the beaming shrunken man dropped the pack of napkins in his hand, grabbed her arm and joined her in a cheerful dance—surprisingly smooth and graceful for his advanced age. Soon, they were surrounded by a group of delighted patients and staff, watching them and clapping.

Joy couldn't remember the last time she'd been in such a good mood. Her first work meeting with Richard had left her exhilarated. She'd delighted in their conversation and relished discovering what was inside his mind—this time without fake identities. Every new glimpse of him fascinated her more.

And of course, there was also the constant anticipation, wondering if—or when—she'd lose the battle of resisting him. From a casual touch to a stolen kiss… if that man only knew the power he had over her.

The song came to an end and Joy and Malcolm bowed and threw kisses in the air, while the small crowd clapped and cheered.

Joy picked up her purse. As she headed to her office, Ava, the office manager, handed her a phone message. Joy scanned the pink paper in confusion.

"What's that?" Dr. Patel asked, approaching at that moment.

"Apparently, it's a hospital consult," Joy replied, still in disbelief. She hadn't gotten one of those in ages.

"I thought you don't round on the hospital anymore."

She groaned with frustration, remembering something. "I agreed to cover the hospital's Ethics Committee while Dr. McDevitt attends a medical conference." She resumed walking toward her office and the doctor followed her. "He reassured me it was very unlikely they'd ever have a consult."

Patel chuckled. "And of course, the minute he leaves, a consult arrives. Isn't it always like that?"

As she entered the office, she read the details of the message. *Rachel Hayes, ICU bed 3. Consult regarding withdrawing ventilator support.* The name didn't ring a bell.

"Changing subjects, you're not going to believe this," Patel grumbled. "I ran into Levenstein at the coffee shop earlier and he said that he'd be stopping by Friday 'to bring a donation for the Hospice House'—he's got a lot of nerve, joking about that!"

"It's not a joke." Joy left her purse on the maroon recliner in a corner of her office and sat behind her old L-shaped desk. She liked this office, decorated in soft pinks and rose gold, so much more than the fancier one at the private center. "Josh made a generous contribution last quarter."

Patel flopped onto one of the office chairs facing the desk. "I'd rather see this place collapse than take anything from that man!" His dark eyes fixed on Joy. "When are we going to meet again about our fundraising plans and our grief campaign?"

Joy tensed up. That project was the last thing she wanted to do right now—or ever. She paused reviewing the pile of mail on her desk to look at him. "Actually, Venkat, I've been having second thoughts about that."

Worry lines creased his forehead. "I sensed you might be hesitant to pursue that project."

Joy exhaled. "I just don't want to have to talk about Michael in public again."

"I'm sorry, maybe it was insensitive on my part to suggest it." He patted her hand resting on the desk. "You've put on such a brave face sometimes I forget all that's been going on in your life."

"Don't worry. We'll find another way." Joy returned her attention to the mail and, noticing an envelope without a return address, her pulse sped up with anticipation. Had Richard mailed her something again? Her excited fingers tore up the envelope.

"If I were in your situation, I would've left town a long time ago," Patel commented. "I can only imagine how every corner of this city reminds you of your late husband."

Disappointment turned into dread as Joy extracted a floral greeting card from the envelope. The moment she opened it and read the words, ice filled her veins and fear gnawed at her stomach.

"Michael is watching you, and he's closer than you think."

CHAPTER 12

RICHARD FOLLOWED LEVENSTEIN TO A ROOM THAT SEEMED TO be a man cave, judging by the pool table, the wet bar, and the large screen TV. After his beefy bodyguard searched Richard for hidden microphones and confiscated his cell phones, Levenstein addressed the man. "You, what's-your-face, give us ten minutes then come in." He removed his business jacket and threw it at the man, who caught it midair. "In the meantime, go tell the cow in the kitchen to take this to the dry cleaners."

Richard was still musing on the man's rudeness toward his employees when Levenstein leaned over a dog bed in a corner of the room and patted an ancient beagle with affection. "How's my good boy?"

The dog seemed old and tired—maybe sick, as it made no effort to get up from the bed—but it moved its tail joyfully in response to Levenstein's touch and licked his hand. For a moment, the man transformed from the arrogant doctor Richard knew into a loving dog owner, worried about the health of his pet.

Faint compassion trickled in Richard's heart, but he bottled it up. His success as an agent depended on keeping emotions in check.

The doctor walked to the wet bar and reached for a bottle of brandy. "Do you want a drink, since we've established that you are off duty?"

"Let's cut the pleasantries and get to the point." Richard moved in front of Levenstein and pierced him with his infamous glare. "A few months back, you saw me working undercover with Dr. Clayton.

Later on we met again and you learned I was an FBI agent, but you pretended not to recognize me. You didn't want to bring attention upon yourself because you *are* involved in O'Hara's death."

Levenstein snickered. "Or maybe you're less memorable than you think." He served himself a drink. "I see over a hundred patients a week. I'm so busy making sure I don't kill any of them, I don't even look at people's faces."

Without transition, Richard said, "You had personal reasons to want O'Hara dead. You wanted his wife."

The doctor froze and his eyebrows flicked up in surprise.

Richard continued, "I'm not blind. I've seen you flirt with Dr. Clayton."

Gathering himself, the man paced away. "You're wrong. I'd never dare to aspire to a woman like Joy Clayton. Angels don't play with demons like you and me." He held eye contact for a moment and Richard wondered if he knew about him and Joy.

Levenstein continued, "Joy is a different species than you and I are. She's a new... gold standard in love and compassion. Something I have no intention to ever become, but that I respect. Compared to her, you and I are nothing but scum."

"I can't disagree with that," Richard conceded. "But answer the question. Do you admit that you had a personal reason to see Michael O'Hara dead?"

Before answering, the doctor took a long sip from his drink. "Michael!" His lips twisted in a cold smirk. "You remind me so much of him."

That felt like a gut punch. "Never compare me with that monster," Richard spoke between his teeth.

"You do. You have the same attitude he used to have." He waved his free hand vaguely around Richard's body. "You have his same arrogance. His narcissism. His two-faced tendencies."

Richard chuckled. "Arrogance? Narcissism? Look who's talking. At least I'm not a murderer, like you."

"Really?" Levenstein gave him a once-over. "I heard you killed two men in the operation rescuing Dr. Clayton. Doesn't that make *you* a murderer?"

Richard took a step back and gaped at the man without an answer.

The doctor clicked his tongue. "You think you're so morally superior to me, just because you carry a badge. Let me tell you, my friend, most cops I've ever met—local or federal—took that job for the pleasure of hurting others. You want the legal blessing of walking around with a gun, intimidating people."

Rage boiled inside Richard. He summoned Joy's words and dug in his memory for anything good he could find in Levenstein. He focused on the image of the loving dog owner. He grasped for some feeling of compassion.

He got nothing.

As he tried to recompose himself, he remembered his recent talk with Joy and had an idea. "You might be right; maybe that's why I became a law enforcer. After all, our conscious thoughts are only the tip of an iceberg. And our mind is a labyrinth..." He stopped, as if trying to recall a word.

Levenstein filled in. "A labyrinth with more rooms and hallways than we can imagine."

I got you.

With his answer, the man had just confirmed Richard's suspicion that he was or had been part of the LOTU.

At that moment, the door opened and Levenstein's bodyguard entered the room. The tall, blond man stood next to the doctor with his arms crossed.

"Well, I guess time's up. You have to go," Levenstein said. "But to show you I have nothing against you—"

He extended his hand in offer. Richard hesitated for a moment, then shook it.

To his surprise, Levenstein gestured as if to hug him. He wrapped one hand around his shoulders and patted his back. Placing his mouth near Richard's ear he whispered, "Don't mess with me, Bond. I'm a powerful man and I know where your son lives."

A burst of horror wrenched Richard's stomach. Before he could react to the words, the bodyguard clasped his arm and dragged him away.

～

Construction cranes and scaffolding were an eternal presence at Holloway Medical Center—the latest project being replacing all windows for hurricane resistant ones. Yet, for all the millions the hospital had invested on renovation, they still kept the same ancient elevators that drove Joy crazy. Even when they were in service, the elevators moved so slow that half the patients would've died if the doctors waited for them.

Not the most athletic person, Joy had to stop mid-stairwell to rest during her climb to the ICU on the fourth floor. This Ethics Committee consult had thrown off her whole day. She didn't have time for lunch or getting in touch with Richard. She needed to talk to him about those two greeting cards she'd received. Should she call the police? Or was she overreacting to a bad practical joke?

After Joy swiped her ID to enter the ICU double doors, she stopped at the physicians' workroom. She logged into the computer and read the patient's records.

Rachel Hayes, fifty-three-year-old woman initially admitted with a cardiac block, then complicated with hospital-acquired sepsis. A neurological evaluation by Dr. Patterson suggested brain death, but no family was available to authorize removing her from the ventilator. Reportedly, she had a daughter, but they hadn't been able to trace her.

What a heartbreaking case! Joy now remembered why she'd resigned from the ethics committee; these were the most depressing cases in the hospital.

Joy knew to be careful with the "brain-death" diagnoses at Holloway. The hospital's neurologist, Dr. Patterson, already had a reputation for being lousy at his job before he started getting old and senile. With that information in hand, she braced herself internally and headed to examine the patient.

The swollen blond woman attached to the ventilator seemed familiar to Joy. She had to disagree with the assessment of brain death. Her pupils were still partially reactive. She returned to the desktop to write her assessment and decided to browse the older records. Opening an old, scanned document, she found a picture of the woman before the admission and her breath caught.

Oh my God!

She did know that woman. She'd been admitted under a different name, but she'd been Joy's client and also a friend of Michael's.

Could this be related to Michael's murder case?

On impulse, she went back to the admission records and reviewed them in more detail.

CHAPTER 13

"Y OU'RE DISTRACTED TODAY. ARE YOU OKAY?" IN HIS backyard, Carl sat in half-lotus on a yoga mat on the grass.

Next to him, Richard stretched on his own mat. Their attempt at meditation hadn't been successful that morning. "Sorry, I didn't sleep very well last night."

It was an understatement. Richard had turned in bed all night, obsessing about his disturbing conversation with Levenstein.

After the unpleasant meeting, Richard had rushed to check on his son and kept him overnight. He sensed Levenstein was only messing with his mind, but he wondered if he should send Ray to New York with his uncle and join him there later. Still, he knew that wouldn't be far enough away if the LOTU ever decided to go after him.

After dropping Ray off at his mother's house the next day, Richard joined Carl, who was making a brief stop in town before heading to his new destination.

"Is there something worrying you?" Carl asked.

A text message dinged on Richard's phone and his stomach clenched when he saw it was from Blair Sanders.

"Meet me Friday at 6:00 p.m., at the abandoned Arcade on US-1."

He texted an agreement and excused himself from Carl to make a phone call using his burner cell.

The person picked up after the first ring. "Hello?"

"This is Guardian," he announced.

"This is Pitbull. Everything's clear here."

"Pitbull" was even more desperate than Richard to hide what had really happened the night the LOTU leader was killed. Richard might be facing a couple of years in prison for lying under oath while taking the blame—but Pitbull would face a much longer sentence for breaking parole.

"We're meeting Friday at six p.m.," he said. No need for further explanation. When the two men had met to brainstorm a couple of nights back, they'd decided that, while Sanders was away meeting Richard, Pitbull and his gang would search her home for the alleged cell phone.

"My boys and I will be there. Just keep her entertained."

Richard disconnected the call and a twinge of a scruple tugged at his heart as he walked back toward Carl. By having people break into Sanders' house, he was digging himself deeper into a pit of illegality. It seemed as if the only way to cover for a lie was to get tangled in others even worse.

He strolled back to Carl. "Sorry, where were we?"

Apparently giving up on meditation, Carl rose from the grass and led the way to the porch chairs facing the river. Gray clouds filled the sky, robbing the Indian River from its usual blue hue. A strong wind disturbed the waters and crashed waves against the shore.

"Is there something on your mind you'd like to talk about?" Carl asked, claiming a seat and inviting Richard to imitate him.

Levenstein's words running through his memory, Richard let his eyes get lost on the horizon. "Carl, do you remember Michael O'Hara?"

"I remember him a little," Carl answered. "Only recently I made the connection of who he was. He attended the Co-Creators meetings for a while, using the pseudonym Phoebus."

"How was he?"

"Meh." Carl shrugged. "People talk about his charm and charisma, but I remember him as a repressed man of constricted energy."

Richard busied himself removing burrs from the hem of his tan work pants, avoiding eye contact. "Would you say I'm like him in any way?"

"You tell me." Carl scrutinized him with a hint of amusement on his face. "Do *you* think you're like him?"

Richard tried to organize the thoughts haunting him since the night before. "Well, I've been accused of being selfish and narcissistic many times—like I've heard he was. Joy brought to my attention once that, like him, I'm paranoid and jealous. My mood swings and temper explosions are infamous. And I may not attack people on the basis of race, like he did, but I do tend to reject people who think differently than me."

"Congratulations, my friend." Carl placed his hand on Richard's shoulder. "You've just proved you're nothing like him."

Richard was surprised. "What do you mean?"

"You are aware. Michael was not." Carl smiled. "From what I know, he died without any knowledge of the darkness in him."

Interested, Richard leaned forward.

"Richard, darkness is nothing but the absence of light," Carl continued. "Light is love, understanding, awareness, and compassion. The moment you shine the light on your own dark side, acknowledging it, its power diminishes dramatically. The more you ignore, or fight, or deny the darkness, the more it grows."

Richard thought about the secrets circling his life. His lie under oath to the FBI. Sanders' blackmail. "What if there are parts of our darkness we can't reveal to others? For example, what if you once told a lie out of love, trying to help someone, and now you can't reveal the truth because you'd hurt that person?"

Carl's eyes twinkled. "You just contradicted yourself. Love and fault are antonyms. By definition, anything you do from real love can't be wrong."

"So you're saying that the same action can have a different meaning when one person does it out of love and the other one out of hate?"

Carl raised a hand. "As long as it's true. People have done a lot of damage justifying selfish motives in the name of love." He rose from the chair and walked back to the mats. "But I have to get ready to leave now, so I guess you'll have to continue this conversation later with your *tutor.*"

The words lit up Richard's spirit, dispersing some of his blues. He followed Carl and mumbled, "Speaking of someone who doesn't have a dark side."

Carl leaned to pick up the mats. "Darkness is in all of us, even Joy is not exempt from it."

"I disagree." Richard shook his head. "Joy is the most luminous being I've ever met."

"If she didn't have any darkness to clear—anything to learn—she wouldn't be here. She would've awakened from the dream already."

To Richard's inquiring look, Carl added. "If everyone else's battle is not letting their dark side dominate their lives, for her it's even finding that dark side she represses. We all need to confront and embrace our darkness. Only then we can forgive ourselves for it and let it go—then, it can no longer hurt us or others."

Richard narrowed his eyes. "Is that why you have her working with me?"

Carl had an enigmatic expression. "That. And because *you* need to find your light." He started rolling the first mat. "And also because if you saved her life and she saved yours that day, it must be because you have messages to deliver to each other."

Remembering the day he'd rescued Joy from the LOTU, an idea sparked in Richard. "Carl, you said that doing something out of love can never be wrong. So, then, when I shot the man who was pointing his gun at Joy, trying to save her life, it's not the same as him trying to murder her, right? Because I did it out of love."

Carl stopped picking up the mats, to think about it. "I'll never endorse shooting and maintain that there's always an alternative to violence. But if you can honestly say there was no other way to save her life, I understand what you mean and I'll agree."

Feeling like a clamp had been released from his chest, Richard exhaled. "I'm so glad we had this conversation. I should've known not to listen to that a-hole, Levenstein." He chuckled. "You'd never believe the things he said."

"Like what?"

"He said the only reason I became a law enforcer was to have the power to hurt others."

Distracted rolling the mats for storage, Carl answered, "Oh well—that part is true."

Richard gaped at Carl. "What?"

"I've always known that you're a sublimating sociopath."

"A what?" Richard asked, frowning.

Carl rolled up the second mat. "It's a psychological defense mechanism called 'sublimation.' For example, a pyromaniac fascinated with fire channels his destructive tendencies and becomes instead a firefighter. Or someone who fantasizes about cutting others with a knife instead becomes a surgeon."

Richard had trouble formulating a reply. "Wait. Are you agreeing that I became a cop because I wanted to carry a gun and shoot and beat up people for a living?"

Pressing his lips, Carl shrugged with feigned innocence.

Richard stared and deadpanned, "Thank you, Carl."

"No, no. Don't get me wrong." Carl rushed to clarify. "That's a *good* thing. Being a sublimating sociopath is much better than being one who's acting out."

All Richard could do was laugh.

He was still laughing when his phone rang with a call from Samuel and he picked up. "Hello?"

"Richard. I'm calling about Hayes."

The grave tone in Samuel's voice immediately set off an alarm. "What's going on?"

"Her Power of Attorney lawyer resurfaced from New York with her living will," Samuel replied. "She's going to be taken off the ventilator tomorrow."

CHAPTER 14

"I N THE DREAM OF LIFE, OUR THOUGHTS AND preconceptions alter everything we see," Joy said, sitting in Richard's dining room. "Two people can witness the same scene and interpret something completely different."

That evening, Joy was having a hard time focusing on the chapter of the day. Sprawled on the chair next to hers, Richard seemed determined to throw off her concentration by the intense way he looked at her. When she'd gotten him to agree to a no-touch policy, it didn't occur to her he'd find a way to caress her with his eyes.

"That especially applies to our opinions about people. We tend to project on others our own qualities and thoughts—mostly those we dislike about ourselves."

She felt relieved when Richard's attention moved from her for a moment and fixed on his phone on the table. "And three, two, one…" Richard slid his chair back, and used his foot to push Joy's chair away from the table. Startling her, he scooped her out of her seat, glided her onto his lap and grinned. "Guess what? We're off the clock now." His mouth captured hers.

His sudden move caught her off guard, delaying her reaction an instant. But a second later the familiar feeling of warm honey spreading through her veins took over, boosted by every caress of that expert, sensual mouth against hers. His large hand ran through her hair to then caress her face, her neck, and her back, leaving a path of goose bumps and fire on the way. Darn it. What was with that man? How could he make her mind cloud like that, awakening in her that wild woman she didn't recognize?

Gathering herself, she pressed a hand to his chest to gently push him away. Breathless, she said, "Off the clock or not, don't you feel any remorse about doing this?"

He squinted and looked up, pretending to think about it for a moment. He then gave her a devilish smile. "No." He nipped at her lower lip before delving into her mouth again.

She softly pushed him away and rose from his lap. She wanted to be firm, but all she could manage was giggling. "Aren't FBI agents supposed to be disciplined, with tons of restraint?"

"I think you got us confused with the Army guys." He smirked. "Me? I've been told I have the impulse control of a toddler."

He stood up and guided her by the hand to the backyard. "I got us dinner from your favorite Italian restaurant so we can have a picnic in the backyard later. It's not the beach, but—" He winked, as he indicated for her to sit on a blanket he'd laid over the grass. "I guess I set the bar quite low that day when the highlight of our evening was jumping off a running truck."

She ignored his joke about the day he rescued her from the LOTU. "But don't you feel even a little guilty?" Settling on the blanket, Joy lifted her face to gape at him. "You're practically lying to the FBI right now. They assume you're working."

"No, I'm not lying. They gave me protected time to become an expert on Carl's principles, and that's exactly what I've done for the past two hours. Now I'm off the clock."

She studied him as he spread his long limbs across the blanket. "And you're using that protected time to facilitate meetings with me? The same woman they'll fire you over if they ever learn you're seeing her?"

"It's just too convenient to pass up." Propping himself up on one elbow, he rested his head on his hand and lay sideways to face her. "It's not my fault that my consultant happens to be the same woman I was planning to see after work."

Giving up, Joy tried to relax and push away her worry about his lack of remorse.

It was a warm but pleasant evening, after the excruciating August sun had finally relented. The air smelled of freshly cut grass and the summer soundtrack of the cicadas surrounded them. Joy had exactly one hour left before the time she'd agreed to pick up her kids from her friend Fe's house—God bless that angel, always willing to take Joy's boys on the spot, "so Joy could rest."

"Come on! Why do you have to be so scrupulous?" Richard caressed her arm with a finger, flushing her and making her ache for more touch. "My point is, you're not hurting anybody with a small white lie. In the same way, you're not hurting anybody by taking a couple extra days off."

He sat up on the blanket, resuming the conversation they'd put on hold to work on the documents. "It's only two extra days. You were already taking Friday off before Labor Day. You just have to get your new partner, Dr. Harris, to cover you Thursday and Tuesday, and we'll have six nights at this vacation house in Pineapple Beach." He held her elbows and shook her lightly. "Six days in a row! When will we ever have another chance like that? How often do your kids go spend a whole week with their grandma O'Hara?"

She sighed; at least this time the kids were excited about going to a Disney hotel with Grandma. "Once a year, if ever."

"Exactly my point!" He tugged her against him. "Wouldn't it be wonderful? Six days taking beach walks together, swimming, watching sunrises on the ocean…"

She had to admit it did sound tempting.

Sensing her hesitation, he shot her the piercing look she now recognized as his attempt to hypnotize her. "You need the time off. It's your responsibility to recharge *your* batteries, so you can keep taking care of your children and patients." He placed her cell in her hands. "Come on. Send the text."

She slanted him a look. "Is this how you manage to lie so well in undercover missions? You convince yourself it's for a morally good cause?"

He nodded, unapologetic. "That's number one. Number two is: give tons of details, and mix in a bit of truth, so you sound convincing. And number three is: you throw in something the other person wants to hear, so they'll *want* to believe you. There. Now you have my fail-proof formula for the perfect lie."

She stared at him in disbelief, wondering how many of the sweet words he often told her were untrue.

What can you do when the man you love is a born actor and a professional liar?

Yes, the thought had been haunting her for weeks. Joy wondered if that question also troubled all the women of undercover FBI agents. Maybe also the women of lawyers and used cars salesmen.

When she didn't make any attempt to move, he took the phone back from her hands with a groan. "For goodness' sake! I'll do it myself."

He typed something on her phone, then extended it to her for her review.

She gasped at the expertly crafted message. "You're good! This even sounds like me. You even called her 'sweetie.'"

Smiling with pride, he hit send, then tossed the phone away on the grass to take her in his arms again.

He scooped her up to cradle her. "Angel, you don't do the world any service by being so excessively good. All you're doing is putting the rest of us to shame."

There it was again. The compliment hidden in a reprimand.

If Michael had been the king of the left-handed compliment, Richard was the king of—how to explain it? *The right-footed insult?*

Michael would say something with a polite air and a gentle tone that would leave Joy feeling vaguely insulted, yet wondering if she was supposed to say thank you. *"Joy, that haircut is so flattering—it takes away attention from your long face and your large mouth."* *"You're a fine physician—considering you're a woman." "You're in great shape— for a mother of three, past her prime."* That was Michael O'Hara *on a good day.*

Richard? He'd start a comment rolling his eyes and sighing in exasperation, then finish it with a twinkle that melted her away. *"Joy, you exasperate me—by being so beautiful." "You should be ashamed— for making every other woman feel bad about herself by comparison." "Your coffee sucks—What a relief! I was starting to worry there was nothing in the world you didn't do perfectly."*

And there she was, equally confused. It was as if Richard knew she refused to accept compliments and believe anything good anyone said about her. By starting the sentence with a scowl and a reprimanding tone, he'd get her to open the gates and pay attention. And then—surprise! He'd ambush her with a judo hold of sweetness.

The answer popped up on the phone and he glanced at it. "Dr. Harris said yes! We're going to have six days at Pineapple Beach!"

Her heart pranced. The prospect of spending six days with him was exciting and terrifying at once. Especially the part about spending *nights* together. They hadn't had one since that weekend before his return to work from his leave.

As if sensing her tension, he softly traced her lips with his finger. "You're going to miss all the fun in life unless you stop trying to be so freaking perfect and embrace your dark side a little—Carl says we have to."

She laughed. "Keep Carl out of this. I'm pretty sure he doesn't endorse lying."

He studied her in silence, his countenance sobering. "Carl is right; you've banished your darkness too much. You spend your life sacrificing yourself for others, rarely thinking about yourself; you defend unredeemable people, like Levenstein; and you haven't even allowed yourself to hate O'Hara."

Tense, she slipped out of his arms to put distance between them. "There's no point in hating. I've forgiven Michael."

His hazel eyes drilled her, as if trying to gauge her sincerity. The intensity of his scrutiny agitated her. "Sometimes I think you're an angel, too good to be true. But you must be human. You must have at least some anger inside you about the way O'Hara treated you for years. At least a twinge of desire for revenge."

Deep shame washed over Joy. If he only knew how many times she'd fantasized about seeing Michael dead. She'd never forgiven herself when he died for real.

"Remember, we're all cells in the same body," she said, changing the conversation to a safer, philosophical discussion. "We can't hurt someone else without hurting ourselves."

He frowned. "But you and I know there are people around who missed that memo. They *are* hurting others and need to be put down." He paused, as if thinking of an analogy. "When a cell turns cancerous, it needs to be removed from the body."

Joy blinked rapidly. Darn it. Every time she thought she was teaching Richard something, she was learning at the same time.

Glad to shift the argument away from Michael and herself, she shook her head. "That happens less often than you'd imagine. Most of the time what we reject in others is not 'evil' in them. It's something that reminds us of a part of *ourselves* we dislike."

"You taught me that term. It's called 'projection,'" he remarked. "But I disagree."

She realized he was starting to get upset for real and moved behind him to offer him a conciliatory back rub. She massaged Richard's shoulders—the left one slightly lower than the right ever since a work injury—gently rubbing in circles. "All I'm saying is that darkness is in you and me just as much as it is in the criminals you put in jail."

He relaxed and seemed to get lost in her touch for a moment. But then, he grabbed her hands off his shoulders and tugged her around to face him. He seemed unusually serious. "I disagree again. You're the exception. *You* are purely good."

She freed her hands with a groan. "I'm *not* purely good."

"You're a freaking angel!" He rolled his eyes. "Do you think it's easy for me?" Clicking his tongue, he shook his head as in disapproval. Then, slowly, a mischievous grin took over, bringing out the laugh lines she loved. "I'm not used to dating good girls. There's a lot of pressure to strike a balance between being a gentleman and doing the nasty things I really want to do." He nibbled at her neck.

The usual wave of pleasure floundered beneath the painful shyness she always felt when someone complimented her.

"I'm not that good," she mumbled.

He tapped her forehead with his index finger. "Get it in there, you're a freaking saint. You're a superb doctor and a wonderful mother."

Wonderful mother. She cringed, feeling the familiar guilt stab her soul. "I'm not! Those poor kids spend the whole day with their nanny while I work. And look at me now, leaving them with a friend to come here. And now apparently I'm getting ready to ship them off to their grandmother so I can spend a few nights out with my lover. I'm a *terrible* mother."

His good humor vanished and a disturbed expression she'd never seen before took over his face. Apprehension flooded her. Had she angered him? Sometimes she couldn't help being afraid he'd snap at her like Michael used to do.

A long silence fell between them, broken only by the cicadas.

He slowly lifted his shirt and showed her a scar on his torso. "Do you see this? When I was a kid, my mother burned me with her cigarette a couple of times—on purpose."

Shock slowly gave way to horror as she assimilated his confession.

Although his voice remained calm, she could read the tension in his hardened muscles and tight jaw. "She used to beat me and my brothers all the time. With wooden spoons, belts, her shoes… She used to lock me in the coat closet as a punishment and sometimes forgot about it and went to bed—usually passed out on

Percocet—leaving me without food or water until she remembered I was there."

Joy's heart clenched at the image and she bit her lips not to answer with *I'm sorry*. The last thing he'd want would be commiseration.

He forced a smile. "My point is, compared to that, I think you're a pretty decent parent." He kissed her forehead and wrapped her in his arms, resting her head against his chest. His deep regular breathing made her wonder if he was more upset by the memories he'd shared than he was willing to admit. She battled tears on his behalf, struggling to find something to say to comfort him.

Cupping her face in his hands, he finally concluded, "And my other point is, remember you said I should imagine the criminal as someone who was abused in childhood? Well, *I was*. And I didn't allow that past to make me into a criminal. Why should I have compassion for anyone else who did?"

She didn't try to argue anymore. She kissed him, nestled him in her arms and imagined her love flowing, healing the little boy he'd once been.

His phone dinging with a message forced them to release the embrace. The way his features darkened when he read the text implied something bad had happened.

He mumbled an excuse and rose from the blanket, while dialing someone on his phone. Despite his precautions, she caught a few words as he walked away.

"Let me guess," Richard said. "Xenos is dead."

The long silence seemed to confirm that Richard had guessed correctly.

CHAPTER 15

RICHARD SAT AT THE FBI RESIDENT OFFICE, TALKING TO Young and her attorney. "You can't continue to refuse cooperating with us. Two witnesses have died."

The husky lawyer's hands shook slightly as he removed his reading glasses from his rounded nose. "My client admits that she was *temporarily* involved in the New Age Spirituality group 'The Lords of the Universe.' Her participation in such society cannot be considered grounds for arrest, since it falls into freedom of association."

"Her right to associate freely with the LOTU is not illegal, but refusing to cooperate with law enforcement is," Samuel said.

"She's not refusing to cooperate," the lawyer contradicted. "She's exercising the Fifth Amendment."

By now Richard felt sick of hearing those same words from Levenstein's attorney.

The lawyer's tone was tense and overly polite. "My client had no knowledge about the plot to murder her cousin, Congressman O'Hara. She was remotely aware of a plan to take him to the presidency."

At least this was more information than they'd been able to extract from Young or her lawyer so far. Richard searched in a folder and extended a picture of Levenstein. "All we need is for your client to identify this man as part of the LOTU group."

"Before she agrees to talk, we want assurances of complete immunity," the lawyer said.

Samuel scoffed. "Of course, we can't guarantee that."

"Then there's no deal."

Richard raked his fingers through his hair, losing his patience. "It's in your client's best interest to cooperate with us. Otherwise, her life could be in danger."

"Oh, please, sugar babe, skip the drama!" Young spoke over her attorney for the first time ever, startling all three men in the room with her shrill voice.

Ignoring her lawyer's warning glance, she rose from her chair and popped a hip, one hand on her slender waist. "Honey, you can't scare me," she addressed Richard with forced levity. "I was smoking, drinking, and getting my first tattoo when you were still in diapers. But on top of that, I'm a physician. I've spoken with Xenos' and Zimmerman's widows and learned everything about their deaths. They died from natural causes."

The ways the LOTU had terminated targets in the past while leaving them with a negative autopsy was confidential information Richard couldn't share. "Dr. Young, two men ended up dead within days of starting a conversation about cooperating with us. Don't you think that coincidence is too big to ignore?"

"Zimmerman was a diabetic and died from hypoglycemia. Xenos was a middle-aged man with an extensive past medical history. He obviously must've had a coronary event."

"So you're not afraid *at all* about your own safety?" She had to be bluffing, hiding how worried she really was.

Unless her relative lack of concern meant *she* was involved in those deaths.

As if reading his thoughts, she placed both hands on her hips, squared her shoulders and tilted her head. "You're not going to intimidate me by insinuating that I'm guilty of something. Sugar, your tough guy attitude doesn't scare me."

"Okay!" The lawyer cleared his throat. "I'll regroup with my client and let you know what she decides." He ushered Young quickly from the office, as if afraid she'd say something compromising.

Richard blew out his frustration in a long exhale.

Samuel patted his back. "Come on, let's go to my office."

As Samuel sat at his desk, Richard settled on an office chair rubbing his temples. "Should we review one more time what happened to Xenos?"

Samuel opened a folder. "His wife found him unresponsive on the floor. The paramedics found his blood pressure very low."

"Similar to Hayes," Richard pointed out.

"Yes, but they were able to reanimate him with IV fluids. They admitted him initially to telemetry and ran all forms of cardiac tests, and they were all fine. They moved him to a regular floor and he was found dead the next day."

"Just like Zimmerman," Richard mused. "It's urgent we figure out how they're doing this; we've lost two major witnesses."

"Make that three," Samuel clarified. "Hayes was just disconnected from the ventilator."

Richard cussed under his breath. "They succeeded. The best informant we could've ever gotten is gone."

"My bet is that Levenstein is behind all three deaths. It was a matter of time before they confirmed he was a LOTU leader, and he must have something to hide about how involved he was in O'Hara's murder plot."

"We'd better assign security to protect Young at all times or she'll be next."

"I agree," Samuel said. "But there's one more person I'm worried about."

It might be denial, but Richard couldn't come up with an answer at first. "Who?"

"Dr. Andrews."

Richard's stomach clenched. Samuel was right. If this criminal—Levenstein or someone else—was determined to eliminate anyone who could potentially help the FBI, Carl could well be next. "I've been begging him to reinforce his security. I'm going to need to talk to him again."

Richard noticed the time on his cell phone, already almost six. He had to run to make it to his meeting with Sanders. "I have to go, Sam."

Samuel frowned. "What's your deal, Richard? Are you doing this on purpose?"

"What do you mean?"

"You resist it when I ask you to stay working late. You're spending more time than ever with Dr. Andrews and his tutor, yet you're barely making progress on Hayes' manuscript. You seem to be doing a half-assed job lately." Samuel crossed his arms. "Richard, it wouldn't be the first time you've shot yourself in the foot. Are you trying to get away from the transfer to New York by getting yourself fired?"

Richard wished he could deny it, but he had to admit it had crossed his mind. "You're talking nonsense, Sam."

His phone chimed with a text from Blair Sanders.

"I'm already at the Arcade. Don't keep me waiting. Remember, I'm the one woman you don't want to upset."

Richard mumbled an excuse to Samuel and left the office.

～

The night Richard opened up about his childhood, Joy cried in her car all the way home. After that, she'd been more affectionate and patient with her children than ever. If Carl was right, and any happiness poured into the universe could benefit everyone—maybe her love could reach and heal other suffering children in the world, balancing the love-hate scale of humanity a little.

And now something had shifted inside her about Richard. The image of him as a vulnerable child followed her around all day and mixed with the image of the majestic adult he'd become. Imagining everything he'd had to overcome to be who he was today made her admire him more, if possible.

After she finished the last case of the afternoon at her private practice, she stopped at the front desk to pick up her mail and phone messages. Only then did she realize she'd forgotten again to talk to Richard about the bothersome greeting cards. She'd been completely absorbed in their work with the documents and Richard's confession. On top of that, Michael's voice in her head kept reprimanding her for blowing a bad joke out of proportion. She was relieved to see no suspicious envelopes among her mail.

"Good morning, babysitter of corpses."

Josh Levenstein's voice jerked Joy from her musings. He stood at her office door with his bodyguard. Despite his mocking tone, Levenstein's eyes studied her with appreciation.

"Good morning, Josh, how can I help you?"

"I just came to drop this." He entered and extended an envelope to her. "It's my donation for the Hospice House."

Joy accepted the envelope and started to open it.

"Don't open it until I'm gone," he said.

It was too late. She'd already removed the contents and was shocked to find how large the amount on the check was.

"Wow, Josh. This is very generous. Thank you."

"I told you not to open it!" A light blush tinted his cheeks and he squirmed in place.

"Thanks again, Josh. The Hospice House appreciates it."

He forced a smirk. "Don't thank me. It's in my own selfish interest that it stays open—so I can keep sending you uninsured patients."

She knew he was bluffing. Josh would never admit it, but he believed in her work. Though his claim to fame was his activism on legalizing euthanasia, he was also a supporter of early termination of futile therapy on behalf of quality of life. "You know, Josh, I see through your façade," she said softly. "The years of seeing your patients die every day have hardened you. But I know you're kinder than you show."

The smugness disappeared off his face and, for a brief moment, he seemed moved. "That's how you make your money, right? You've capitalized on your ability to see the best in people. You force your patients to see themselves through your eyes as lovable and good, and they end up buying it." He scoffed. "But your spell has no effect on me." His eyes didn't look as convinced as his voice sounded. He shot her one last glance and walked away without saying goodbye.

She winked at the bodyguard. "He's something else, isn't he?"

The man sighed and looked up to the ceiling before giving a single nod and taking off behind his boss.

Joy returned her attention to her mail. The top message was from the hospital, notifying her that Rachel Hayes had expired. She sent a small prayer for that poor woman who must've had a very unhappy life to end up on the path of crime and hate.

She sat at her desk, still processing the case as she opened her email. She was aware that the woman was connected to Michael's murder case, and she had the deep gut feeling that her health crisis had been provoked. HIPAA laws didn't apply to law enforcement, but she had hesitated to bring Richard a theory that was a big stretch. Michael had always warned against her wild imagination.

She was so absorbed in her thoughts she barely heard the knock on the door.

"Hello." Allison stood at the threshold.

"Good afternoon," Joy greeted her with a tense smile. Darn it, she'd forgotten to reschedule her canceled therapy appointments.

Allison handed her a folder. "You asked me for the list of women's shelter sponsors?"

Oh, yes. She accepted the folder with thanks and invited Allison to take a seat. "I'd forgotten about it. I guess I've been too distracted lately to make any progress on my own fundraising projects."

As she settled into the office chair, Allison commented, "I stopped by yesterday and Dr. Harris said you'd left early for a therapy session. Obviously she didn't know I am your therapist."

Joy blushed. Her partners had continued to assume that the days she left early she was attending grief counseling and she hadn't bothered to correct them.

"Would you like to fill me in on why I'm covering for you?" It was difficult to read Allison's immobile features, but Joy guessed she felt displeased.

Joy winced in apology. "I'm sorry. I didn't mean to put you in an uncomfortable position."

"So, you're still seeing him, huh?" Allison crossed her arms and leaned back. "I'm worried about you, Joy. You're not thinking clearly right now."

"I've never thought more clearly in my life, Allison. I love him." Joy was the most surprised to hear those words stated aloud.

Despite Allison's Botox mask, Joy could sense worry in her flat voice. "I told you, infatuation was unavoidable after the intense bonding experience—"

"You keep forgetting that I already had feelings for Richard before that happened. For months." Joy sustained Allison's gaze.

"And I thought we'd already established that you can't 'have feelings' for someone who doesn't exist. The man you fell for was a fictional character."

Losing the staring contest, Joy looked away and fixed her attention on the pile of mail on her desk. "But over the past few weeks, I've gotten a glimpse of the *real* Richard and… I like him even more than the fake one."

Allison rose from her chair and walked around the desk to place her hands on Joy's shoulders, making her look at her. For a moment her eyes filled with compassion and her expression softened, but then it hardened again. "Joy, your dating experience is, literally, that of a fifteen-year-old. You think the only man you ever had, Michael, was evil—but you have no idea how low men can be. They'd do and say anything to get a woman in bed."

Joy knew there was little point in arguing with Allison. Her mistrust for all men was rooted deep in her own history, watching her mother suffer abuse at the hands of her stepfather.

And this was why it was so hard for Joy to find a therapist. She'd start as the client and then invariably shift the roles and try to help *them.*

Avoiding Allison's scrutiny, Joy fixed her eyes on her computer screen. "I hear you, but—"

The next words died on her lips as she caught a glimpse of a recent email in her inbox.

Her heart plummeted and her veins filled with ice. It couldn't be. The message came from Michael's home email address and the subject was: *"I am alive. And I'm coming to get you."*

The sound of her own scream reached Joy's ears before she realized it had escaped her. The room darkened, and the next thing she knew she was lying on the floor, her legs up on a chair, hyperventilating, while Allison held a paper bag against her face. She must've blacked out, because she had no explanation for the tears dampening her cheeks.

"It's all a cruel joke. Michael is not coming; he's dead!" A desperate Allison squeezed her hand and tried to reassure her.

Joy couldn't control the terrified sobs convulsing her body. "Michael is coming to get me. Michael is coming!"

CHAPTER 16

S ITTING IN HIS CAR IN FRONT OF THE ABANDONED ARCADE building at 6:10 p.m., Richard waited impatiently for his burner phone to go off. When it did, he picked up at the first ring. "Hello?"

"This is Pitbull."

"And this is Guardian. It's all clear here," he replied, sticking to the routine.

"Me and my boys are in Sanders' house," the man said. "We ain't finding no cell phone so far."

Damn it. "She said she'd made a copy of the video. Take any discs or memory drives you can find."

"Her computers too?"

A tiny scruple flickered through Richard. Breaking into Sanders' house was reprehensible enough. Instructing this gang to steal her computers—crossing the line into larceny—was a different thing.

Tapping sounds on the car window startled him. Sanders stood next to the car, flashing a self-satisfied grin.

"If you can, just reset the hard drives. If not, do what you have to do," he mumbled before disconnecting the call and exiting the car.

"Good evening, handsome. Are you hiding from me?" Sanders' countenance radiated smugness and flirtation as she hooked her arm with his and walked him to the building. "I thought you and I were overdue to touch base, since it seems you're not taking me seriously."

She guided him into the abandoned brick structure. The wide space had no dividing walls and only an occasional column for support.

Once inside, he shook her arm off. "Sanders, let's cut the pleasantries. Why am I here?"

She settled on an office chair near a dusty pool table and signaled him to take another one in front of her. "Even if you're not being nice to me, I've decided to be a good girl and help you out. I have some information for your case."

Richard claimed a seat, but slid his chair back, increasing the distance between them. "I'm listening."

She grabbed a folder from the table and extended a black-and-white photo to him, apparently a printout from an old news article. He immediately recognized Michael O'Hara, yet it took his photographic memory a second longer to come up with the name of the dark-skinned man standing next to him. "Venkat Patel?"

"I've recently found out he might've had some interest in eliminating O'Hara."

Richard raised his eyebrows.

In the picture, Michael O'Hara's fake smile was tenser than usual. Richard knew O'Hara had been covertly racist and xenophobic, and chances were he was posing with Patel as a way to flaunt to voters an openness he didn't have.

"My informant claims he and Patel had an ugly argument six months before O'Hara's death," Blair continued. "According to my source, Patel was trying to convince O'Hara's wife to partner with him and travel all over the country for speaking engagements. O'Hara didn't like it at all."

No surprise, considering that O'Hara was a pathologically jealous and controlling man. "What kind of partnership?"

"He wants to turn Dr. Clayton into his 'sidekick' as he becomes the next 'it' celebrity doctor of holistic medicine. Being a woman, light-skinned and well-liked she's his perfect complement. Add to that the name recognition she has now since O'Hara's death, which guarantees instant media attention. He's in a hurry to seal the deal; from what I gather, he's deep in debt and this plan has become more and more urgent."

Richard pondered the words. Had they missed a suspect all along? Patel's name had come up on the list of local authors who wrote about New Age topics. "Thank you; I'll look into this." He slanted Blair a look. "But I'm curious why you would try to help me."

She extended her hand to caress his arm and he flinched at her touch. "This is just a small sample of what a great team we'd be working together." She drew circles on his forearm with her thumb before releasing it. "Which reminds me…" She picked up a yellow envelope from the pool table. "Here's a draft of a contract, so you can see how generous my client's offer is."

Richard's jaw clenched. "I will not do business with someone who works for the O'Hara family."

"…And here are a few interview date options so you can choose which one works better for you," she continued, ignoring his protest. "Would you like to meet your future boss tomorrow, next weekend, or after the Labor Day holiday?"

What nerve. "What I would like to do is tell you and your client exactly what you can do with your contract."

"Oh my." She tittered. I can tell you don't like me much right now."

"How could I?" He stood up and glowered at her. "You're a blackmailer. And I'm starting to suspect, a liar too."

Head tilted, she rose from her chair with an amused look. "Are you surprised that I'm a liar? I'm a sensationalist reporter. Half of what I say is questionable."

And that was precisely why he had to find that evidence she had against him. Her sensationalist past ensured the FBI was unlikely to believe anything she said. But things could turn out differently if she had proof to back up her story.

He needed to get her to reveal where she had that cell phone, so he could pass the information to Pitbull. Taking a step forward, he scowled at her. "I'm starting to think you're lying about that video you say you have against me. You have nothing." He leaned toward her. "How about you show it to me?"

She clapped twice and, out of nowhere, someone clasped Richard's wrists behind him.

"What the f—" He shot his elbow back, hitting his captor in the chest with force and heard him groan; but the man still managed to immobilize his arms. Richard kicked back, aiming for the man's shin, but before he could free himself, a second muscular man appeared and the two of them pushed Richard back onto the chair. While the first man held him, the second handcuffed Richard's hands together in the back and then iron cuffed his ankles to the chair. Heart racing, Richard fought them all along while exhausting his whole repertoire of cuss words.

When it became clear that he couldn't escape, Richard searched Sanders' eyes with a wordless question.

"Sorry if this seems over the top." She gave a small shrug. "My client lent me his bodyguards for my protection while I do this." She addressed the men, "Thank you, guys, now excuse us; this will only take a minute." The men exited the room, leaving them alone.

Richard glared at Sanders. "What is this about?"

"Just in case you felt tempted to attack me when you see this." She reached for her purse on the pool table and extracted an old-fashioned flip phone. She pressed a few buttons and played a video for him.

The image was shaky and low definition. Yet, Richard was identifiable in it as he engaged in a physical fight with the LOTU leader. Despite the technical limitations of the video, it clearly showed that the shot killing the man had come from behind Richard. The video had also captured the real shooter—aka Pitbull—approaching to help Richard up from the floor, while still holding the gun; though it had shown mostly his back.

No wonder the gang couldn't find the phone; she had it with her.

"You didn't have to restrain me; I have no plans to attack you," he lied. He was desperate enough that he'd consider it.

"I didn't mean to be dramatic." She returned the phone to her jacket pocket and slid the back of her hand over his face. "But I couldn't resist this sexy image of you, literally tied up and unable to resist me." She pulled his head toward her and kissed him.

Tensing up, he tightened his lips and jerked his head away.

She huffed in frustration. "Richard, why do you keep pretending nothing happened between us?"

Richard froze, sensing danger, and eyed her with caution. *Something happened between us?*

She continued, caressing his jaw. "Richard, I swear this is not like me. But all these years I've never been able to stop thinking about you after that night."

His pulse sped up. Had they ever slept together? For the life of him, he couldn't remember. But it would explain the vicious persistence she'd been following him with.

A flash of vulnerability crossed her face as she searched his features. "You do remember that special night, don't you?"

Waves of adrenaline flushed him. He couldn't risk insulting her, so he limited himself to a nod. But how low had he fallen in his life to get involved with a woman like Sanders—and not even remember it?

"Let me go. Right now." He shot her his most glacial glare. "I want nothing to do with people like you."

"Oh please!" Rolling her eyes, she released his neck and paced away. "You're worse than me and you know it." She pivoted to face him, a hand on her narrow waist. Her previous soft expression had been replaced by defiance. "You think you're so much better than the criminals you arrest, because you carry a badge. But, maybe you aren't. You call me a liar; but you're the one lying to the FBI, aren't you?"

She had a point. And she didn't even know half the story about his lies to the FBI. Starting with his forbidden affair with Joy.

"You say I'm a blackmailer," she continued. "But I'd rather be a blackmailer than a murderer. You might not have killed the LOTU leader, but you did shoot that gang member in the head during the same operation, didn't you? And we both know that wasn't the first time you'd killed on duty."

Damn it. She's right. Levenstein's words returned to his mind. Maybe he wasn't any better than the criminals he fought.

Blair opened the door, and the bodyguards returned with the keys to free him. "Guys, give me a head start, to discourage him from following me," she said, and then addressed Richard. "Unless I hear from you, I'll assume we're having your interview the weekend after Labor Day. You have my number if you have any questions."

After blowing him one last kiss, she exited the place.

Richard invented new cusswords to yell at Sanders' bodyguards, as he had to wait for minutes before they released him. He was still boiling and fuming when he made it to his car and turned on the engine.

But the anger mixed with something else. It was a deep feeling of shame, guilt, and self-doubt he'd fought all his life to push away.

His phone rang and he gathered himself before picking up the call from Samuel.

"Richard." The cautious tone of Samuel's voice worried him.

"Oh, no. Who died now?" Richard asked.

"No one." The pause on the other line seemed like an eternity before he answered, "But someone sent a threatening message to Dr. Clayton."

CHAPTER 17

R ICHARD HAD NEVER BROKEN MORE TRAFFIC LAWS AND SPEED limits than that evening, as he rushed to Joy's office. No wonder the FBI didn't allow agents to work in cases where they had personal involvement. The terror of seeing Joy hurt, or of losing her, blunted his ability to think logically.

Had the LOTU group targeted her for elimination again? Had he been worrying about Carl as a potential victim and neglected to protect *her*?

Calm down. This is not the LOTU's modus operandi.

Still, he felt nauseated, weakened with terror when he arrived at the Masden Center, which housed Joy's private office. He jogged across the luxurious two-story ceiling lobby, at risk of slipping on the shiny marble floors. He rode the golden elevators to the CeMeSH on the fourth floor and found a small crowd of people gathered in the waiting room. When Samuel saw him arrive, he stopped his conversation with another agent and went to meet him.

Richard skipped the greetings. "Where is she? I want to see her."

"She's fine. She was pretty rattled at first, but she's bounced back quite quickly." Samuel extended a few pages to him. The top ones were photocopies of greeting cards with the common message, "Michael is watching you." The bottom one was a printout of an email reportedly sent from O'Hara's address. *"I am alive. And I'm coming to get you."*

A chill raced down Richard's spine.

"We're working on tracing the IP address," Samuel said. "But I'd be surprised if the sender was reckless enough to leave a trace."

"Why didn't she tell me?" Richard mumbled, clasping the sheets.

"As you can see, the cards weren't really threatening but more a form of harassment. They could've come from any creep with a bad sense of humor who's followed the news and heard of her. Now, this email either came from someone close to O'Hara who knew his email password, or it required professional hacking work. Either way, it's more worrisome than the cards."

Richard mused. "But you said the cards had no postmarks. Someone must've had access to her office to drop them off." If that person had taken the trouble to personally deliver the messages, he or she must be quite obsessed. And if they had access to enter Joy's suite, they may've potentially had access to hurt her. Filled with a sudden urge to see her, he headed for her office.

Samuel followed him down the hallway. "We're still not sure if the cards were dropped here or mixed with the building mail. We recommended she install security cameras."

Richard was about to open the office door when Samuel grabbed his arm. His warning glance revealed his apprehension. "I don't recommend that you enter."

Richard understood. He trusted his own ability to conceal his feelings, but Joy could give away to others what was going on between them.

"I have to, Samuel," he whispered. "I need to see she's okay."

He slowly opened the door and came in. Joy sat at her desk with another agent and a couple other people. When her eyes met his, he was afraid he'd lose it in front of everyone at the despair on her face. It took everything he had not to break character and take her in his arms.

He limited his greeting to a bow of the head. "Dr. Clayton."

"I'm okay, Agent Fields," she rushed to say. Despite the tremor affecting her hands and lips, she seemed to reassure him with her eyes.

As relief settled in, he noticed someone next to her; Venkat Patel sat in the role of supportive friend, holding her hand and mumbling soothing words.

"Dr. Patel, where were you when this happened?" The tone of the question came out harsher than Richard intended.

Surprise crossed Patel's features, followed by indignation. "I was here at the clinic, still seeing patients. When Dr. Connors called me I came as soon as possible."

Richard read the man's body language, his clenched jaw, his tense shoulders, his balled left fist. His eyes slid to Patel's right hand, still holding Joy's and something in Richard's expression must've worried Samuel, as he rushed to intervene. "Hey, Fields, how about you speak with Dr. Connors while Keith and I ask Dr. Patel some questions?"

Richard glared at Patel and sent one last longing look toward Joy before signaling the woman Samuel had called Connors to follow him.

He guided Connors to one of the small examination rooms and, after they exchanged business cards, he listened to her summary of what had happened and took some notes.

"So, Ms. Connors—"

"It's *Doctor* Connors," she interrupted him in a stern voice.

He raised one eyebrow. "Sorry, *Doctor* Connors. Can you think of anyone who could've sent these messages? Maybe someone who's interested in keeping Michael O'Hara's memory alive?"

"I didn't have any mutual acquaintances with Michael O'Hara. Actually, I rarely had contact with him; I avoided him on purpose."

Richard found that strange. "How come?"

"He offended my feminist sense." She scoffed. "Michael O'Hara liked flaunting his wife in the press, using her as a shield against critics who called him anti-feminist, but it was all an act. He secretly wished she'd stayed in the kitchen barefoot and pregnant."

He gave a sour chuckle and mumbled almost to himself, "O'Hara seems to have been a very unlikeable man."

Connors pierced him with her blue eyes and deadpanned, "Yes, poor Joy has very bad taste in men."

The disapproval radiating from her was undeniable. *Does she know about Joy and me?*

He searched his mind for what he knew about Allison Connors. She had a PhD in psychology and was a therapist and self-help author. Her name had come up on the FBI list of New Age authors to screen because her first two books had been on goal-achieving through Law of Attraction. However, her writings after that had focused on quite misandric feminist self-help, unrelated to Carl's or the LOTU's teachings, so they'd ruled her out.

But now, after learning her dislike for Michael O'Hara he wondered if they should revisit her as a suspect.

He studied the blond woman in a gray skirt suit, sitting straight, with her long legs crossed. "How do you know Dr. Clayton?"

"We met years ago in college, at University of Florida. But we only re-connected in the past few years."

"Did you ever meet Mr. John Zimmerman or Dr. Rhodes Xenos?"

Her face was motionless; she seemed to be loaded with Botox. "This is a small town and everyone has met everybody at one time or another."

Vague answer. "Yes or no."

"Yes. We coincided a few times in the Fort Sunshine social scene."

"How would you describe your relationship with them?"

"I don't use that word."

His photographic memory returned to a passage of her last book, which he'd reviewed when screening her. "That's right." With a grave tone, he quoted, "A woman should only care about one relationship in her life, and that is with herself."

Even if her eyebrows were unable to move, the lift in her eyelids betrayed her surprise. Her voice was as sarcastic as monotone. "I'm impressed. So charming of you to have read the *first page* of my last book."

"You seem to be quite tense around me," he observed, vaguely indicating her crossed arms and legs. "After browsing your book, I would've attributed it to a general dislike for the male gender." He narrowed his eyes. "But you seemed okay with Agent Elliott. This seems almost personal against me; would you like to fill me in?"

Uncrossing her arms, she leaned forward in her seat and whispered, "I know about you and *her*."

His pulse sped up. He immediately went into undercover mode, keeping his body immobile and his face impassive. "Excuse me?"

"You know who I'm talking about."

He scanned his brain files and remembered seeing her at the press conference. A previous conversation with Joy jumped into his mind. He put two and two together. *She's Joy's therapist.*

Richard had to be extremely careful. "I'm sorry. I have no idea what you're talking about."

They locked eyes for a while, she then said, "I know this is a game for you, but for her, this is serious." For a moment, her gaze softened and reflected sincere worry. Her eyes seemed to beg. "She has suffered enough already; have mercy on her and leave her alone, before you damage her even more."

Richard was out of words for a moment, then finally said, "That will be it, Dr. Connors."

She rose from her seat and kept eye contact until the last second when she turned and left the room.

Richard stayed in the examination room for a while, processing Connors' words. They mixed with Sanders' words and Levenstein's accusations.

Is she right? Is my insistence on continuing to see Joy doomed to hurt her?

CHAPTER 18

WHAT A DAY!

After answering the FBI's questions for what felt like hours, Joy was glad to accept Allison's offer to drive her and her car home. Hope and Tom were already there, alerted by Joy's phone call, and insisted on taking Joy and the kids with them for the night to Tom's house in Winter Park. Joy accepted gladly; she felt much safer out of her house.

But around eight, with the boys tucked in with their future cousins and Joy settled in Tom's guest room, Richard's text messages started escalating. They'd begun as anxious requests for reassurance that she was doing okay and had evolved into frantic pleas for company.

"I need you. Please come over," the last message had begged, not sounding like the usual Richard.

Worried when he'd abruptly stopped answering her texts, she decided to go check on him. She threw on a pair of yoga pants, a T-shirt, and a hoodie, left a note for Hope claiming a patient emergency, and drove to Richard's house.

Following the usual precautions, she circled the block first to make sure no one was following her before pulling into his garage using the opener he'd given her. She passed through the garage door into the house.

"Hello, anybody home?" she announced herself on her way to the family room. "I got worried when you stopped answering the—"

She stopped in her tracks when she found the house in complete darkness. "Sweetie? Are you home?" She felt her way around a wall and turned on the lights.

A mess of dirty clothes covered the family room floor and, for an instant, her stomach clenched in fear that someone might've robbed the house.

Then she noticed the pile of dirty dishes in the kitchen sink as she moved past the breakfast bar and followed the sound of groaning into the living room. She found Richard lying on the couch, an arm covering his eyes. Next to him on the carpeted floor rested an empty liquor bottle.

"Sweetie, are you okay?" she asked from a distance, still trying to process what was going on.

"You made it, goddess!" He uncovered his eyes and flexed his fingers, summoning her closer. "Come here. Have a drink with me."

She reluctantly approached him. "You know I can't drink."

His laugh sounded hollow as he staggered off the couch. "I forgot. You're such a lightweight! If I want to get you drunk I just have to kiss you after *I* have a drink."

With clumsy hands, he captured her face and tried to kiss her, but she pulled back with a grimace. "Buddy, I could get drunk right now just by smelling your breath."

Worried, she surveyed his wrinkled work clothes, his disheveled hair and thickening stubble. "What's going on? Why did you ask me to come over?"

Distress shadowed his countenance for a moment. Softly, he touched her cheek. "I was planning to break up with you; but now that you're here I'm so happy to see you I'll never manage to do it."

She recoiled in surprise. "You wanted to break up?" For days she'd been debating with that idea herself. But hearing his words felt like a punch in the ribs, making her realize how much he'd grown on her.

He flung himself back on the couch and remained silent for a while. Finally, he slurred, "I don't even have the decency to do what's right; I'm too selfish to let you go." He lifted his glassy eyes to hers. "But the truth is that a scum like me has no business with a nice woman like you."

"What?" She studied him, confused. "Sweetie, how much have you had to drink? Do you even know what you're saying right now?"

He reached for a glass on the coffee table and emptied the remainder of its contents in one gulp. He grimaced at the burn of the strong alcohol. "Maybe you were right and I'm a hopeless liar." He set the glass back on the table just a little too hard. "Maybe Carl is right that I'm a sublimating sociopath. Maybe Samuel is right that I'm a half-assed agent acting recklessly on purpose, trying to get himself fired." He rested his elbows on his knees and buried his face in his hands.

She sank beside him on the edge of the sofa and placed a hand on his back. "Where is all this coming from?"

He uncovered his face. His bloodshot hazel eyes were loaded with pain as they searched hers. "Do you remember the gang member I shot the day I rescued you?"

She couldn't find any words to reply. Of course, she remembered the terrifying moment when that man's blood had splashed her. It had taken her many debriefing sessions to be able to talk about it calmly.

He continued, "I reviewed his files. Did you know that he had a fourteen-year-old son—the same age as Ray? And that boy is now an orphan because of me."

She felt tightness in her throat and chest but limited herself to caressing his back. "That's sad."

He nodded. "I wish I could say that he was the first and last person I shot. But it's not true. Carl says it's not the same as murder, because I did it out of love, trying to save you. And that lying as an undercover agent is not the same as lying just for lying. But I don't know what to believe anymore."

Because I did it out of love. A corner of her mind captured the vague declaration, but at the moment, all she could think of was how to make him stop hurting.

He gave a mirthless snort. "I kill and lie for a living. Maybe I'm not much better than the criminals I chase."

She hugged him and tried to communicate love and acceptance with her embrace. "Don't say that; it's not the same."

"Do you remember that day you said we're all parts of the same body?" he asked. Without waiting for her response, he continued, "What if *I* am the cancerous cell?"

"No, you're not!" She held him tighter, desperately thinking about what to say to lift him up. Having an idea she released him to hold his face "You are a white blood cell."

He frowned at her, working hard to focus. "A what?"

She nodded effusively. "If we're all organs of the same body, law enforcers are cells in our immune system. You are a cell that circulates in our blood, fighting infections, fighting cancer cells. Yes, sometimes you have to kill another cell that has turned malignant, and sometimes a benign cell gets accidentally hurt too… but it's your job. And without you, the body would've died long ago."

He stared at her without visible emotion. The silence dragged for so long she wondered if he hadn't registered what she'd said.

But then she noticed a suspicious shine in his eyes. "You're an angel. *Damn it.*" With a growl, he slouched back on the couch. "You're a freaking angel. And I'm a damned demon who's going to hell for having seduced you."

"Stop it!" She mock punched him on the arm, feeling relieved he'd finally reacted. "I'm as human as you are."

"You're not," he grumbled and covered his eyes with his hands. "You're an effing celestial being. And if there's a hell, I'm so going there for profaning you."

Joy hesitated. What could she do to soothe him? How could she make him see that she was just as human and imperfect as he was?

Her own dark secret emerged from the depths of her

thoughts—that terrible side of herself she'd always kept hidden. Could she tell him? The guilt had been building inside her for so long, and a part of her longed to confess.

"I'm not an angel or a saint," she muttered. "Trust me, I'm very capable of hate."

He lowered his hands and looked at her intently.

"Back when you confessed you were an undercover agent, I got upset because you lied to me, not because you thought I had killed Michael." She paused and averted her eyes. "Because I wanted to. You have no idea how often I used to fantasize about his death." The guilt choked her, drowning her words.

"Oh, my sweet Joy!" He scrutinized her. "Your biggest sin is what the rest of us call a moral victory: hating someone so badly you want to kill them, but managing not to do it." He laughed, then he tipped her chin to lift her face. "The man was a bastard. He treated you like garbage. It's not surprising that sometimes you wished he'd die."

His unforeseen understanding astonished her, making her self-disgust grow. "You don't get it. I spent hours and hours imagining plots; it turned into an obsession." She struggled to meet his gaze. "My outlet became writing crime stories. In those stories, a woman used medical means to murder her husband and make it look like natural causes."

This seemed to sober him up. All sorrow vanished from his face, and he leaned forward, mesmerized. "Tell me more."

This was the most difficult confession of Joy's life. That shameful secret was something she'd expected to take with her to the grave. But his attentiveness encouraged her to talk. "For example, Michael was severely allergic to peanuts. He had to carry an epi-pen for emergencies and be sheltered all his life, because any minimal contact could be life threatening."

He nodded. "I remember hearing that."

Even though she knew they were alone, she looked over her shoulder and glanced around instinctively. "Well, I used to fantasize about replacing his morning allergy medicine with metoprolol pills—that's a medication used in patients with cardiac issues which happens to block the effect of epinephrine. In my fantasy, I would bring ground peanuts with me to the restaurant the next time we went out for dinner. I would wait until he was distracted, and sprinkle the peanut powder on his food. When he developed a full-blown anaphylactic reaction, the epi-pen wouldn't work."

She paused, feeling again the excitement that fantasy used to bring her. "His throat would swell, preventing him from breathing. He'd choke to death in front of dozens of witnesses ready to confirm that his poor wife had desperately, unsuccessfully, tried to save his life by giving him his shot and starting CPR. I knew CPR was useless in a case like that—he would've needed an emergency tracheostomy—but nobody could blame me for panicking at the time and not thinking about it. By letting everyone know I was a doctor, they'd hold off on calling nine-one-one. I'd wait until he lost consciousness before finally calling. By the time the paramedics arrived, it would've been too late. All they'd find would be his lifeless body."

She stopped, trapped in a confusing net of exhilaration and shame. Back then she'd felt so powerless and been so desperate to escape Michael's mistreatment. But how had she ever allowed herself such lowly thoughts?

Mortified, it took several moments for her to meet Richard's gaze. She expected to find him looking at her with disgust.

Instead, he gaped at her, his expression a mixture of wonder, admiration, and… was that desire?

"Maybe Carl is right and I have a thing for bad girls," he said at last. "But you have no idea how turned on I am. I need to have you right now."

As he took her in his arms and reached for a kiss, relief burst in her soul and bubbled out in the form of giggles. She placed a hand on his chest, keeping him at arm's length. "Well, buddy. The only thing you're going to have tonight is a good sleep."

CHAPTER 19

Hangovers had once been Richard's perpetual companions. But he must've been out of practice, because this particular one was worse than ever. He hadn't realized how much he'd cut down on alcohol lately.

He wasn't sure how he'd made it to his bed. He noticed his work clothes and shoes had been removed and he lay under the blanket in his briefs and an undershirt.

His memory tortured him with a sharp recollection of the embarrassing state in which Joy found him the night before. He tossed aside the blankets, trying to work past the headache and nausea as he eased out of the bed and headed to the kitchen.

Thank God someone had made coffee. He served himself a mug and drank a few large bitter gulps, trying to clear his mind.

Joy's purse lay on the counter, confirming she was still there, and he felt both relieved and worried—both longing to see her and dreading to face her. The thought of confronting her made his headache threaten to evolve into a full-blown migraine. Then, he heard cheerful voices and, mug in hand, followed them to Ray's room.

Joy and Ray were engaged in a video game battle. The screen, split in half, showed cartoon characters driving racecars.

"You're worse than Dad, Joy!" Ray trash-talked. "You have to at least *try* to win."

"Now I can't sop giggling; my arms are so weak I can't manage the controls!" Joy laughed uncontrollably. Normally, any noise would've worsened Richard's headache, but the refreshing sound of her laughter seeped through him, soothing his pain.

He wasn't sure why Ray was there instead of at his mother's, but he felt pleased, watching him and Joy in silence and enjoying their playful banter.

The game-over music sounded and Ray clapped. "I win! I wish I could be more excited about it, but this victory was too easy."

Drying tears with the edge of her T-shirt, Joy shot back, "Well, I guess we're even now, since my baseball team creamed yours last night."

Ray snorted. "They only won because the umpire was blind! That was so not an out!"

"Still, we won!" Joy clapped once and pointed at Ray. "Five points to four!"

Richard entered the room and joined the conversation. "In baseball it's called a run, Joy. Not a point."

She whipped her head toward Richard, making her long hair fly, and the grin that brightened her face warmed his soul. "You're awake!" She rose from her seat to greet him with a hug that felt as good as oxygen after near drowning.

Ray limited his greeting to a wave.

"When did you get here?" he asked Ray as they walked to the kitchen.

"You were asleep when I came to grab dinner. By the way man—" He clicked his tongue and shook his head in mock disapproval. "You have to shop for groceries more regularly; your fridge was emptier than my piggy bank." He perched himself on a barstool at the kitchen counter. "But don't worry; Joy ordered us pizza."

"I had him call through the landline and paid cash," she clarified, reassuring him she hadn't forgotten the usual precautions. "And this morning he rode his bike to the store and got a few supplies for breakfast."

Richard took a long sip of coffee while making a mental note to reimburse her. "How come you stayed last night?"

The question was directed to Joy, but Ray answered, "Well, it started raining like crazy. Then we got busy cleaning up in the kitchen and the living room and then having pizza while watching the game…"

"It was raining too hard," she interjected. "Even Hope and Tom agreed it wasn't safe for me to drive back to Winter Park, so I crashed on the couch." She glanced at the clock on her phone. "I'll be heading out soon to join them and the kids at a water park."

Ray leaned his arms on the counter. "Did you know Joy feeds her kids pizza twice a week? Her kids are so lucky!"

She busied herself searching for something in her purse, seemingly ashamed. "Yeah, I know; I'm a lazy cook." She handed Richard a few tablets. "Here. Tylenol, antacid, and nausea medication." Familiar with his kitchen, she grabbed a glass from a cabinet and filled it with water from the fridge dispenser. "And here, start working on your hydration. I can make you some breakfast while you go change." She winked. "Just keep your expectations low and don't get used to it—since we've established I'm a lousy housekeeper."

He smiled. "Thank you. I'd love to shower and shave first." His eyes refused to move away from her. Caught on their uncertain present, he'd never dared to imagine what life would be if they could be a normal couple. But how wonderful it would be to have her here every day.

By the time he finished showering, shaving, and brushing his teeth he felt like a new person. He threw on an olive T-shirt and cargo shorts and returned to the kitchen where he found Joy alone. "Where's Ray?"

"He said he was meeting some friends to go surfing. I imagined you didn't feel like driving him, so I sent him in a taxi—don't worry, I had him call for it himself." She handed him a fresh mug of coffee. "It's not as good as yours, but it's something."

He thanked her and took a seat at the counter.

She presented him with a tray. "Anti-hangover breakfast. Eggs, avocados, and bananas. And more water."

He eyed her with curiosity. "How do you know so much about hangovers if you never drink?"

"My sister Hope drank enough for the two of us. I used to rescue her from parties and take care of her afterward."

While she made small talk, he nibbled at his breakfast, savoring her presence even more than the food. When he finished his plate, he sipped the last of his coffee and commented, "I'm surprised you're still here after the show I gave you last night."

Her voice carried a playful tone as she sat on the stool next to his. "You thought you'd get rid of me that easily?"

Relief flooded him, and a jolt of joy and gratitude overpowered him. He wanted to take her in his arms, kiss her and tell her how much he loved her.

Instead, he tentatively joked, "If I wanted to get rid of you I'd just stop watching you when you cross the street."

Chuckling, she rolled her eyes and shook her head. "Well, I just wanted to make sure you were feeling better before leaving." She reached for her purse. "I'll see you for our trip to Pineapple Beach at the end of next week, right?"

His heart filling with light, he reached for her hand. "Do you still want to join me even after you saw me shit-faced drunk?" The sheepishness in his own voice surprised him.

She seemed shy too. "Do you still want to hang out with me after I told you about my murder fantasies?"

"Are you kidding? I loved that!" Beaming, he tugged on her hand to get her closer and encircled her waist with his arms. "I can't wait for you to tell me more!"

She tittered and wrapped her arms around his neck, letting him hold her against his chest. He wished he were more able to express his feelings. He wished so hard he could say aloud how much he loved her, but the words were stuck in his throat. He didn't deserve this wonderful woman; but he was selfish enough that he'd enjoy her for as long as it lasted.

His voice was almost a whisper. "I know I babbled many stupid things last night. But the worst of all was saying that we should stop seeing each other." He kissed her hair. "If I don't say it enough, I'm a very lucky bastard to have you."

She tightened her embrace. He could feel the waves of soothing energy flowing from her, restoring him. He drank up the feeling, smelling her hair, and relishing her touch.

After moments in silence, she mumbled, "Okay. Let's try that experiment."

He gently separated her from his chest to look at her, confused. "What?"

"Let's try that positive-negative reinforcement plan you offered. If I ever psychoanalyze you, I'll reward you and take a punishment. You'll do the same for me if you get mean or paranoid on me again."

As he caught the deeper meaning hiding under those words, the room seemed brighter. She was surrendering. She was agreeing to take their relationship to the next level. All the worries previously burdening him, from the case to Sanders' threats, dissipated, and he felt like clapping and cheering.

Cupping her face, he kissed her lips softly; then he caressed her cheek with the back of his hand. "So what's my punishment going to be if I ever flunk my end of the deal?"

A flash of childish playfulness sparked in her eyes. "If I'm going to strip my body, I want you to strip your soul."

Frowning, he removed his hand from her face. "What do you mean?"

"Your punishment is going to be to tell me one story from your childhood. Something significant enough to have made you who you are today."

Every muscle in his body tensed at the unexpected request. "Why?"

"Because you know everything about me and I know very little about the real you."

He groaned with dread. "I know what you're doing; you're going to use those stories to psychoanalyze me."

Shaking her head, she placed a hand on her chest and raised the other one. "I promise I won't. But if for any reason I do," she gave a weak shrug and her mouth curved up, "I guess someone's getting a striptease."

He cracked up.

"Deal?" Joy extended her hand.

After a brief handshake, he tugged her to his chest and kissed her.

Richard took his time, slowly tasting those soft, plump lips he loved so much. He kissed her with reverence, feeling undeserving of the treasure he had in his hands. Holding her like that—feeling her petite body, her small bones, her delicate hands—he relived the fear of being a mortal profaning an angel.

But then her mouth responded to his kiss, and when her tongue met his, the switch flipped in his brain. His body lit up in flames. He turned into a cloud of desire.

He moved his kisses to her neck and asked in a hoarse voice, "Can you stay just an hour longer?"

Her nod was so subtle he would've missed it, if all his attention hadn't been on her.

That was all he needed. He picked her up in his arms, startling her. Her small yelp, followed by giggles, was drowned by his mouth.

Without breaking the kiss, he carried her to the bedroom.

CHAPTER 20

J OY DIDN'T REALIZE SHE'D DOZED OFF UNTIL KISSES ON THE back of her shoulder woke her up. She was lying in bed in Richard's arms, her head tucked between his neck and his chest. The ear she pressed against his body could feel, more than hear, the beating of his heart, now slowing down after its previous frantic race. He had both arms and his right leg wrapped around her, her own legs weaved and tangled with his free one. Every piece of her body fit with his, like a perfect puzzle. She inhaled his masculine smell with every breath, half consciously, half drowsing, lost in the deep relaxation her body experienced.

She'd once believed she was a soul which just happened to have a body attached to it, and that such body was nothing but a necessary evil in the path of spiritual growth. Richard was making her reconsider that. *Maybe the body can also be a gateway to the highest heaven.*

Floating in her cloud of bliss, she barely had the energy to lift her head and meet his eyes. He gazed at her with a tender expression.

"Hi." It was all it occurred to her to say. *Darn it, I'm so unsophisticated.*

What she really wanted to say was that she loved him. That their mutual opening had left her feeling closer to him than ever before; that their lovemaking minutes ago had been wonderful; and that it felt so real she had trouble believing they could ever part from each other.

His answer wasn't much cleverer than hers. "Hello." The longing in his eyes transmitted shared emotions.

He kissed her shoulder again, then her neck, then her jawline. "I wish you didn't have to go."

To go. She whipped her head toward the alarm clock on the nightstand and jerked up straight. "Oh shoot! I have to go get the kids."

She slipped back on the underwear and T-shirt she'd dropped on the floor before tossing the blankets aside and jumping out of the bed.

He flopped back against the pillow, looking like a kid asked to relinquish his favorite toy at bedtime. "Will I see you again before the trip? You know, so we can keep... working on the documents?"

She couldn't help chuckling as she pulled up her yoga pants. "I have the feeling that we're not going to make much progress. Maybe you should get yourself a new consultant."

He shot her an innocent, wide-eyed look. "Why?" Then he pulled her arm, making her fall back in bed and kissed her.

She squealed, then giggled and pushed his face gently away. "*That* is why." She slipped out of his arms and searched for her hoodie on the bedroom floor.

"I can't wait to get to Pineapple Beach so you can keep telling me all the different ways to murder Michael." He moved to sit on the side of the bed.

"Oh, please!" She shuddered before throwing on her gray hoodie. "I shouldn't have told you that story."

He worked on replacing his cargo shorts. "No, no, it was great! Very educational."

She laughed and retrieved her flip-flops from under the bed. "Really? *Educational?*"

"Seriously. I'm constantly reading medical and forensic articles while working on my cases. I'd love to discuss some of that with you. In fact, with that wild imagination of yours combined with your medical knowledge you could really help me—" He stopped mid-sentence with his olive T-shirt in his hands and looked at her.

"Joy, did I see your name on the list of providers who saw Rachel Hayes in the ICU?"

Her fingers stopped working on tying her hair up and she became serious. "It's interesting that you mention her. I reviewed her records and..." She hesitated. HIPAA laws didn't apply when talking to law enforcement, especially about someone who was already dead. She finished tying her ponytail. "I know she's connected to Michael's murder case and I've been debating whether I should throw a theory your way."

He raised an eyebrow, then slipped his shirt back on. "I'm listening."

She sat on the bed next to him. "Any chance someone could've tried to kill her?"

A flicker of surprise crossed his face, but he immediately covered it up with an unreadable mask. "I'm not allowed to deny or confirm that statement. But for theoretical discussion, let's assume that's right and... go on."

She took a deep breath. "Her records said they found her unconscious and with a very low blood pressure. What if someone had been feeding her blood pressure medication? That would be something that doesn't show in a normal drug screen. The drug screen can show opiates, benzodiazepines, cocaine, and such. But it doesn't test for most prescription drugs."

Richard leaned forward, seemingly interested. "I'm not allowed to give you any hint about whether what you're telling me matches the case or not. But if you were an anonymous informant calling in a tip, what would you say?" He reached for a notepad and pen lying on the nightstand.

She moved to the reading chair next to the bed. Lately, she'd been mostly practicing the psychiatry portion of her medicine-psychiatry training, but her internal medicine skills were still fresh. "Despite renal function being impaired, her potassium levels were low—that's unusual. Adding to that high bicarbonate levels and signs of dehydration, I suspect someone was giving her diuretics. That would've caused her to urinate frequently, mimicking a urinary infection and matching the information given by the jail infirmary."

He gaped at her for several moments before scribbling a few notes. "Go on."

She continued, "Then her slow pulse is unusual for someone with low blood pressure, and I'm not convinced about the heart block diagnosis. I'd also have tested her for beta-blockers, like metoprolol."

His fingers rushed to take notes while his quickening breathing revealed his excitement under his poker face. "You're going to need to explain some of these terms in more detail."

Her eyes flicked to the clock on the nightstand. "But I really have to leave. I'm already late to get the kids."

Slowly putting down his notes, he nodded. "Let's make an appointment to keep talking about this."

～

Monday, Richard had annoying, syrupy love songs stuck in his head—from '50s rock, to boy teen bands, to lately Jesse McCartney's "Beautiful Soul." Only years of practice concealing his emotions—from navigating his unstable mother to the FBI training—prevented him from grinning like an idiot all day long.

What a lucky bastard I am. I can't believe this woman.

If he weren't obsessed with Joy's divine mouth and body—or addicted to the energy of her soul—Richard would've still been unable to leave her just because of her incredible brain. She was proving to be the best weapon he ever had in solving his case. He had to be careful when phrasing his medical questions, to avoid revealing confidential information. But he had no doubt that if someone could help him figure out how the LOTU had murdered their latest victims, she could.

But now he had much work to do. He suspected the harassing

messages Joy had received weren't connected to the case. It wouldn't make sense that the LOTU would try to scare her instead of just eliminating her.

The moment he arrived at work, he sent the request to analyze Hayes' stored blood for the drugs Joy had suggested. Next, he called Venkat Patel for an informal meeting, reportedly to ask him more questions about the greeting card incidents. But what he really wanted was to read his body language and search his speech patterns to see if he might be involved with the LOTU.

He met Patel at his office at the CeMeSH, in the Masden Center, and after a few simple questions, Richard charged without transition. "I understand that you didn't get along well with Michael O'Hara."

Frowning, Patel leaned back in his chair and crossed his arms. "Everyone who got to know him beneath the surface knew his charm and charisma were limited to the cameras. And he always struck me as a racist."

With a chuckle, Richard casually commented, "Some would say you're glad he's dead."

Patel's jaw clenched and a muscle twitched on his temple. "I would never wish for anybody's death."

"That didn't come out right," Richard clarified. "It's not a big deal, right? After all, what is death but waking up from an illusion?" He stopped and searched Patel's eyes. There was no hint of recognition at the words. He tried again. "You know, there are some people who even believe in instant reincarnation." The man didn't even blink.

"Well, not me," Patel said without intonation.

Richard decided to change strategies. "Is it true that O'Hara was the one thing stopping Dr. Clayton from helping you propel your speaking career?"

This time Patel couldn't hide the flash of surprise in his eyes. This could suggest his early lack of reaction didn't come from great skills concealing emotions. Maybe he wasn't with the LOTU after all.

Patel shot Richard an offended glare. "If I'd known you'd invited me here to insinuate that I had something to do with O'Hara's death, I would've brought my lawyer." He uncrossed his arms. "You're wrong, Mr. Fields. I would never kill. I'm a pacifist, and unable to use violence against other people."

That would be a typical answer for a LOTU leader—they'd be blind to their own destructive tendencies until they snapped. "I have an informant who claims you're interested in making Dr. Clayton your 'sidekick' as you become the next holistic medicine media personality."

"All I want is to help Dr. Clayton."

"So you admit you have a personal interest in her?" The two men locked eyes.

Patel's tense jaw and clenched fists tightened further. "No, I don't. Joy has three small children to support on her own, and a morning job which is commendable, but destined to go bankrupt any time. She's a fine physician who's done a huge service for this town and has never been compensated adequately."

Richard raised his eyebrows. "And since when do you have such a generous interest in compensating fine physicians?"

The man didn't blink. "Since Joy took care of a dear friend who died in her Hospice House."

Richard recoiled in surprise. The grief in Patel's eyes hinted this person had been more than just a friend. A lover maybe? He seemed sincere.

Patel continued, "My way to say 'thank you' to Joy, is to make sure that she's taken care of financially. And once she accepts my business offer and is discovered as a mind-body-spirit star, she'll have nothing to worry about."

Richard took pride in his ability to read when someone was lying; and something told him Patel wasn't—at least in that last sentence.

"Good morning, am I late?" Allison Connors' voice brought Richard back from his thoughts.

He rose to shake her hand. "Dr. Connors. What a surprise."

"Since you mentioned you wanted to talk about the card incidents, I invited her too," Patel said. "She was with Joy when she received the first one." His lack of enthusiasm hinted he now understood the meeting had a different purpose.

Richard didn't have any more questions for Patel. "Actually, I was on my way out. I don't need to talk to Dr.—"

"But I do want to have a word with you, Agent," she interrupted him. "Would you mind coming to my office upstairs for a minute?" Something in her severe expression reminded him of a stern schoolteacher.

He followed her out, but then had second thoughts. He couldn't risk her mentioning his relationship with Joy in a place he hadn't checked for hidden cameras or microphones. "I'm going to have to request we have this conversation somewhere else."

A few minutes later they sat in his SUV, windows up, the engine running, the AC blasting against the heat. Despite her protests, he'd checked her for hidden microphones and made her turn off her phone.

"Do you have anything to tell me about the cards, or that email Dr. Clayton received Friday?" he asked.

"No. I needed to continue our conversation." She seemed to hesitate. "I'm aware that I shouldn't have disrespected authority."

"Apology accep—"

"Do not interrupt me; I'm not apologizing."

He did a double take at her defiant tone.

Without moving a facial muscle, and with no intonation in her voice, she enunciated every word carefully. "I meant everything I said. I will not sit quietly and witness you break Joy's heart. She has suffered enough."

In the privacy of the car, this was an unrepeatable opportunity to clear things with her. "You're Joy's therapist, aren't you?"

She tensed up. "I can't confirm or deny that statement."

He half-smirked. "You just confirmed it. Allow me to remind you that, this being a murder case of national security, you're exempted from your professional secrecy. If there is anything I need to know for anyone's safety—"

"As Joy's therapist I don't have much to discuss." She leaned forward. "But as Joy's concerned colleague, I have a lot to say."

He raised his eyebrows. "So that's how it's going to be?" *To hell with it.* He searched for his badge in his jacket pocket and slammed it on the dashboard. "If you're not the therapist, then I'm not the agent. Speak, Connors, I have the feeling you don't like me."

"Listen to me." She narrowed her eyes. "I gave up long ago the idea that any man in the world is worth a rotten potato. But I also know Joy could do better than you."

You're preaching to the freaking choir. He concealed his agreement with a snort. "That's not for you to decide."

She continued as if he hadn't spoken. "The only reason why Joy felt attracted to you in the first place is because you're just like Michael O'Hara."

The words felt like a slap on the face and a punch in the ribs rolled into one. His jaw clenched and he took his time biting off each word. "Never. Compare me. To that monster."

"You are. Like him, you seem put-together but deep inside you're a mess. You boss her around, imposing your will over hers. You don't appreciate her—you don't even value her enough to be seen in public with her."

Her words swirled in his brain making him take a cold hard look at the past weeks.

At his silence, she continued, "The only difference between you and O'Hara is that *you're worse.* At least Joy was the only woman in his life since they started dating in high school. But you? You're the man who screwed every woman in a fifty-mile radius."

How would she know that? The busy romantic history he wasn't proud of flashed in his mind; from the poisonous ex-wife who'd made him swear off marriage, to his alleged one-night stand with Sanders that was now costing him his peace—and every other drama queen in between. Connors had the dangerous gift of making him doubt himself.

"Why do you hate me so much, Connors?" he asked surveying her face. "Did I sleep with you and forgot to call you back or something?"

She pretended to put a finger in her throat and fake-gagged. "Please. Don't make me lose my breakfast. I have better taste than that. Unfortunately, more than one woman I know doesn't."

An idea sparked in Richard's mind. *Damn small town. She must've also been the therapist of one of my ex-girlfriends.*

Connors straightened in her seat. "You're used to women falling at your feet without resistance. And then you find the one gal who pushes you away, and the challenge is too good to pass. If that woman is also forbidden, then she's even more enticing."

"So, you have me all figured out. You know even better than me why I went after Joy." He crossed his arms. "Then answer this question, Connors. If all I wanted was the challenge of chasing a forbidden woman, how come I'm still with her after I got her?"

"Because just as you are her type, she's yours," she shot back. "You gravitate toward the broken woman. And Joy may have a high-paying job and a seemingly balanced life, but deep inside she's as wounded and unstable as those women you used to go for."

Richard had wondered more than once why he had fallen so hard for Joy when she was so different from his usual type of woman. Could Connors have a point? Was this just another instance of his unconscious mind playing games with him? Would he wake up one morning realizing the magic was gone and the love he thought he felt for her had vanished?

The tactile and olfactory memory of having Joy in his arms in his house Saturday flashed in his mind. The sound of her laughter when she played video games with Ray re-played in his brain.

No.

He shot Connors a cold once-over. "If you can't understand what a unique human being Joy is, and why I fell for her…" He scoffed. "You're wrong to say you know her at all." They stared at one another for a moment, then Richard said, "Have a good day, Dr. Connors."

She flushed, but her expression remained frozen. "Just be aware that I'm willing to go to any extreme to protect Joy if you try to hurt her." Her eyes turned to slits. "Even if that means calling the FBI to fill them in about your relationship with her."

Richard's pulse raced. She wouldn't carry through with that threat, would she? He pushed back. "You can't break your professional secrecy unless someone is in danger. If you expose me, I'll make sure you lose your counseling license."

Fear flashed briefly in her eyes, but she didn't move a muscle. "It might be worth it."

He struggled to keep his face immutable despite the adrenaline rushing through his bloodstream. "Have a good day, Connors," he repeated.

She picked up her phone and exited the car. She sent one last glare in his direction before slamming the door, then sauntered away.

CHAPTER 21

Nestled between the Indian River and the Atlantic Ocean, the "island" of Pineapple Beach boasted fantastic sunrises and sunsets. After so many weeks of confinement, the past three days had been a dream for Joy. She'd savored every minute, from starting the day with lovemaking alongside the rumbling of the ocean through the open windows, to ending it with beach walks under the stars after homemade dinners.

Sampling a taste of domestic life felt wonderful, like having lazy morning chats over Richard's delicious coffee, or shopping for groceries at the local market—always hiding behind hats and sunglasses to blend in among the tourists. She treasured the "normal couple" experience of having small arguments about the thermostat—she was always freezing, he was always burning up. She even relished the new routine of taking breaks from each other while he surfed and she read—only to miss each other soon and happily reunite.

But the best part was getting to know Richard better through his childhood stories.

"I can't believe this!" Dissolving in giggles, Joy sat cross-legged on the blanket they'd laid on the grass at the riverside, where they were watching a sunset. "I spent my childhood obsessed with good grades, killing myself to make straight As—and you were failing tests *on purpose*?"

Next to her, he lounged on the blanket with his hands clasped behind his head. "Yup. Tanking my grades was the safest way to fly under the radar of the bullies."

Like a mirror, the Indian River lagoon reflected the intense mixture of gold, orange, and red the cloud-sprinkled sky had turned into. The scent of mosquito repellent mixed with the mild swampy smell of the lagoon waters. Along with the warm breeze, Joy's body felt the lingering relaxation after their most recent lovemaking, a short time ago.

She ran her fingers through Richard's hair, gently scratching his scalp with her nails the way he liked it. He closed his eyes and a groan of pleasure escaped him, making her smile. Being with Richard was so effortless compared to being with Michael. Getting constant positive feedback made it much easier to be a good partner.

"You were saying?" she asked.

"Well," he continued, "when I was about ten, after one of my multiple trips to the principal's office, the school counselor gave me a life-changing piece of advice." He got up on his elbows and, imitating the man's serious voice, shook his head and clicked his tongue. "'Richard, don't you get it? Having a work ethic is the self-serving thing to do if you want to have fun in life. If you pass your tests and stay out of trouble now, you get to enjoy your summer off, instead of going to summer school. And as a grown-up, if you show up to work and do it right, you can have a blast when you get paid and have money to spend.'"

"Interesting!" She chuckled.

"The poor guy was probably just out of ideas when he threw that one at me, but somehow it clicked. It transformed my outlook."

A flock of birds in perfect synchronization crossed the last hint of the sun sinking into the horizon. He sat up, facing her, and leaned his forearm on his bent knee. "See, I'd learned early in life that I might as well do whatever I pleased, because I'd get in trouble regardless of what I did. Even the days I was on my best behavior, if my mother happened to be PMSing or cranky about something, she'd beat my brothers and me—so what was the point?"

Her eyes followed a pelican diving in free-fall into the water surface to catch its dinner. Gosh! Did she know what he meant! Michael hadn't beaten her physically, but he did emotionally. And the harder she tried to please him, the unhappier he got, like he resented her efforts to disturb his misery.

"But if I previously didn't have any guidance or encouragement to behave well or do my job," Richard continued, "now I had a reason. It was the self-serving thing to do to maximize my fun later."

She ran her hands over the eagle tattoo on his muscular right arm, exposed by his short-sleeved T-shirt. "I'd always wondered how you can balance your self-indulgent side with the strict discipline required for your type of work."

"My self-indulgent nature saved my life—literally," he pointed out, smiling. "I grew up in the perfect brew to become a juvenile delinquent and end up dead in my teens, like many of my pals in the Bronx."

"You're right!" she reflected. "You had all the risk factors: the risky environment; the mostly absent, alcoholic father; the physically abusive mother…"

"Who was hooked on pain pills," he completed the idea. "In my teenage years, I did follow my older friends around after school in amateur acts of vandalism and petty crime. But the pleasure-seeking view of life made me realize that the fun of breaking a window just because wasn't worth the breathless run, being chased by the angry neighbor—or worse, the police. And the brief thrill of a knife fight wasn't worth the trip to the ER for stitches. I narrowly escaped the gang life and got my first after-school job at age sixteen, so I could always have my own money to buy myself food when my mother was passed out again—and to get my own beer."

She pondered his words in silence, purposefully ignoring the part about underage drinking.

He glanced at his watch and gasped. "We have ten minutes to moonrise! Let's go!"

They jumped off the ground, rolled and picked up the blanket from the grass and climbed on their rented beach cruisers. He pedaled ahead, holding the rolled blanket under his arm, and she followed behind him.

"Can you smell that? Isn't that divine?" he asked, cruising for a moment to allow her to catch up.

She admired how he could smell the ocean from blocks away. Contrary to her oblivious self, who ran into walls constantly, Richard had an amazing ability to attune his senses and pay attention to detail. Before him, she'd never noticed the tracks on the sand from giant mother and tiny baby turtles finding their way to the water. She'd never glimpsed the invisible ghost crabs, camouflaging themselves at the shore. Seeing the world through his eyes was a wonderful experience.

In just minutes they covered the few blocks separating the west from the east coast of the island, returning to the beach access closest to their vacation house. They left their beach cruisers at the bike rack and held hands as they descended the wooden steps to the sand.

The last of the afterglow in the west tinted the clouds over the ocean, but darkness grew by the minute. They spread the blanket on the sand and, with fingers laced, listened to the symphony of the crashing waves. As some clouds on the horizon dispersed, a huge reddish moon made its debut over the water. Joy watched it in silence, feeling an ancestral connection to every human being before them who had witnessed that miracle.

He kissed her head. "Why so quiet?"

"I'm still thinking about the last story you told me," she replied. "It's admirable that after a childhood like that you became a policeman and then a federal agent, instead of a criminal."

He played with her fingers. "Carl says it was a case of sublimation."

"He's probably right," she agreed. "You found a way to channel your violent energy in a positive way."

His face lit up. "Gotcha! You just psychoanalyzed me again!" Laughing, he released her hand to clap. "You owe me a striptease!"

Squeezing her eyes shut, she tapped her forehead. "Darn it, I did analyze you!" She opened her eyes. "But don't you ever get tired of those?"

Raising his eyebrows, he tilted his head as if the answer was obvious. "What do you think?"

Sighing in resignation, she leaned on his shoulder to get up from the ground. "Well, then let's get back to the house," she grumbled. "You blasted that AC so much the house is freezing enough without me taking my clothes off."

His large hand on her forearm stopped her. "Wait, maybe you're right. Never mind."

She wasn't expecting that. "What do you mean?"

"How about today you also 'strip your soul' instead of your body."

The surprise was so much she stumbled and almost tripped over. He coaxed her back onto the blanket and rested her head on his lap to gently caress her hair. "Tell me about *your* childhood, Joy. How did you become a compulsive overachieving super woman? When did you first become obsessed with straight As?"

She'd answered that question many times before, during therapy; but she took her time, making sure her reply was sincere.

"I guess it was after my mother's death," she said, settling for her stock response. "My father fell into depression and withdrew psychologically from my sister and me. Grades and awards were my desperate attempt to get his attention."

The moon kept rising, turning its color from reddish to golden. Its light reflected on the water, mimicking a path across the restless waves. "No matter what I did, my depressed, emotionally absent father would never notice me," she continued. "Straight As, perfect scores, honor society endowments—nothing worked. I was invisible in his eyes."

His tender manner touched her. His voice was as soft as his caress on her hair. "I remember you said your mother died of breast cancer when you were only nine. Was she sick for a long time?"

A knot formed in her throat. "I was seven when she was diagnosed the first time. She had a break after the first round of chemo, but then it spread."

"Only seven? You were so young."

She swallowed, feeling a sudden desire to cry.

His eyes were full of loving compassion, devoid of pity. "That's why you can't stop taking care of others. It's now your second nature."

The tightness in her throat and chest grew. She knew that, but there was something in the gentleness of his touch and his voice that deprived her of her usual armor of intellectualization. "I still remember the day I realized she wasn't putting me to bed anymore—*I* was putting *her* to bed, when she was sick from the treatment." She stopped, trying to gather herself. "After she died, I spent the rest of my childhood holding my father's hand and being his cheerleader, trying unsuccessfully to lift him from his depression. I also had to watch my younger sister, Hope."

He nodded slowly. "No wonder you continued the pattern and married Michael, an unstable man in constant need to be protected from himself."

She lost the battle with the tears. In a way, she'd always known that. But she'd used the information mostly to beat herself up. Richard's tenderness made her see herself with a light of compassion for the first time.

She dried her eyes with the back of her hand. "I've been so angry with myself for marrying Michael. I'd almost forgotten that the woman who married him was the same broken fifteen-year-old girl who first started dating him around the time her father died—and the same heart-broken little girl who'd watched her mother die."

He guided her to sit up and wrapped her in his arms. She savored his embrace, delighting in his warmth while he infused her with his strength.

After a while hugging in silence, he spoke with a hoarse voice. "Okay, you win," he tightened his hold. "I'll turn off the AC."

CHAPTER 22

WHO WOULD'VE KNOWN THAT PLOTTING MURDER WAS SO much fun? And who would've known that killing someone could be so easy for a doctor?

For the duration of the drive to Pineapple Beach, and on and off during the trip, Richard had brainstormed theoretical medical scenarios with Joy. They'd even managed to make it a fun activity by inventing a game about killing O'Hara over and over again. Sneaking blood pressure medication into someone's dinner. Switching their pills without their knowledge. Changing the strength of a pill or someone's insulin doses.

It seemed every inch of a drugstore shelf was loaded with potential deadly weapons. Richard would never look at a pharmacy the same way.

"I assumed it would be hard to kill someone in the hospital," he commented during their sunrise beach walk. "I'd expect the patients to be under surveillance, on monitors, or surrounded by staff."

"Only if they're in ICU or a telemetry floor," she replied, moving away the hair the wind blew on her face. "Once someone is in the hospital, the possibilities to kill them are endless. For example, Hayes' sepsis would've been easy to provoke. They just had to inject bacteria into her IV."

He shot her a dubious look. "Where can you find lethal bacteria?"

"Where can't you? Hospital counters, saliva, toilet water… Our bodies carry bacteria that would kill us if they get injected directly into our blood. They're innocuous only because of our natural defenses and because they're balanced by the good bacteria in our normal flora." She stopped and smiled with a hint of defiance. "Like in the body of the Universe, where so-called evil and good constantly compete in balance."

He chuckled. Typical of Joy to reel any conversation back to their philosophical and ethical debates—which he loved just as much.

The past four days had been the happiest days of Richard's life. Sleep didn't seem necessary when he and Joy were absorbed in their mutual explorations—physical and intellectual. They'd reached a magical balance where they were still new to each other, but were comfortable enough to let down their guards and live in shorts, T-shirts, and flip-flops. He delighted in this new side of her, no fancy clothes or makeup on. He was also enjoying that new side of himself, able to join her singing loudly to an old tune on the car radio, or let her give him ballroom dancing lessons in the bedroom without self-consciousness.

He inhaled the scent of the ocean and relished the sensation of the sand between his toes, small pleasures that seemed multiplied by her company. If he could have this in his life permanently—her small hand in his—it would be worth any sacrifice. Even abandoning his dream of working for the FBI.

Could Sanders' job offer be the answer to his problems?

"This is so beautiful! I can't believe I live so close to the ocean and I never take the time to visit it!" She stopped briefly to point at the fire-like colors in the sky, then kept on walking. "Do you know that the east-facing offices at the Masden Center have an ocean view? I've beaten myself up for years because I didn't think of that when I leased my office space. If I could see the ocean from my office window, work would be so much easier."

A corner of his mind followed her words, but the rest absorbed how beautiful she looked bathed in the sunrise colors. He wasn't sure what had possessed him when he decided to pursue her, but now he thanked the stubbornness that prevented him from giving up.

He stopped walking and tugged on her arm to spin her around and surprise her with a quick kiss. "You're so cheerful, you remind me of upbeat music that gets stuck in my head and I can't help but sing all day. Something like ABBA, or Neil Diamond, or happy rock-and-roll from the fifties and sixties." That's what he was hearing in his head right now, annoying oldies love songs. What was happening to him?

She giggled. "I love all that! That's what I listen to all the time in my car."

"Of course you do." He kissed the tip of her nose with adoration.

He wished so badly he could say how much he loved her, but those words had only come out easily for him one day, when he was still anesthetized by the shock of finding out himself. Instead, he kissed her lips softly, almost with devotion, hoping to communicate that way what he was too cowardly to admit aloud.

The glee leaked out of her features and, gently, she freed herself from his arms. She scanned his face and, a flash of fear crossed her eyes. "The breeze is getting chilly. Let's get back to the house."

She picked up the pace, leaving him behind, and headed for the wooden beach access.

Baffled, he watched her stride away. *Chilly?* It was at least eighty-five degrees.

Scowling, Richard took off behind her and caught her arm to make her stop. "What the hell is going on?"

His abrupt question startled her and her dark, thick eyelashes fluttered. "Excuse me?"

"You're doing it again. You're withdrawing from me."

She released a nervous titter. "I'm not."

"I can tell when you're getting caught in a loop of overthinking or PTSD. Your muscles get tense, you avoid my touch, your voice changes… And most importantly, you complain about feeling cold."

She gaped at him. "You know it freaks me out when you go agent on me." She marched away.

She arrived at the beach access as he caught up with her and pulled her arm to make her face him. Searching her eyes, he asked again. "We were having a great time, goofing around, and out of the blue, you're withdrawing. What's going on?"

She focused her attention on the blanket they'd laid on the sand earlier. She picked it up and rolled it into a tight cylinder. "Maybe that was the problem. We were having *too much* of a great time." She strolled to her rented beach cruiser and stuffed the blanket into its basket. Her eyes finally rose to meet his. "I don't want to get used to this... because I know it's going to end soon."

He understood. Closing the space between them, he wrapped her in his arms. Without her usual high heels, her head rested on his chest. "I know what you mean. The idea of going back to our normal lives in only two more days is painful."

She shook her head. "I don't mean the trip. I mean... *us*."

Frowning, he separated her from his chest to study her face. "And why are you so sure *we* are ending?"

She moved a hand between them. "I should never forget what's really going on here."

He imitated her hand gesture. "Please fill me in. What exactly is going on here?"

Avoiding his eyes, she shrugged. "We're two adults having an adventure. And that's okay. I've never had an adventure before, so sometimes I get carried away and forget that we have an expiration date. That's why you've decided not to say anything about us to the FBI."

Every muscle in his body tensed up. "There are some things you don't know. Coming clean about us means risking more than my job; I'm risking my freedom."

Closing her eyes, she nodded. "You've been clear that you have no intention to tie yourself to a woman ever again."

How could he explain he wasn't talking about freedom symbolically, but literally? Coming clean about them to the FBI could open an investigation about his behavior in the case and send him to jail.

But he couldn't tell her about his lie under oath without dragging her down with him if he ever fell.

She touched his arm. "Richard, I have no intention of pressuring you to marry me. All I want is honesty."

"I'm honest with you when I say I want you in my life. I told you I'd never lie to you ever again, and I meant it."

Her dark eyes drilled into him. "Really? Well, to me lying and withholding information is the same. You keep avoiding my questions about your transfer to New York."

He couldn't answer.

Her hand slid from his arm to his shoulder. "All I need is a little notice to brace myself for the impact. I know we're coming to an end sooner than later. All I want to know is when."

~

Joy surprised herself with her own words. All this time, she'd refused to think about the future. But the last few days together had been painfully wonderful. If that was what life next to him could be, it would be forever harder to settle for less.

He held her arms above the elbows, mesmerizing her with his hazel gaze. "Some days I'm tempted to send everything to hell. Come clean, resign from the FBI, find a different job... But you have to admit you haven't exactly given me much reassurance that taking that risk will be worth it—that I won't go through all that, hoping for a happy ending, only to have you run away and leave me with nothing."

She jolted, taken aback by his words.

Maintaining eye contact, he said, "I'm putting the ball in your court, Joy Clayton. If I took the biggest risk of my life—a risk that's much bigger than you can imagine—do you guarantee you'll be there for me?"

His words caused panic to rise in her. Michael's image surfaced in her memory and for the first time she realized she'd been projecting on Richard a refusal to commit, when the truth was that *she* was terrified of seeing herself tied to a man again.

Allison's voice whispered in her brain, *He's manipulating you. He's only putting the ball in your court so he can avoid responsibility.*

A range of conflicting emotions flooded her. Her love for him. Her terror of being at the mercy of a man again. Her fear of scandal if their relationship became public knowledge.

And something else she couldn't describe. Inexplicable terror that propelled her to run away without looking back.

"Nobody can give you an assurance like that," she replied. "Fifty percent of couples end up splitting—and that's before the challenges you and I face."

With a frown, he released her arms. "I didn't ask for statistics; I asked for your thoughts. Can we please put Dr. Shrink away and bring my woman back?"

Disproportionate anxiety rose in her. "What I mean is, no one knows better than I how challenging it is to make a relationship work, even in the best of circumstances." She paced away from the bike. "I have more knowledge about the human mind and couples' dynamics than I wish I had." All her energy leaked out with her long exhale, and despair filled her soul. "And still I wasn't able to make my own marriage one tiny bit less excruciating than it was."

A long silence fell between them until he finally broke it. "Oh, I see. So everything goes back in a circle. This *is* PTSD. All this is just another version of Michael O'Hara's ghost messing with us."

She felt the sudden impulse to push him, jump on the bike and sprint away. But she breathed through it. He deserved more than that. If she was asking for absolute honesty, she had to start by being honest herself.

Before she could change her mind, she blurted out, "Richard, do you love me?"

If she'd thought he was tense before, now he looked like a rubber band about to snap. "I told you, and I don't remember you saying it back."

She avoided his eyes. "You told me once, on impulse. And then you never said it again."

"Don't ignore my question." He pulled her chin to make her look at him. "I said it once and I never rescinded the statement. I think it's your turn to say it next."

Of course I love you, dummy! I wouldn't be with you otherwise.

"And don't say, 'I love everybody,'" he added, releasing her face. "I know you're a bottomless well of love and compassion and keep throwing them at people around you by the handful." He rolled his eyes, and she almost smiled through the sadness. There he was again, hiding a compliment in a reprimand. He concluded, "I'm talking about... romantic stuff."

What am I doing? Why can't I stop running away from the man I love?

His phone interrupted, flooding her with relief.

Cussing under his breath, he picked up. "Samuel. I'm on vacation. I told you not to call me unless the world's coming to—" He stopped abruptly. His grave expression told Joy something terrible had just happened.

He held up one finger, asking for a minute and walked away. But before that, and despite his usual precautions, she did get to hear two words pronounced on the other side of the line in a worried tone of voice.

"It's Levenstein."

CHAPTER 23

AT HOLLOWAY HOSPITAL'S ICU, RICHARD STARED AT LEVENSTEIN unconscious on the narrow bed. He looked almost alien, his face ghostly pale beneath the tape and tubes, one from his mouth and another out of his nose.

The ICU attending and Richard's friend Dr. Shawn McDevitt sanitized his hands for the third time as he answered Richard and Samuel's questions. "The GI doctor says he'd never seen such an angry bleeding ulcer and so many erosions at once. He couldn't cauterize them all."

"Why is he on the breathing machine?" Samuel asked.

"For airway protection. He was practically spouting blood from his mouth and we didn't want it to get into his lungs."

"Wasn't the amount of bleeding unusual, Shawn?" Richard asked, searching his mind for some of the medical scenarios he'd discussed with Joy. "I heard he'd lost half his blood by the time he made it to the ER."

"He was on Xarelto, a blood thinner, for an irregular heartbeat—that made the difference." Dr. McDevitt adjusted the cuffs of the white coat he wore over his scrubs before continuing. "Unfortunately, this blood thinner doesn't have an antidote. All we can do is keep pumping blood into him to make up for what he's still losing until the Xarelto gets eliminated by his body over the next few days. The hematologist is trying to get NovoSeven, the only drug that can help with this type of bleeding. But it's just a temporary fix."

Richard pondered. Had that been just Levenstein's karma—like Carl would say.

Or was it another murder attempt?

~

Richard and Samuel sat at the Resident Office, still processing the news. Richard sank motionless, sprawled in the black vinyl chair while Samuel drummed a pen on his desk over and over, making a sound that echoed the rattling of questions in their minds.

"I guess this supports our theory that Levenstein was involved with the LOTU. But this is the worst thing that could happen," Richard muttered. "This means there must be someone else above him we need to be concerned about. We have to apprehend Young, even if only for her own safety."

"But this is so different from what happened to the others." Samuel released the pen to pinch the bridge of his nose. "Is this just a coincidence? And if not, how are they doing it?"

"I have a few new theories," Richard said cautiously. He didn't want to mention Joy's help. "Before I left, I ordered some pharmaco-logical tests on Hayes' frozen blood samples. The results are delayed due to the holiday weekend, but I expect them some time this week."

Samuel shot him a curious glance. "I'll look into it. But, before I forget—" He extracted a card from a drawer, then handed it to Richard.

Only a few words disrupted the blank interior: "Michael is com-ing to get you."

Richard jerked up straight in his chair. "What is this?"

"It's another card to Dr. Clayton her secretary intercepted Friday. No stamps and no fingerprints—just like before," Samuel replied. "I also have the report from the IT department about the email she got the previous week."

"Were they able to track down the sender's IP address?"

Samuel nodded slowly. "It was sent from her own computer. Either Clayton sent it herself, which I consider unlikely..."

Richard completed the idea. "Or the sender was physically in her office." Cold fear settled in his chest and he felt the urgency to return to Pineapple Beach and make sure Joy was safe.

"I'm officially on vacation time. I'll look into this after I return." He sprang up from his chair.

Samuel frowned at him. "Richard, something is going on that you're not telling me. You don't seem to take work seriously lately."

Richard waved him off. He was no longer sure if his slacking attitude arose from his current state of being brainlessly in love, or from depression over feeling powerless about keeping that love going.

Throwing his hands out, Samuel grunted. "You've never done something like this before—taking a week off in the middle of a critical point in our investigation, and after you just returned from a leave. And now you insist on taking off again despite what just happened?"

"I'm supposed to be off through Tuesday."

"For goodness' sake, man. What's all this secretiveness about? Are you interviewing for jobs?"

Richard recoiled. Only someone as astute as Samuel could've come up with a guess like that. He decided to be as honest as possible with his friend. "I admit that I've considered tendering my resignation—for the reasons we talked about in the past."

"You mean *her*?" Samuel whispered and rose to lock the office door, even if the place was nearly deserted on a Sunday of a holiday weekend. "Man, have you lost your mind?"

Richard raised a hand to signal him to stop. "Let's not start again."

"Richard. Are you planning to commit career suicide?" When he didn't answer Samuel sighed in resignation. "Where are you planning to go?"

The thought of leaving the FBI hurt. He shrugged. "I have nothing yet. There's... an informal job offer; but I'm not feeling it. Still, I'll hear it, just to have an idea of what I can start looking for." As he said the words aloud, he made the decision to go to that interview with Sanders' client.

"Man, I know we're an unlikely match…" Samuel seemed to struggle with words. "If someone had ever told me I'd care so much for a snarky, bratty white boy from the Bronx, I'd never believed it. But you grew on me. And I had many dreams for you here at the Bureau. I hope you reconsider your decision."

Richard swallowed a knot in his throat. Being part of the FBI had once been a dream come true for him. He resisted the idea of saying goodbye to it.

~

Joy was used to Michael punishing her with long bouts of silent treatment after any disagreement. She could hardly believe how quickly she and Richard had bounced back from their argument and how smoothly their last two days at Pineapple Beach were. They wordlessly agreed not to mention the future for the rest of the trip.

But Joy knew that an irreversible change had occurred during the past days together. Saying goodbye and returning to their separate routines now seemed inconceivable.

A traffic accident prolonged the bittersweet drive back to Fort Sunshine on Tuesday afternoon. Richard's house being on the other side of town, they drove straight to Joy's to exchange her car for her van. The plan was that she would drop Richard at home on the way to pick up her kids.

But what was meant to be a quick pit stop took longer because she couldn't find the van keys. "Where on earth are those keys?" she mumbled while searching the catchall kitchen drawer, after trying the basket on the coffee table and the wall hooks in the laundry room.

"Don't worry, we still have time," Richard commented, claiming a stool at the breakfast counter.

Michael's voice scolded her from inside her head. *"You always lose everything. You live on another planet."*

"I'm sorry," she apologized while probing the slots between the cushions of the tan sectional in the family room. "They have to be somewhere—here they are!" She shook the keys in the air, relieved. "Let's go."

"Didn't you say you wanted to change?" Richard offered.

"But I'd hate to keep you waiting even longer."

"That's okay, angel. Take your time."

Despite his reassuring words, she couldn't help feeling anxious. "I'll try to be fast," she apologized and headed to her room.

She went straight to her walk-in closet, shed her silk beach dress and changed into jeans and a T-shirt.

"You take too long getting dressed. Why can't you ever be ready on time?" Michael's voice berated her. She breathed through it, reprimanding herself. She had to remember that the man by her side wasn't Michael.

From the closet, she heard Richard's muffled voice say something at a distance.

"What was that, sweetie?" she asked, exiting the closet. She stood in front of its large mirrored door and tied her hair up in a ponytail.

"There's a note from your cleaning lady on the kitchen counter, "he answered. "She says there was a delivery for you and she had them put it in—"

She didn't hear him finish the sentence as her eyes collided with the reflection of a man in the mirror, standing behind her.

Her blood turned to ice and her heart sprang out of her chest. A scream escaped her throat against her will.

It was Michael.

CHAPTER 24

J OY'S SCREAM DRAINED THE LIFE FROM RICHARD'S BODY. Terrified, he bolted to her room, his mind consumed with possible scenarios.

He found Joy huddled on the carpet, shaking uncontrollably. Her back against her closet door, knees up to her chest, arms covering her head, she sobbed.

"What's going on?" He knelt down and tried to help her up, but she flailed her arms, eyes squeezed closed. He finally immobilized her against his chest and could feel her heart fluttering.

"It's Michael!" she cried. "Michael is here!"

Afraid she'd lost her mind, he cast around the room to find the cause of her distress. A chill jolted him when he found it.

Against the opposite wall of the room leaned a life-sized portrait of Michael O'Hara. It was the freakiest thing he'd seen in his life.

"It's a picture." He exhaled in relief while rubbing her back.

It took him a few moments to convince her to open her eyes. Shaking, she finally peered up. "Oh my God, you're right." She pressed a hand on her chest and tried to control her panting.

She struggled to recompose herself and he didn't rush her. Finally, she accepted his help getting up but still hesitated to approach the picture. "That was the biggest scare of my life!"

They stood in front of the portrait, which seemed to be a mixture of photograph, painting, and computer-generated image. The incredibly realistic business suit-clad figure looked vaguely like a 3D hologram, with eyes so alive they seemed to be staring straight at them.

"What kind of psycho would send you something like that?" he asked.

Joy snatched a card from the bed and opened it. "Ugh. It's a present from Maureen, Michael's mother."

"A present? I'd call that more like... a curse! Let's burn it." He wasn't kidding.

"I can't. If Maureen doesn't see it when she comes to visit the kids next week, she'll freak out."

"Ugh. Let her freak the hell out."

Joy braced herself, studying the monstrosity from a distance. "I guess after she sees it, I could donate it to his old campaign office. And in the meantime, keep it covered with a sheet, maybe?"

An irrational territorial feeling possessed him. "I don't want him in your bedroom—not even his picture." He picked up the large, framed portrait, which proved heavier than expected. He lugged it out of her room and she followed him.

Not satisfied with getting it out of the bedroom, he had Joy open the sliding glass doors in the family room and made his way to the backyard. He carried the picture as far as he could from the house and set it against the back fence.

"We can't leave it here, sweetie. What if it rains?" she said. "I can't let it get ruined before Maureen comes over."

He glanced around and noticed a tool shed a few steps away. Besides tools, inside he found sandbags and some blue tarp. "What's that for?"

"For hurricane season. Donna's husband brought those over, in case my roof leaks during a storm."

He tented the tarp over the picture, using the sandbags to press it in place. "There." He addressed Joy, "Whenever you confirm his mother is coming over, call me and I'll carry it back into your living room. Then after you fulfill your duty and let her see it, I'll be right over with an ax to shred it into splinters." He meant that. He hated the idea of any memory of that man near Joy.

She gave a single nod, but seemed more rattled than she admitted. The signs of PTSD showed in her trembling hands, her agitated breathing and her muscle tension. But this time there was more; her tremors had turned into full-blown shivering. "I feel so cold," she said. "I think I'm coming down with something."

~

Joy opened her eyes and, for a moment, her groggy brain couldn't remember anything that had happened. She felt achy, as if she'd slept for a long time in the same position.

She stretched under the blankets and Richard sprang off the carpeted floor and sat on the bed. "Are you okay?"

She blinked away her sleepiness. "Why were you on the floor?"

"I didn't want to scare you if you woke up and found a man in bed with you." He caressed her cheek with his thumb. "I should've known the minute I dozed off you'd rouse."

"I feel like I've been sleeping for hours."

"You have. I had you take some cold medicine, thinking you might've caught something, and you were out like a light a minute later." He adjusted her pillows and chuckled. "I guess alcohol is not the only thing you're hypersensitive to."

The memory of Michael's portrait resurfaced in her mind and resurrected the bone-deep chills.

Richard noticed her shivers. "Give me a sec." He disappeared through the door.

She closed her eyes, breathing through the waves of fear to stop them from turning into panic. Flashbacks raced through her mind: Michael exploding when she least expected it; Michael yelling at the children; Michael threatening her with suicide if she ever left him.

When would she be free? When would his ghost stop chasing her?

Her eyes still closed, she felt the most exquisite warmth over her skin and caught the pleasant scent of fabric softener. Richard covered her with a plush quilt, hot and fresh, just out of the dryer.

"This feels amazing," she said, melting into the cozy feeling.

"I know your PTSD makes you feel cold, so I've been warming up your covers in the dryer and changing them every hour." He finished removing her cold blanket, leaving the hot one in place.

She moaned in delight. "You're a genius! I think I died and went to heaven."

Laughing softy, he finished tucking her in, sat on the edge of the bed and kissed the tip of her nose. "I never get over how easy it is to make you happy."

She relished the appearance of his adored laugh lines. Was she imagining the adoration radiating from his eyes? She felt the heat of the quilt—and his loving gaze—permeating deep into her bones, relieving the cold ache. If she'd always felt invisible before, she'd never in her life had felt as seen as in that moment.

Then her eyes caught a glimpse of the nightstand clock and she startled. "I can't believe I slept so long! I was supposed to pick up the kids—"

She shoved the blankets aside but he grabbed her arm to stop her. "It's taken care of. The kids are sleeping at your sister's."

"What?" Astonishment cut her breath.

He gently pushed her back in bed and covered her again. "I didn't want you to have to face your mother-in-law in that house filled with… his memories. I texted your sister from your phone, passing for you, and asked her to get them because you weren't feeling well. She brought them here and came to check on you, but you wouldn't wake up."

Joy blinked rapidly. "So… Hope saw you here?" *Shoot.* Did Hope remember him from the press conference?

"I told her I live nearby and was helping you with your hurricane preparations when you felt sick. But judging by the way she stared at our matching tans, and by the two million personal questions she shot at me, I doubt she believed me." He shrugged. "But somehow I don't care anymore. We fed the kids dinner and got them ready for bed before she took them to her place. They remember me very well and kept asking about Ray."

The image of him getting her kids ready for bed melted her. It was the first time since she'd learned who he really was that she'd dared to imagine him becoming part of their lives.

And then, noticing her pink cotton pajamas, another memory hit her. "You got *me* ready for bed, too." It was the first time since age seven that someone had put her to bed.

As if reading her thoughts, he ran his fingers through her hair. "You've been taking care of people all your life. It's okay if you let me take care of you sometimes for a change." He kissed her face, then tucked her in with the thick, warm sheets.

And she knew beyond any doubt. She'd known it for a long time, but only now gave herself permission to admit it. Richard wasn't the passing adventure she'd been telling herself about.

She wanted to spend the rest of her life with him.

∼

Richard stayed in a chair until dawn, sometimes dozing off, sometimes watching Joy sleep, but he knew he had to leave before the neighbors woke up. He used his burner cell and a fake name to call a taxi, giving them an address a block away. Before leaving, he went to the laundry room one more time to replace her covers with warm ones from the dryer. As he did, she opened her eyes.

"Good morning, angel. I'm about to head out." He leaned to kiss her forehead and she wrapped him in her arms, preventing him from leaving. The tightness of her long embrace surprised him and he sat on the bed, holding her.

"You have no idea how grateful I am to have you." She released the hug and met his gaze. "I'm sorry for being so difficult sometimes. I promise things will be different."

His heart jolted, sensing a deeper meaning in her words.

"Forget about anything I said at the beach," she continued. "You don't have to give me any answers until you're ready. You've given me so much I couldn't possibly ask for anything else from you." She extended her hand and caressed his jaw. "The only thing I ask for is honesty."

The memory of his lie under oath reached him, tightening his chest. He swallowed. "Angel, my work will always come with secrets. And there are some things it's better you don't know for your own safety." He reached for her hand. "But that aside, I promise I'll always be honest with you." He let his eyes communicate the message of love that still refused to leave his lips. He kissed the top of her head and finished tucking her in. "Now go back to sleep."

Within minutes, she was asleep again. He took in her soothing image one more time, donned his cap and sunglasses and headed out.

As he walked to meet the taxi, his thoughts returned to Michael O'Hara. He knew he'd never have the whole story to fully understand the damage that man had done to her. He hated him so much he almost felt thankful for the people who had killed him—yet he knew they were monsters as evil as O'Hara had been.

As he entered the taxi, Richard realized that searching for a different job was not an option. He could never quit his job as an agent.

He was a white blood cell. His mission in life was ridding the planet from people like Michael O'Hara.

And his mission was bigger than his personal happiness.

CHAPTER 25

Since the episode with O'Hara's portrait Richard poured himself into work with more vehemence than ever. And in the face of Levenstein's health crisis, the first priority was meeting with Young. That Thursday morning, during the meeting with her and her lawyer, the slight tremor in her hands and lips hinted at her worry.

"This is now a matter of life and death. *Your* life and death," he said. "Three witnesses have died and a suspect is in critical condition. You can't continue to refuse cooperating with us."

"You are bluffing," Young answered, squaring her shoulders, but the quaver in her voice betrayed her confidence had decreased since the last interview. "Sugar babe, you may've succeeded at scaring my lawyer. But I'm very aware of the details of Levenstein's health crisis—the rumors are all over the hospital. He had an overdose of Ibuprofen that re-activated his ulcer, and took too many blood thinner pills—probably in a suicide attempt after his dog died."

He leaned forward, getting his face close to hers. "Dr. Young. You're an intelligent woman; you know that the coincidence is too large to ignore. Three men related to this case ended up in the hospital within weeks."

"Three middle-aged men with known medical issues. Three men who, by the way, were under unprecedented amounts of stress, being harassed by *you*. If someone is to be blamed for those men's death it's you, the FBI."

"So, you're not afraid *at all* about your own safety?"

She placed a hand on her hip and tilted her head. "You're cute, worrying about me, honey. Normally, I would say 'hot' instead of 'cute,' but you're a little too old for my taste."

Unbelievable. With a grunt, he signaled another agent to take over and stalked out of the interview room.

As he headed for Samuel's office, dwelling on his frustration, Richard glanced at the schedule on his phone. He'd blocked his afternoon for a session with Carl before he'd learned Carl was leaving town again for a speaking engagement. He could try to work on Hayes' writings on his own, or tackle his paperwork.

Or...

Or he could work on the case *and* see the woman he couldn't get off his mind and hadn't seen in two long days.

He grabbed his burner phone and texted Joy. *"I need to talk to my anonymous consultant. I have a three-hour block free from two to five. You?"*

He held his breath as the three periods on the screen showed she was answering.

"Let me see if I can move some appointments around."

He returned the phone to his jacket's inner pocket and suppressed the grin threatening to spread over his lips.

I'm pathetic. I'm like a freaking kid who can't think about anything but the girl he has a crush on.

Samuel's voice brought him back. "I'm glad you're here." He signaled Richard to follow him.

Once in his office, Samuel closed the door. "I just got back the results on Hayes' stored blood." He took a seat at his desk. "You were right; they did find beta-blockers and diuretics in her blood. What does this mean?"

"Well, this is my theory." Richard dropped into the office chair. "They feed the victims prescription medications. In the case of Zimmerman and Xenos, drugs to plummet their blood pressure or blood sugar; in Levenstein's case, an overdose of his blood thinner. If they're lucky, the person dies instantly. If not, they seize the opportunity while the person is in the hospital, to finish them off."

"How?" asked Samuel.

Richard described some of the possible scenarios he'd discussed with Joy, including the possibility that Hayes' sepsis could've been provoked.

At the end of his explanation, Samuel leaned back in his chair, processing it. "So, if this were true, our murderer must be someone with access to the hospital, or have helpers among the hospital staff."

Richard nodded. "Being a doctor, with a hospital ID, able to move freely around the wards, Young is at the top of my list of suspects."

"I'll order to investigate the staff working at Holloway the day of each death."

"I would also add Dr. Venkat Patel. He came up on our list of local authors who write about Law of Attraction."

"I'm impressed, man," Samuel said. He rubbed his chin, then asked, "Any updates in translating Hayes' journal?"

Richard reached for his laptop carrier and pulled a folder from it. "With guidance from Dr. Andrews' helper, I organized what's likely to be the first chapter of Hayes' writings, 'the world of illusions,'" he explained. "The first two characters at the bottom of the pages are the numbers one and three." He passed some pages. "Going over a different section later we found a chapter where the characters spell 'FTSUNS' and another one spelling 'F-L-3-2.' I suspect that stands for 'Ft. Sunshine,' the abbreviation of 'Florida,' and the beginning of a zip code, which mean Hayes might've been trying to leave us an address."

Samuel's eyebrows shoot up. "So it's a matter of organizing the rest of the pages in order to get it."

Richard assented. "I assume the numbers should form a street address and zip code and the letters should rearrange to form the street and city name. Give me a sec." Having an idea, he opened his laptop and typed the letters he had copied from the document. *neShWoSpodSuringsbrisindgeDrFtFL,* then, he eliminated the characters for Ft. Sunshine, FL ending up with *SWoSpodDrEGSbringsrid.* He typed those in the search engine along with, *"street names, Ft. Sunshine, Florida."* He hoped the server would offer suggestions of street names but it didn't. He then tried an online word unscramble program, but it generated hundreds of possible combinations. "I guess we can run the letters through a database, or a more powerful word unscramble program to figure out possible combinations of street names. I will focus on the number portion of the address for now."

Samuel gawked at him. "Please remind me to never doubt you again. I thought you'd been slacking off, but obviously, you just had to work at your own pace." Samuel placed his hand on Richard's shoulder. "You *are* becoming indispensable on this case. As much as I've resented it, I have to agree that you're wasting your talent in this small-town resident office. You belong with the team in New York, and you have a bright future at the Bureau."

With slow movements, Richard stowed away his laptop. "Don't worry, Sam. I've changed my mind about leaving."

A flash of satisfaction sparked on Samuel's face and he offered his hand for a soul shake.

Yup. Sometimes you have to do the right thing even if it means digging your own grave.

Richard's burner cell rang. Joy would never call him at work, so that could be only one person. He sent the call to voicemail and excused himself.

He had one more huge task to take care of before he could even dream of a future at the FBI—eliminating the proof Sanders had against him.

He waited to be inside his car before calling back. "This is Guardian," he said, sticking to the usual routine.

"And this is Pitbull. Everything's clear here."

"Were you calling me?"

"We broke into her car. There was nothing there either."

Damn it. Over the long weekend, the gang had searched Blair Sanders' office looking for the phone and they hadn't found it. Her car had been Richard's last hope.

"She might be carrying it around all the time," Richard mused.

"Could fake a mugging and steal her purse?"

Richard felt unsettled. They've done questionable things already, but having the gang assault Sanders crossed a different line. "Not a good idea. The last time I saw her she was surrounded by bodyguards."

"Me and my boys don't mind a fight."

Bloodshed. Exactly what I need on my conscience. "No, Pitbull, we had a deal. I helped you because I expect you're done with the life of crime."

The man on the other line went silent, apparently ashamed. "And I *am* committed to a new, honest life; but if she shows that video to anybody I'm going to rot in jail!"

"I know, I know." Richard tried to calm him down. "But I have the feeling she's not going to do anything yet." *Not if that eliminates the only leverage she has with me.* He remembered his upcoming interview with her and her client. The night Pitbull and his gang had searched Sanders' house they still hadn't known what the phone looked like. Could they've missed it? "We'll have to split up. Tomorrow night, you'll search her house again and I'll search Sanders myself."

A text message from Joy popped in his burner cell.

"Done. I'm free at three."

The sun shone brighter, and worries shrunk in his mind. *I'd better enjoy this for as long as it lasts.*

He ended the call with Pitbull and considered his reply to Joy. They had only a couple of hours and he needed to maximize their time together. It was a stretch from their usual precautions, but if he could pick her up from work, they could save nearly half an hour each way and talk in the car.

That was it. He still had the keys for Carl's car after dropping him off at the airport—a car not traceable to him. He texted back. *"I'll pick you up at the Masden Center main entrance at 3:00. Look for a gold Audi."*

~

Ready a few minutes earlier than expected, Joy busied herself with paperwork, while waiting for Richard's message to meet him at the Masden Center front door. As she browsed unsigned medical records on the computer, her hand trembled in barely controlled excitement.

We're only meeting so I can help him with the case. She knew she was lying to herself; the thought of something else happening while "off the clock" was an exquisite possibility that had kept her going throughout her workday.

As Joy settled back into her routines that week, her mood was un-improvable. Maybe she'd been wrong to be so hard on herself about leaving the kids with sitters in order to meet with Richard. Lately, she'd been the most patient and loving mother her children had ever seen. And thinking about it, they were in a better mood than usual too. It was as if her boys were getting secondhand expo-sure to her happiness.

"Almost there." The text from Richard popped up on Joy's phone and she jolted in anticipation. He'd agreed to text her when he was a block away—about the time that it would take her to make it from her office to the entrance. The less time he spent waiting, the less attention they'd draw upon themselves. She picked up her purse and headed out.

As she locked her office, Venkat arrived, extending a manila envelope to her. "Good afternoon, Joy. Dr. Byrd gave me this. It was delivered to his office next door by mistake."

"Thank you." She accepted the envelope and tossed it in her tote bag, hoping Patel didn't delay her.

"Have you had a chance to read the proposed marketing plan I emailed you Monday?"

"Sorry, I haven't finished reading it yet." As she spoke, she passed through the clinic reception area to the waiting room.

He followed as she exited the suite. "I was thinking we could have a series of lectures on your favorite topic, the mind-body-spirit connection. And it ties together with the work I've been doing in holistic medicine."

Barbara Young's high-pitched voice grated in their ears. "For goodness' sake, Patel! Would you let Joy be?" Young intercepted them in the hallway and they had no choice but to stop. "Joy has better offers in her hands than becoming the sidekick for a Deepak Chopra wannabe."

Patel's eye muscle twitched and suddenly an Indian accent crept in. "For the hundredth time, I'm not copying Deepak Chopra."

Ignoring him, Young placed a hand on Joy's shoulder and spoke with enthusiasm. "Sugar babe, you won't believe the ideas I've had to kick off this fundraiser. We need a Sponsor's Spa event. A weekend where I offer free samples of my skincare services as bait to attract donors."

Joy maneuvered around Young and resumed her stroll toward the elevator. "That sounds interesting. We should catch up some-time." She took off.

Please, guys, don't follow me! She had to get out of there soon, so Richard didn't risk too much time waiting for her. She entered the golden elevator and pressed the button to the lobby repeatedly, in a hurry for the doors to close.

But just as the two doors nearly touched each other, a manicured hand blocked their contact, making them re-open. Joy cringed inter-nally as Young and Patel joined her in the elevator.

CHAPTER 26

A's THE ELEVATOR DESCENDED, PATEL'S EXPRESSION TURNED glacial and his British accent became thicker than usual. "Young, I know what you're doing. Cooperating with Joy is your excuse to advertise your... *cosmetic* activities to wealthy women in town."

Young's tightened lips advertised her annoyance. She shoved her hands in the pockets of her pinstripe suit pants. "*Sweetie pie*, my proposal can make a huge difference in Joy's income."

"And mine can change Joy's life," Patel countered. "By increasing her reputation she has a much wider audience with whom to share the ideas she truly believes in."

Her stomach knotting with worry someone might recognize Richard, Joy mentally begged them to both go away.

Young huffed, impatient. "Patel, honey, what do you have against me?"

Patel's British accent slipped away again. "Your work is based entirely on exploiting the low self-esteem of women and fomenting vanity."

"Oh, sweetheart, look who's talking." She gave a sour chuckle. "Your motives are not that high either. All you want is to make money from endorsing supplements."

Joy's eyes bounced from one doctor to the other in disbelief. They seemed to have forgotten she was there. "Uh, guys, I think that—"

"Young, your goals are entirely selfish and you don't care about helping Joy," Patel accused.

"That's not true, *sugar*." Young stomped toward him clenching a fist and for a moment Joy thought she would punch him. "Joy is a beloved physician in this town. If she joins you in your... celebrity-status-seeking plans, the patients at Hospice House will miss her terribly."

"Joy is done working in hospice," Patel replied. "She's spent years doing slave work and getting paid pennies. She's better off quitting that useless place and joining me."

A corner of Joy's brain caught the contradiction. *Useless place? Then why did you offer to help me save it?* "Enough, you two! I'm starting to feel like a prize you're competing for." The elevator arrived at the ground floor and she exited, but they both followed her. Joy picked up the pace with the hope of leaving them behind, her heels and Young's clicking on the multi-color marble floor. "Do you mind if we continue this conversation later?"

"That's a great idea," Young exclaimed as they passed the fancy gift store. "Let's meet for dinner tomorrow, all three of us, and each will present our offer to you."

Patel huffed. "Why do you assume we have time to—"

"Uh, guys." Joy stopped in the middle of the spacious, two-story ceiling lobby. "How about you two agree on the details and text me later? Now I'm in a hurry to make it somewhere." She headed for the exit.

"How come you're leaving from the front lobby? Aren't you parked at the staff garage as usual?" Patel asked.

Shoot. Joy stopped abruptly at the automatic sliding glass door. She couldn't bring attention to the fact that someone was picking her up.

She spotted the gold Audi approaching the carline and in it Richard wearing a hoodie and sunglasses. Quickly, she texted, *"Don't stop. I'm not alone."*

Seconds later the car drove away from the entrance. She sighed in relief.

Patel's attentive look showed he was still waiting for an answer. *And I'm the worst liar in the world.* "Uh… my car is at the shop, so I'm taking an Uber," she improvised.

"Oh, dear, why didn't you tell me?" Patel raised his hands. "I'll be happy to give you a ride home. Cancel that car and I'll drive you, so we can talk on the way."

Darn it. Joy hated lying with all her being, but she was now too deep in it to turn around. She paced around the entrance. "Uh, actually, Venkat, I have some errands to run on the way."

"I don't mind."

She stopped pacing and fixed her eyes on him. "It's about some… woman's, girlish… female stuff."

Joy had no idea what that was supposed to mean, but Patel's rapid blinking and sudden stuttering showed he had no desire for an explanation. "O-okay, then. W-we'll c-catch up later." He waved goodbye and dashed away.

"Well, well, sugar babe!" Barbara clapped once. "*I* am a girl, so it seems that I am your perfect driver today."

Joy thought quickly. In a theatrical movement, she tapped her own forehead. "Oh, I must be losing it! My car was at the shop *yesterday*, not today! I'll be canceling that Uber after all." With a quick wave goodbye, she buried her face in her phone to send Young the message that she was busy, and headed for the parking lot.

Young followed her. "Well, let me tell you about the ideas I've had since our last talk."

While walking, barely paying attention to the outdoor heat and Young's chat, Joy texted Richard. "*I don't think I can make it.*"

"*Where are you?*"

"*On my way to the staff garage. But someone is with me.*"

"*I can circle the block and meet you in five minutes. Can you ditch them by then?*"

"Joy, you're a mother of small children," Young said, ending her sales pitch as they arrived at the garage. "Your time is too precious to follow Patel around all over the country. You need to partner with someone who would understand your needs. I consider you my family and will take good care of you."

Joy thought how ironic it was that she now had more help than she'd ever dared to dream of, for a project she no longer felt compelled to pursue. "You've given me a lot to think about, Barbara. Let me process it and I'll get back to you."

Holding Joy's hand, Young shot her the *poor-widow* pitying look. "I know times have been hard. I'm here for you if you need anything."

She mumbled a "Thanks," and walked to her Prius.

She pretended to search for her keys in her bag for a while, to kill some time until Young was gone. Her hands trembled as she unlocked the door and got in her car.

This is never going to work.

All the peace she'd derived from their time away seemed to have deserted her. She couldn't keep living like this.

Another text from Richard came in. *"Where are you? I'll meet you there."*

Despite her recent promise to herself to lower her barriers, she couldn't stop shaking. *I can't take this anymore.*

Why was she putting herself through this torture? The fear of being caught, the constant anxiety?

While gathering her thoughts, Joy glanced at the cushioned manila envelope in her bag for the first time. The sender's information consisted of only one word; *Guardian*. Her spirits lifted, realizing it came from Richard. Carefully, she opened it.

It contained a gallon-sized Ziploc bag enclosing smaller re-sealable bags. The smaller bags held seashells and sand.

Confused, she searched the envelope and extracted a page.

The page read. "If you can't see the ocean from your office, now at least you can smell it."

The memory of their sunrise beach walk during their trip reached her, making her lips curve against her will. She hadn't even thought he was listening when she talked about longing for an office ocean view.

She opened one of the small bags and took a whiff of it. *Wow!* He was right. The salty scent of the ocean, still attached to the seashells, was intense. For a second, she was transported back to Pineapple Beach.

Tears of happiness brimmed in her eyes. That was Richard. Always paying attention. Always so thoughtful.

She enjoyed the ocean aroma a moment longer, then stowed the bags away.

Joy's hands no longer trembled when she reached for her phone and texted Richard. *"Please come get me."*

CHAPTER 27

S ITTING AT HIS KITCHEN COUNTER WITH JOY, RICHARD MADE an effort to focus on the pages in front of him and ignore the feeling of his leg brushing hers from the adjacent stool. He was dying to touch her, yet didn't dare interrupt the turning wheels of her unbelievable brain.

They'd been going back and forth between Hayes' writings and the medical plots, switching whenever they hit a dead end. Since their trip together, when these discussions became something they did for pleasure more than work, he had trouble reminding himself he was on the clock.

"I'm finally getting the hang of this handwriting; I just had to imagine I'm reading another doctor's notes," she said, rearranging some pages of Hayes' manuscript. "This chapter I understand, and the order of the topics is: first, know what you want; second, focus on the gratitude; third, detach from the outcome. Now the characters at the bottom of those pages spell 60-S-W-O." She bit her lower lip while shuffling another set of papers. "And in the chapter on detachment the characters spell D-R-#19... and from the labyrinths of the mind chapter we got R-I-N."

He watched her in silence. Was it delusional to dream they could find a way to stay in touch after his transfer? If he could only silence Sanders, then he wouldn't be so worried about confessing he'd fallen for a former suspect. Only then could he and Joy have a shot at a long-distance relationship.

Joy settled the sheets down on the gray Formica counter and

picked up another pile. "Now, these other pages are giving me a hard time. I don't understand what this writer means about 'exercising the muscle' and 'desensitizing from the fear.'" She exhaled through pursed lips.

"I think we hit a roadblock again with this." He forced himself to redirect his attention to work. "Should we switch back to the medical plots?"

Nodding, she put away the manuscript pages and picked up the four sheets where Richard had summarized the medical cases while concealing the identities of Xenos, Zimmerman, and Levenstein. He'd been afraid at first that she might've heard the hospital rumors Young referred to and would guess that "victim number four" was Levenstein. But so far Joy seemed oblivious.

"We're missing something." He pondered. "If we're theorizing that all victims were attacked by the same group, how come victims number two and three died within hours, while Hayes and victim number four lingered? Why would they kill Hayes and victim number four slowly and kill the two others fast?"

She scanned the medical histories. "The only thing in common I see is that both Hayes and victim number four were admitted straight into the ICU. The other two victims went to regular floors. What does the ICU have that the regular wards don't have?"

"More vigilance, I assume," he offered.

She drummed her fingers on her delicate chin. "And monitors."

He raised one eyebrow, interested. "Monitors?"

"Yes. Screens constantly displaying the patient's vital signs and recording their EKG." She twisted a lock of long, dark hair. "Maybe, the way they killed the others wouldn't work on them because it could've been detected by a cardiac monitor and set off the alarms."

Richard reflected. That would also explain why Xenos was fine as long as he was on the telemetry floor—another floor with monitors—and died shortly after he was moved to a regular ward. "Any guess what that could've been?"

She answered so quickly he wondered if she referenced one of her fictional plots to kill O'Hara. "KCl—Potassium chloride."

They'd discussed the topic in the past. "You mentioned once that potassium would mess up the electricity in the heart and make it stop." He mentally reviewed the details of Xenos's and Zimmerman's deaths. "Would that be fast enough that the victims could be fine one moment but gone the next?"

"Oh yes. It would cause the patient to die instantly."

"Is it reversible?"

She nodded. "If it's detected in time, an injection of calcium carbonate can reverse the effect. But it only takes minutes of no heartbeat for the brain to suffer permanent damage. By the time the nurse or CNA found them, it might've already been too late to resuscitate them."

"And potassium chloride shows on the monitor?"

"Peaked T wave—classic exam question."

He took some notes, feeling glad they'd had security watching Levenstein's hospital room at all times.

"The code blue team routinely draws blood during resuscitation efforts," she added. "Those potassium levels would read super high, can you check those?"

He used the temporary password on his laptop to log into Xenos's and Zimmerman's medical records. It took him a while to find the levels. "They were not; the potassium was in the low range of normal." He wrote the values on the pages with the case summaries.

She studied the pages and pointed at Xenos's case. "His were *suspiciously* low for a patient taking lisinopril and aldactone. Those blood pressure medications raise potassium levels."

"Are you suggesting this is a false result?" He eyed her intently. "How could they fake it?"

She closed her eyelids and seemed to draw in the air with her hands. "I'm trying to visualize the chaos going on during a code blue. While one person does chest compression and another one tends to the ventilator bag, someone else draws the blood, and someone else handles the medications." She opened her eyes. "If you have an insider in the hospital staff, that person could switch the blood sample before it makes it to the lab. Or alternatively, someone could hack the hospital computers and change that value in the laboratory report."

He made a note to talk to the IT team.

They brainstormed for a while longer, trying to come up with ways someone could've sneaked potassium chloride into the victims. Then, noticing the time on his cell on the counter, his mouth slid into a sly grin. "I guess we're off the clock now. As much as I've enjoyed this chat, I'm ready for a break." He closed his laptop and tugged on her hand to bring her closer.

She pressed a palm to his chest to gently keep him away and chuckled. "I'm afraid that a stolen kiss is not going to do it anymore."

He knew what she meant. After having tasted how wonderful life together could be during their trip, these efforts to steal a minute together felt pathetic.

"I'm sorry," she apologized—she seemed to do it constantly. Then she cheered up. "Tomorrow night, I'll have to get a babysitter to watch the kids while I attend a dinner meeting." She caressed his arm. "How about we try to sneak some time together after that? It would definitely be off the clock."

Damn it. The idea was incredibly tempting, but tomorrow night he had his interview with Sanders and her client. "I can't. I have… something to do."

"With Ray?"

It was easier to go with that than trying to make up an excuse, so he nodded once.

She blew out a disappointed breath. "It would be so much easier if we didn't have to hide all the time."

He caressed her hand with his thumb. "I'm working on it.

Angel, nothing would make me happier than showing you off to the world on my arm."

Nothing would make me happier than never having to say goodbye.

An idea jumped into his mind; it was so crazy that he felt mildly lightheaded. Slowly, he released her hand. "This is just a theoretical question." His pulse sped up and he leaned away, tense. "Would you consider someday… moving to New York?"

She jolted up straight in her seat. "Gee, I don't know. I don't have a New York medical license."

"You could get one—hypothetically speaking." He had no idea where this was coming from; but he carried on.

Squinting in concentration, she rested her elbow on the counter and cupped her chin in her hand. "Well, hypothetically speaking, just for the sake of brainstorming… I have no family or friends there, no one to help me with the children…"

"If other working mothers there have figured that out, couldn't you? I mean, in this theoretical scenario." He cleared his throat and crossed his arms to disguise the subtle trembling of his hands. "Wouldn't it be great to be somewhere new, where nobody knows you, and leave this town and all its bad memories behind?"

After considering it for a while, she ran her fingers through her long hair and shook her head. "It's more complicated than that. Michael's mother would never let me leave town and take her grandchildren away, unless it was to move in with her. And she has ways to discourage me from leaving."

He nodded. "It's fine. It was just a theoretical question." He returned his attention to his notes, but his racing heart and thoughts were far from settled. Considering his marriage to Sandy had been a shotgun wedding, this was the closest thing to a proposal he'd ever made. The fact that it had been turned down was almost irrelevant next to the realization hitting him.

This was the first time in his life he'd considered a long-term future with a woman.

CHAPTER 28

T HE DINNER INTERVIEW WITH SANDERS'S CLIENT PROVED MORE
pleasant than Richard anticipated. He expected an associate of
Sanders to be a thug, or shady character. Instead, he found a
cheerful middle-aged man with a firm handshake, good eye contact,
and an easy grin. The man had insisted on treating Richard at the most
expensive restaurant in town and reserved them a private alcove so they
could talk. Over the extravagant dinner, he extolled the advantages of
working for his company, putting down pitiful government salaries.

But Richard's interest was fake; the main purpose of the dinner
was to distract Sanders. While Pitbull and his men searched her house
again for the flip phone, he focused on her. Her tiny purse seemed to
contain nothing but makeup, as far as he could glimpse the few times
she opened it. And the skimpy red dress she wore had no pockets and
no room to hide anything.

At the end of the dinner, Sanders' client left first, having some
other meeting to attend.

"I have a little present for you," Blair said, once she and Richard
were alone.

"A present?" He raised one eyebrow.

"It's a clue for your case." She extended a folder. "This is a copy of
the O'Hara family trust, and I think you'll find it interesting."

He scanned the pages, skipping the legal jargon, until he found
a highlighted segment. "So, Michael O'Hara was supposed to inherit
the family fortune after his mother's death. But he died before her and
couldn't, so what's your point?"

"You would expect that now his children would be his heirs. But at the moment the will was drafted, Michael O'Hara still had no children. So the way the will is currently written, the money would go instead to his cousin."

A light immediately went on in Richard's mind. "Barbara Young?"

"Yup. Sounds like a motive for murder to me."

Richard considered it. This might end up being an important clue; but how had Blair gotten it? "You're acting as a double agent, aren't you?" he asked. "You're dipping your fingers in the O'Hara family's business while you and your client are working with them."

Her mouth curved up, smug. "Anything to please my man." She ran the back of her hand down his arm.

Something didn't compute. Why was Sanders so invested in helping him with his case if the better he did with the FBI, the less likely he'd be to accept her job offer?

Could she be trying to mislead him? Was she covering for someone?

Maybe herself?

A text message reached Richard's burner phone from Pitbull. "*We found nothing. We took an old desktop and a couple of CDs and flash-drives, but ain't no videos in them.*"

Damn it.

"So, what do you think about my client's offer?" Sanders asked after taking a sip from her wineglass.

Returning the phone to his jacket pocket, he shrugged. "I'll have to mull it over for a few days."

"When you do, I want you to call me with your answer."

He glared at her. "I'm sorry, Blair, but your role as recruiter ended the moment you got him an interview with me. You can step back now."

She rested her palm on his chest. "What if I didn't want to step back?"

Her lips moved toward him, but before she could kiss him, he rose from his chair. "Good night, Blair."

She caught his arm before he could leave and a flash of rage crossed her eyes. "My patience has a limit. Trust me, Fields, you'd rather have me as a friend or a lover than an enemy."

He freed his arm. "You must be very desperate for attention to resort to blackmail in order to get a man." He marched away.

She caught up with him as he exited the alcove and threw her arms around his neck. "I'm sorry; I didn't mean to threaten you." Her voice was a whisper and contained a hint of tears. Richard tensed up, wondering what kind of unstable woman he was dealing with.

"But you leave me no choice. Why are you torturing me like this?" She sniffled against the lapels of his jacket. "Stop pretending that there's nothing between us."

The only thing worse than rejecting her, would be admitting he had no recollection of ever having been with her. He let her hug him and slid his hands down her back and sides pretending to soothe her, while feeling for some hidden pocket in her clothes where she could be keeping the phone. Finding nothing, he held her hands to disentangle her fingers from his lapels. "I'm too mad at you right now to talk. Maybe when I cool down. Please let me go."

Her face darkened, and for a moment, she looked wounded and vulnerable. He almost felt sorry for his harshness.

"I understand. Please call me later." Before he could move away, she kissed him on the lips. She squeezed his hands for a moment before releasing them and walked out of the restaurant.

The second she was out the door, he exhaled and held his temples.

What am I going to do?

He now felt compelled to investigate Sanders. But how would he confront her? She had proof that could sink him, and also a personal reason to seek revenge and destroy him when he turned against her.

189

Running his fingers through his hair, he looked ahead and his stomach dropped when his eyes landed on a table. Sitting next to Barbara Young and Venkat Patel, Joy was staring right at him.

Their gazes met across the room and he could read the pain and confusion in her eyes. She, no doubt, had seen him with Blair.

Before he could figure out what to do, she looked away, as if she hadn't seen him.

CHAPTER 29

JOY TOLD YOUNG AND PATEL SHE HAD A HEADACHE AND ENDED their meeting. Back at home, her kids seemed determined to punish her for having left them with the sitter. Arthur threw a huge tantrum over relinquishing his handheld video game at bedtime, and the twins used that distraction to escape their cribs. By the time Joy finally left Arthur tucked in, Edward had started the washing machine filled with toys—his Tonka trucks included—while Alex had mixed every powder, oil, and liquid he found in the pantry into a big bowl on the kitchen counter.

At least the commotion prevented Joy from dwelling too much on her misery. But after she kissed the twins good night for the second time and turned off the lamp in their room, her overwhelming thoughts haunted her again.

She felt like crying, yet the tears refused to come out. In her mind, she'd replayed the scene at the restaurant a hundred times—Richard with another woman. Joy hadn't seen much of her, barely the back of a shiny-haired head that, in the low light of the restaurant, seemed auburn or light brunette. But she couldn't ignore the woman's perfect body, highlighted by her strapless red cocktail dress.

"*Now, that is a gorgeous woman,*" Michael's voice pointed out in her mind, as usual leaving open the insinuation. "*As opposed to you.*"

She'd gone over all possible scenarios trying to find a justification. Could Richard have been playing an undercover role? No, he'd told her that after the news breach he could no longer work undercover. Could that woman be only a relative, or a friend showing inappropriate gestures of affection? No, he had no sisters and no relatives in town. And no "friend" kissed a man on the lips that casually—like she'd done it a hundred times before. The way she'd hugged him was too intimate, and he'd caressed her back and waist and held her hands for a long moment. The more she obsessed about it, the more she realized she'd been in denial. Richard had been cheating on her.

As she finished getting in her pajamas, tapping sounds on her bedroom's sliding glass door startled her. She approached cautiously, pulled aside the curtain and found Richard standing on her back porch. Despite the partial darkness, she could see the worry in his eyes. His damp hair and clothes showed he'd been waiting out in the drizzle for a while.

"There's nothing between that woman and me," he rushed to say, his voice muffled by the glass.

She glowered at him in silence, not making any effort to let him in.

"You have to listen to me." He tried the door and it slid open without resistance—the darn lock was finicky and hard to get engaged.

He came in but she raised her hand, signaling him to stop. "Don't even try." The contained rage in her own voice surprised her.

He took one more step and opened his arms. "Angel, listen to me."

All the feelings she'd tried to suppress during the past hours by focusing on her self-deprecation sprouted in her. Anger. Jealousy. An irrational desire to slap him. An unlady-like desire to scratch the woman's face. "You told me you were spending the night with Ray!"

"It was a business meeting," he replied. "It wasn't much different than the dinner you were attending with Young and Patel."

"Then why did you kiss her?" She had to make an effort not to raise her voice and awaken the kids.

Something that looked like regret flashed across his features, but he recovered quickly. "I know you're not going to believe me, but *she* was the one who kissed *me*. I repeat, there's nothing between that woman and I."

What a nightmare. This was exactly like those times Michael gaslighted her, making her second-guess herself; making her doubt her own eyes. Despite the fire she felt inside, she started shivering. "I don't believe you!"

"For goodness' sake, Angel!" With an impatient grunt, he looked up to the ceiling. "Don't you know by now you have me at your feet? How can you even doubt that you are my world and I have no interest in any other woman?"

She hesitated, taken aback by such an effusive statement coming from a man famously stingy with words of affection.

He inched toward her. "And I don't know right now if I should reprimand you for being so oblivious to how crazy I am about you." His lips twitched before curving upward. "Or if I should celebrate, because I'd never seen you this angry and jealous before—and I kind of like it."

Oh yes, I'm angry. You have no idea. Rage she'd never in her life allowed herself to feel boiled inside her, alternating with the feeling of ice in her veins.

She scrutinized his face, trying to read him; he stared right back, weakening her conviction. "Can you swear there has *never* been something between you two?"

There it was again. The flicker of guilt followed by the expressionless mask. Joy felt her heart deflate.

Richard said nothing for the longest time before he raised his hands in a half shrug. "Apparently we slept together once."

She gaped at him confused. "*Apparently*?"

"Angel." Richard's pleading eyes spoke of remorse. "I've done many things in my past I'm not proud of—"

"Have you been seeing her besides today?" she interrupted him.

Richard's acting skills as an undercover agent were definitely failing him today. His apologetic grimace answered before his words. "She has been trying to convince me to take a job offer. We've met a couple other times."

Imagining him with that woman, an unreasonable, uncontrollable fury erupted in Joy. "*I bet she has no stretch marks, loose skin, or cellulite,*" Michael's voice commented in her head. "*But that's not surprising; she's obviously younger and you're a mother of three.*"

"I'm such an idiot." She growled and paced away from him.

Richard sighed in frustration. "Why do women always demand the truth if hearing it just gets you even more upset?"

Balling her fists against her temples, she trembled. "I always knew I shouldn't trust you! I always knew getting involved with you was a mistake." She started shivering again. "You never intended to tell the truth about us, did you? You never planned to stop your transfer to New York."

He groaned. "You promised you wouldn't pressure me about that."

"Don't talk to me about broken promises!"

"Joy, Joy, stay with me; you're not thinking clearly." He stepped closer. "If you just take a moment to remember *one minute* of our time at Pineapple Beach, you'll realize you're making no sense."

Self-doubt washed over her again as the memories of their trip hit her. He was right, wasn't he? Was she going crazy?

When she didn't answer, he extended his hand to touch her cheek. His hazel gaze mesmerized her, holding her in place. "Angel. Goddess, are you really that blind to your own beauty and your own power? Don't you know that you have me in your absolute control and I have no eyes for anyone else?"

Watch out. He's a professional liar.

"Stop it!" She escaped his reach. "You always know exactly what to say to warp my brain. I own a mirror, you know. I'm *not* beautiful and I'm not a goddess. And I should've known what a liar you were the first time you said that."

He flinched at the words. "Listen to yourself. That's not you talking. That's O'Hara's voice still in your head."

She stepped back, blinking rapidly—it was true.

"See?" He waved a hand to indicate her shivering. "This is not about that woman, or about me lying in the past; this is PTSD."

Don't let him change the subject. He's the one who lied. He's trying to confuse you like Michael used to do.

She inhaled deeply to calm herself down. She wiped an angry tear from her face with trembling fingers. "Goodbye, Richard. We're over."

Joy could hardly believe the words she'd just said. But she was in so much pain, she had to end it somehow.

Horror flashed in his expression, but he then tensed up and gathered himself. His eyes communicated a mixture of disappointment and desperation. "After everything I've done to convince you that you can trust me, you're going to let this stupid misunderstanding pull us apart?"

"Leave. Me. Alone."

"Do you realize you're only looking for an excuse to push me away again? That you're breaking your promise to rise above your traumas with Michael?"

His words were a punch in her gut, but she kept her voice calm. "The day I made that promise I asked you for only *one* thing, honesty. And you were unable to come through."

She could see the emotional armor of hardness rise in him. "Okay, as you wish, I'll let you be. I'll walk away and we'll be over— forever. Is that what you want?"

No. I want you to take me in your arms and lie to me again. Please convince me that everything was a dream.

Resisting those thoughts, she bowed her head in affirmation.

Narrowing his eyes, he nodded slowly. "Okay, then." He pivoted on his heels and strode to the glass door, but then seemed to change his mind and turned around. "But if this is it, if I'm never going to see you again, then it's *my* turn to say everything I've been holding inside." He marched toward her.

For a moment, she was irrationally afraid he'd turn violent. His large hands clasped her arms above the elbows. "I'm sick of it!" he exclaimed inches away from her face. "I'm sick of knowing that half the time when you look at me you're seeing *him*. I'm sick of seeing you hold hands with Michael O'Hara's ghost."

He released her so suddenly, she stumbled. "So many times I've regretted that he's already dead, so I can't kill him." A cold mask descended over his countenance. "But that wouldn't do. The one who needs to kill him is *you*."

He jostled her arm and made her follow him through the glass doors, to the porch and then to the yard, where the drizzle continued to fall. Too confused to resist, she had to make an effort to keep up with his fast pace.

They arrived at the back fence where Michael's portrait still rested. He pulled down the tarp covering it and moved away the sandbags holding it in place.

From the toolshed, he picked up a hammer and placed it in her hand. "Here. Kill Michael."

Shuddering, she dropped the hammer on the grass as if it burned her hand. "Are you out of your mind?"

"I'm not. You said you fantasized for years about killing him. Humor me for one last time in our lives. Let out all that anger you've never allowed yourself to show against him."

Shaking her head, she backed away. "There's no point in this. I've forgiven Michael."

He picked up the hammer from the ground. "No, you haven't. If you had, he wouldn't be able to keep hurting you." He extended the tool to her. "Your forgiveness will never be real until you have given yourself permission to admit how much he wounded you."

His words caused a wave of pain to rise from her chest. "He did. But I'm not like him. I'd never hurt him back."

196

"He wants you to, Joy." His voice turned softer. "If Carl is right and there's such a thing as punishment for our unfinished karma, Michael is suffering right now. His tortured soul is trapped here, unable to move on, because he needs to expiate his faults. Do it for us, but also do it for him." He placed the hammer in her hands one more time. "Free him, Joy. Kill Michael."

She stood in front of the life-size portrait, trembling, with the hammer in her hands. Facing that implacable blue stare, waves of terror mixed with surges of anger and grief. Memories of desperate days and tearful nights flooded her, but the ultimate result of the mixture was an unconquerable feeling of powerlessness.

Slowly, she lowered the hammer back to the ground. "I can't." She eased down onto the wet grass, hugging her knees to her chest, and crying quietly; her tears mixed with the faint raindrops.

She was still crying when Richard trudged away from her. He lifted the portrait and hauled it out of the yard, and by the sound of his steps she could guess he took it to the curb. Between her sobs, she heard him drop it on the curb with a slam, and then heard his car engine turn on. The last sound she captured was the rumble of his car fading, as he drove away from her life.

CHAPTER 30

B Y THE END OF HIS FIVE-MILE JOG ALONG THE BEACH, Richard's mind finally started to clear up. As he ran, his thoughts raced faster than his body. He barely noticed the surfers, the seagulls or the pelicans. He didn't see the fishing poles buried in the sand and the crane birds stalking the fishermen, hoping for a free snack. He ran with his eyes fixed ahead, ignoring the scolding of the gorgeous ocean—the same ocean he'd never again be able to see without thinking of *her*.

This morning had been a run; yesterday he'd spent hours swimming and surfing with Ray; the day before, he'd lifted weights until every fiber of muscle in his body hurt. Filling every free minute with physical exhaustion was his best bet to bottle up again the pain threatening to drown him—the pain he'd become an expert at crushing all his life and never should've allowed to resurface in the first place.

He always knew he was better off living in anesthesia. He cursed the moment he learned to feel again.

He barely had time for a shower at the end of his run and arrived ten minutes late for his meeting with Samuel.

"Breaking news!" Samuel announced the moment he entered the office. "A kitchen worker at the jail confessed that she accepted money to grind 'a bunch of pills' and mix them into Hayes' food."

Richard sprawled on the chair in front of Samuel's desk. "So that must've been the blood pressure medications she tested positive for—the diuretics and the metoprolol."

198

"I bet. The kitchen worker is willing to cooperate with our sketch artists and give us the description of the man who bribed her."

"I wonder if it was Levenstein," Richard pondered. "Anything new about him?"

Samuel exhaled through pursed lips. "He's off the ventilator, but still unresponsive. His MRI didn't show any specific area of stroke, but apparently the lack of blood supply to his brain after the bleeding must've caused microscopic brain damage all over. The neurologist just shrugs. He says we'll have to wait a few days and see if he shows signs of improvement. If not, they'll need to discharge him to a nursing home."

"He has no family?"

"His daughters are still minors and his ex-wife is more concerned about the fact that she can't collect life insurance because he's still technically alive. The only person who's visited him at his hospital room besides curious doctors is his bodyguard—probably just trying to find out if he'll wake up enough to give him his last paycheck."

So the man had no one who cared for him. Maybe that's what happened when you treat everyone around you like dirt. "My theory is that whoever was responsible for his attack will sooner or later want to verify his condition—or terminate him."

"We have it covered. He's been under surveillance twenty-four seven and will continue to be when he gets transferred from the unit to the regular floor. We're also monitoring his electronic medical records so we can track down whenever anybody accesses them."

"Agent Elliott," the voice of the secretary came through the intercom. "You have a call from the lab on line one."

Samuel picked up the phone and exchanged a few words with the caller. By the change in his expression, Richard could guess he'd just gotten big news.

"You were right, sonova bitch," Samuel said hanging up the

phone. "They confirmed someone hacked into the hospital laboratory computer system. Someone altered Zimmerman's blood potassium value."

"That supports the theory that he might've received a potassium injection." His chest ached with the memory of the evening Joy had brainstormed that theory with him, and he rushed to bottle up the pain.

Frowning in concentration, Samuel drummed his fingers on the desk. "So they must have an accomplice among the hospital staff."

His photographic memory repeated word for word Joy's answer when he'd asked that question. "Maybe in the pharmacy. If the bags of potassium are mislabeled before they're delivered to the floor, the nurses would think they're administering something else—an antibiotic, for example. They may also have a nurse helping to sedate the patients ahead of time. Apparently, potassium chloride burns the veins and hurts quite a bit, and they must be doing something to prevent the victims from crying for help."

Damn it. How would he ever forget this woman if every step of the case was a reminder of her?

Shaking his head, Samuel seemed to be staring at his childhood hero. "I can't believe how much progress you've made in only a few days. You're amazing, man. You definitely are the FBI's best man to solve this case."

Not feeling like taking credit for someone else's work, Richard didn't answer.

Samuel insisted, "I still can't believe you ever considered leaving us. I'm so glad you changed your mind about that."

What for now? The depression haunting him for the past three days expanded like a cloud of smoke. He'd been burying himself in the case to escape his melancholy, but he no longer cared about its outcome. He no longer cared about Sanders' threats or the danger of ending up in jail. Except for Ray, he didn't care about anything anymore.

~

The twins seemed to sense Mom's blues and were more hyper than ever. They'd escaped the bathtub and ran around the house, slippery wet and buck naked, each one sprinting in a different direction so Joy couldn't catch both at once. It took forever to get them back on track for their bedtime routine. After they were finally asleep, it took Joy a while to put Arthur to bed and pick up the mess from the kitchen and the toys on the living room floor.

She dragged herself to her room and dropped onto the bed, fully dressed, ready to collapse in exhaustion. To her dismay, her thoughts returned to Richard as they had done every second of the past three days she wasn't drowning herself in activity.

It's over. I always knew it couldn't last. She sent a prayer for Richard, wishing him happiness, but that didn't help the stinging pain inside. She followed it by repeating the prayer she'd given that day to Lucía, the last heartbroken widow she had counseled.

"Please, God, help me be thankful for what I briefly had, instead of resentful for what I lost."

Chats over his delicious coffee, picnics in his backyard, sunrises and sunsets at Pineapple Beach… The bittersweet memories followed her all day long like a rain cloud. Was it possible that Richard had never really cared for her? That she had imagined the love between them? Even Michael's scolding voice had been quiet, as every megabyte of capacity in her mind was consumed by the questions.

She rose from bed and headed for the laundry room to get some clean pajamas. As she crossed the family room, she felt more than saw a presence. Someone sat on the sectional couch.

Joy screamed at the top of her lungs. The second the scream left her throat, she realized the visitor was her sister Hope.

Pressing her hand to her chest, she exhaled. "Hope, you almost gave me a heart attack! How come you didn't call ahead?" And darn it. She prayed that scream hadn't awakened the boys. Miraculously, no sound came from their rooms.

Her face unreadable, Hope slowly rose from the couch and strolled to stand in front of her sister. Crossing her arms, she tapped her pointy-toe pump on the floor. "You've been avoiding me since that day I had to pick up the kids from Maureen's house. I've been trying to have a talk with you about that 'neighbor helping you with your hurricane preparations.' That's when it hit me that you've been acting strange lately. Starting with that night you sneaked out of Tom's house to 'go check on a patient.'"

Joy froze in place, unable to reply.

Squinting, Hope lifted Joy's chin and examined her face. Something in her expression made Joy tremble.

"I can't believe I didn't connect the dots before. The glassy eyes. The glowing skin. The great mood..." Holding Joy's arms above the elbow, Hope shook her and exclaimed, "You've been sleeping with Agent Fields!"

Joy's guilty grimace answered for her.

CHAPTER 31

CARL WAS BACK IN TOWN, THIS TIME FOR A WHOLE WEEK, AND Richard seized the opportunity to keep working with him on Hayes' document. But the evening proved quite unproductive; he'd almost forgotten about Carl's tendency to layer riddles and leave him more confused than when they started.

And going over those documents was a torture, as each of those concepts he now understood because of Joy reminded him of her.

"I'm spent. I need a break," Carl announced after a while. "Come to the kitchen and I'll make us a light snack."

Richard picked up the folder of documents and followed Carl. After setting them on the white marble counter, he pulled out a stool and perched on it. "I thought you didn't eat," he deadpanned. "I thought you gather nourishment from the air and the soil."

The spiritual master winked. "I tried that, but I didn't like having to sprout roots and grow leaves."

Carl made small talk as he boiled water in a kettle and retrieved vegan homemade biscuits from his oven. "Do you think they'd allow me to go see Levenstein in his hospital room? I admit a part of me is still hurt about the LOTU deserting my group. I feel the need to get some closure, forgive and let go."

"I don't see why not. I can arrange for that."

As he served Richard mint tea, Carl asked, "So you and Joy split?"

Richard's hand stopped midway to the cup. He whipped his head toward Carl and gaped at him. "Please don't tell me you're a freaking mind reader now like your psychic friend Laura."

"It doesn't take a genius to put the pieces together." Carl shrugged, then pointed at the pile of papers on the counter. "You're here review-ing Hayes' writings with me—instead of with your 'tutor.' You haven't smiled since you arrived. And you haven't shaved in…" He squinted. "I'll guess three days."

Richard gave a sour chuckle and grumbled, "I've always said you should be the one working for the FBI."

Carl poured himself some tea and set down the teapot. "Did you guys have a fight?"

Carl's penetrating gaze weakened Richard's resolve to keep the denial going. "It wasn't exactly a fight. But I had to step away and give her some space," he admitted, lowering his eyes to the biscuit plate. "And I'm not sure I want to try to mend things with her. She has too much baggage to process."

"Who doesn't?" Carl's voice was soft. "Isn't a little baggage worth it if what's on the line is your happiness?"

Richard clutched his teaspoon as if his life depended on it. He swallowed the knot in his throat. "Happiness doesn't really exist. I always knew it couldn't last."

The rumble of feelings he was trying to bottle up threatened to come out full force. Yes, he always knew they'd be saying goodbye at one point. Why did it hurt so much now?

When Carl said nothing, he continued, "The truth is that none of the obstacles in our way would've been unsolvable—the geographical distance when I get transferred, risking getting fired when confront-ing the FBI, risking—" He stopped short of mentioning the danger of going to jail for lying under oath. "I would've gladly risked it all, if I could've trusted she'd be there for me. But I can't." He released the spoon and lifted his hands in a powerless gesture. "O'Hara still has control over her from the underworld. And I'm tired of fighting him."

"There's no point in fighting; what you fight grows," Carl replied. "The way to defeat an invisible enemy is to embrace him. Shine light on the darkness and keep going."

"You're making no sense now." He frowned. "*She* is the one who refuses to let him go. How can *I* shine a light on Joy's issues?"

"You don't. You shine a light on *your own*."

He looked intently at Carl, puzzled.

Carl pulled up a stool and sat across the counter. "Richard, Joy has her own path of growth, separate from yours, and there's little you can do to help her speed it up. She'll arrive at her own conclusions at her own pace. But in the meantime, you keep working on yours."

"I hate it when you talk in riddles." He glowered at Carl.

"It's not that hard," Carl said. "Have you ever wondered why, out of the blue, you stopped seeking the type of toxic woman you used to pursue and became interested in Joy?"

In fact, yes; he'd wondered about that beyond Connors' theories. He waited for the answer in silence.

"*You* changed," Carl explained. "It's a fact. The more enlightened human being you become, the more enlightened the people you'll attract into your life."

As Richard processed his words, Carl added, "Stop worrying about her path. You keep growing. If she's 'it' for you, she'll have no choice but to pick up the pace. If she doesn't, it just means she wasn't."

"But what more light can I shine on me or my issues?" Richard groaned. "You've psychoanalyzed me to sickening levels. You've made me look at my childhood traumas, and screwed up parents, and unconscious patterns…"

"Didn't you just say that 'happiness doesn't exist' and that 'you always knew this couldn't last'?" Carl pointed at him with his open hand. "So, all along, your unconscious thoughts have been telling you there wasn't a point in fighting for your relationship. Maybe—just maybe—the only problem wasn't her issues, but also your conviction that your fight was pointless."

Richard felt his face flush and his ears heat up. "That's not true."

"Are you sure?" Carl narrowed his eyes. "What has happened in your life whenever you've been happy for a long time?"

Richard scoffed. "I never have been."

With a smirk, Carl spread his fingers. "My point exactly."

Richard stared at Carl, trying to assimilate the meaning of his words.

"We human beings say we want happiness," Carl continued. "But the truth is that we run away from it. Your role is to desensitize yourself from the fear by working on being happy right now. Exercise the muscle of happiness by taking in the joy in the little moments."

Exercise the muscle.

Richard's eyes fixed on the documents lying on the counter and something sprang from his memory. "Wait," he blurted, his voice strained with excitement. "I've heard those words before."

His mind racing, he snatched the pages off the counter and scanned them, re-arranging them, as he now understood two previously obscure chapters. His fingers could hardly keep up with his brain, and he risked dropping the pages several times as he organized them.

"Exercise the muscle of happiness."

"Desensitize yourself from the fear."

He got it! This was the way the chapters should read. If this was it, the characters at the bottom of the sheets should make more sense now. He went over them and read them again.

1360 S Woodbridge Springs Dr #19 Ft Sunshine FL 32951

It was an address. And if his memory didn't betray him, it was a storage unit near town. He excused himself and picked up the phone to call Samuel.

He answered at the first ring as usual. "Hello?"

"Sam, I need your help. There's a storage unit we need to get open as soon as possible."

CHAPTER 32

J OY SANK ONTO THE SECTIONAL IN THE FAMILY ROOM AS SHE
listened to her sister's reprimand.

"You deserve for me to slap you!" Hope said for the hundredth time, pacing around the room. "Here I am, worried to death that my poor sister had sworn off men and was letting life pass her by. Here I am, tiptoeing around asking you to consider online dating. And it turns out you're doing very well on your own!"

Shrinking into her seat, Joy covered her hot face with her hands. "I couldn't tell you! Richard's career would be in jeopardy if it ever comes out."

"I knew something strange was going on!" Hope continued. "And you denied liking him when I asked you!"

Joy flopped back onto the seat. "But this conversation is pointless. I told him I didn't want to see him anymore."

Quiet filled the room. Slowly, Hope sat next to her sister. "So you're over him? Did the sparks die?"

"Are you kidding me?" Joy scoffed. "There are no 'sparks' left between us—they exploded into freaking *wildfires*! I'm a disaster!"

Hope pursed her lips to suppress her amusement.

"Yes, a disaster," Joy reiterated. "When he's in the same room my brain short-circuits completely. And when we're not together, I can't focus on anything but when I could see him again. It's been horrible!" She looked at her sister, imploring for help.

Hope hugged her. "Sweetie, welcome to being in love. I knew you had no idea what that was."

A knot formed in Joy's throat as she remembered her talk with Richard in Pineapple Beach about her childhood. Now she understood better why she'd clung to Michael. No therapy in the world had helped her see that more clearly than Richard's attentive ear.

But before Joy could answer, Hope clapped. "My prudish sister is finally sneaking out to meet with *a boy*! I'm so proud of you!" She hugged Joy again, then lowered her voice. "And if Fields is setting 'wildfires' in your bed, I approve of my future brother-in-law already!"

Joy turned away, ignoring Hope's raised high-five gesture. "Stop it, Hope. He'll never be the 'brother-in-law' you invite to family dinners. He was just playing with me." She stopped, not wanting to share about the woman she'd seen him with. Her voice faded. "He just wanted some fun with a forbidden woman before he moves to New York."

"How do you know? Did you ask him?"

"He denies it, but how could I ever trust what he said? He was lying from the first time he met me, while working undercover." She dropped herself back on the sofa. "Allison was right; the man I fell in love with was a fictional character."

Hope rolled her eyes. "Girl, *every man in the world* is playing a fictional character when you first start dating him."

That almost made Joy giggle.

"Sis, for two years I've watched you run away from any man who showed the slightest interest in you." Hope sat next to her and poked Joy's forehead with her index finger. "How about instead of running away you give yourself a chance to figure out if there's a future in this or not."

With a naughty smile, Hope nudged Joy's shoulder and added, "And if this ends up being nothing but a few months of brainless passion with a hot-as-hell, tough FBI agent, well..." She wagged her eyebrows. "I can think of worse destinies than that."

At another time that comment would've made Joy laugh, but not right now. She'd lost Richard forever.

And the worst part? She wasn't even sure she'd ever had him for real.

~

The door of storage unit number nineteen creaked painfully as it opened, its hinges rusted by the ocean mist that plagued the city. Reaching in, the attendant pulled the cord to illuminate the hanging light bulb on the ceiling. "Here you go, agents. All yours."

Leading the small crowd, Richard cast a first glance into the unit he'd worked so long to discover. The five-by-five space was crammed with plastic bins along with a dresser, a few paintings, and an open box filled with trophies and what seemed to be child's memorabilia. He was jumping out of his skin, dying to explore the contents of the unit, but he controlled himself. He took a step back. "Go ahead, team. You know what to do."

Richard waited patiently as the team followed routine security checks, starting with testing for explosive materials or hazardous gases. Then he waited less patiently as another team took pictures, analyzed fingerprints, and swabbed for DNA samples.

That morning, in record time, the FBI had secured an emergency order to open that storage unit, which had been paid for a year in advance by the renter—he suspected Hayes herself using an alias. He had no idea what they would find inside those containers, but it must be something important if it had cost Hayes her life.

It seemed to take an eternity until all routine procedures were done and they could begin opening the boxes one by one. They contained mainly Hayes' family photo albums, travel souvenirs, and an occasional macaroni necklace and hand turkey art that must've been crafted by her daughter in her childhood years. It felt strange to glimpse the personal side of that woman he'd only seen until now as the leader of a merciless group of murderers. She had once loved someone dearly.

"This is going to take forever," another agent mumbled next to him.

Richard opened the dresser drawers. The top drawer contained more travel souvenirs. The middle one contained a collection of old music CDs. The third one contained china and silverware.

The bottom drawer contained a pile of papers and a shoebox labeled, "FBI."

"Guys, I found something!"

He had to wait again until the procedure of pictures, finger-printing, and DNA collection was completed before he was allowed to review the papers; they seemed to be transcriptions of meeting minutes. He held his breath when he recognized the word "Phoebus" in it, Michael O'Hara's pseudonym in the Co-Creators—and probably LOTU—meetings.

He scanned the documents quickly, his pulse racing. Some pages summarized LOTU meetings plotting their plan to take O'Hara to the presidency, some others related murder plots involving several politicians and public figures they considered to be "engaging in morally wrong behavior." Unfortunately, the members were only referred to by one-word names he could guess were pseudonyms. He passed to the last set of pages, a collection of printed emails from communications between Hayes and Joshua Levenstein.

I knew it! A few weeks ago he would've given his right arm to have this evidence proving that Levenstein was the LOTU leader they'd been searching for. But now it just confirmed that his health crisis had not been a coincidence.

He moved his attention to opening the shoebox, which he found filled with more papers and photographs. By the unflattering expressions on the people in them, they seemed like candid pictures, probably taken surreptitiously during a LOTU meeting. He held a gasp. So Hayes had found a way to leave them a clue as to whom some of those pseudonyms belonged. He thumbed through the pictures, finding photos of O'Hara, Levenstein, Xenos, and Zimmerman, as well as the LOTU leader Pitbull had shot.

Damn it! This sucks All of those people were now dead or about to die, so what was the point? And there still must be another leader they hadn't found—whoever had tried to terminate Levenstein. He flipped to the next photograph and the image hit his eyes like an answer to his question. In the background he could identify a blurry figure.

Barbara Young.

CHAPTER 33

" **I**'M GOING TO SAY THIS ONE LAST TIME." AT THE FORT Sunshine police station, Richard used his most menacing voice to address Barbara Young. "We know you participated in the LOTU meetings. We now have evidence of the LOTU's involvement in several deaths. And with every other member of the LOTU ending up dead or in critical condition, *you* are now our biggest suspect."

"I had nothing to do with that, sugar babe." Young's defiance didn't sound very convincing. Reckless as usual, she didn't wait for her lawyer to start talking.

Young and Richard locked gazes. He sent his harshest glare and Young sustained it. He narrowed his eyes and her eyelids flickered. The smugness faded from her features. A suspicious shine moistened her eyes and her lips trembled, then she burst into sobs.

Richard wasn't expecting that, but he hid his surprise.

"I swear I had no idea what they were planning." Young sobbed. "My cousin Michael invited me to those meetings, and I started going only for networking purposes. All I wanted was more clients for my dermatology practice." She cried, shuddering. "I didn't even care about their stupid spiritual theories that never made any sense to me."

Richard studied her. She seemed sincere, but he couldn't lower his guard.

"I had nothing to do with Michael's murder!" she wailed. "And it's not true that I ever had a chance to inherit any money from the O'Hara family like you're suggesting. The only reason Maureen still hasn't changed the beneficiaries in that will is because she's using it to manipulate her daughter-in-law."

At the mention of Joy, Richard tensed. "What are you talking about?"

"The O'Hara Trust is supposed to pay for the college education of Maureen's grandchildren. But she's dangling it over Michael's widow so she agrees to do everything the old witch wants."

"And what does she want?"

"She wants Joy out of this town, to stop fueling the scandal around Michael. She's trying to force her to move with her to the family estate in Connecticut. But I've never supported that!"

"Wait, we're digressing," Samuel intervened. "This is irrelevant, and we should go back to talking about the LOTU."

Maybe this is not irrelevant. Could Maureen O'Hara be behind the threatening cards Joy had received?

And if that was the case, were Sanders and her detective client part of it?

"I swear I had no idea this LOTU group was more than a place to discuss philosophical theories," she insisted. "I only attended a handful of gatherings."

"But you saw the members," Richard said. "You have to help us identify every other person who was at those meetings."

"I didn't know that many people." She sniffled against her blouse's sleeve. "They had this… system. They'd separate into small groups and you would only know the people who met with you."

From Hayes, he knew that was true. It was the LOTU's way to minimize damage if there was a breach of confidentiality. Only the leaders knew more than a handful of members.

She continued, "My team leader was Levenstein, and my group also included Michael, Xenos, and Zimmerman. There were a couple more people, but they used pseudonyms and I don't know their real names."

"You will help us identify those visually."

She nodded.

"What else did you know?"

"I overheard that the leader of the nearest group was a woman, and I assume that's the Hayes person you're talking about, but I never met her."

Richard's stomach clenched with an irrational fear. What if they were not talking about Hayes?

As the meeting ended and officers took Young away, he pondered. Was there another woman involved he should investigate? He'd already wondered once if Blair Sanders had tried to mislead him on the case to detract attention, and now he felt the strong urge to make sure she wasn't part of this. But how could he confront her without shooting himself in the foot?

His phone rang and he frowned to see Allison Connors' number. Why would she be calling him? He took off to the parking lot and picked up. "Fields here."

"I told you not to hurt her." Connors voice sounded glacial as usual on the other side of the call.

He tensed up. He was always afraid phones could be intercepted and really hoped she didn't dare to say anything compromising. "I'm sorry, maybe it's better if we talk in person—"

"I warned you that if you hurt her, I was going to make you pay for it. Now that she's back to her senses, make sure to stay away. Don't tempt me to call your bosses."

Before Richard could answer, she disconnected the call.

Oh great. Richard heaved in exasperation and raked a hand through his hair. *Just one more delightful thing to add to my list of worries.*

~

"Joy, Joy! You're never going to believe this!" Patel burst into Joy's office at the CeMeSH, snatching her out of reviewing her emails.

"What's going on?" she asked.

In front of her desk, he grinned and bounced his weight from one leg to the other, like a fidgety kid. His voice rang loud and joyful as he announced, "Barbara Young is going to jail!"

His words sounded surreal to Joy. "What?"

"The FBI showed up at her medical suite and arrested her. Nobody knows exactly why, but everyone assumes it must be something related to your husband's case—the only famous FBI case in this town."

Lost in her broken heart, Joy hadn't given any more thought to Michael's murder case. Imagining his own cousin could've been involved was too horrific to process. "That's terrible."

"Yes, it is terrible." Barely able to contain his glee, Patel's accent had turned purely American. "I always knew she wasn't trustworthy! Thank God you didn't agree to partner with her!" He clapped once. "Which reminds me. Now that she's out of the way, we should prepare our fundraising project."

Joy studied him, her mind consumed by a question she'd wanted to ask him for days. "Venkat, how come the other day you said the Hospice House was 'a useless place'? If that's what you believe, why would you help me fundraise for it?"

Surprise mingled with guilt on Patel's face.

"So Barbara was right?" Joy asked. "Helping me to save the Hospice House was just a way to convince me to join you in your holistic medicine projects?"

"I apologize for having said that." He looked down at the laminate floor. "I swear I do want to help the Hospice House. But you can do more for it from a distance than from here. The more well-known you become, the more sponsors you can attract." He raised his eyes to meet hers. "Think about it. No more pain in the neck of running a practice. You'd get to travel all over the country to speaking engagements, helping to change the world's view of medicine."

She shook her head. "Venkat, you know I can't do that amount of traveling. I have small children."

"You told me their grandma would be more than glad to move in with you to help you."

Joy cringed internally. Living with Maureen O'Hara was the last thing she'd ever want.

"And you'd have more time off, since sometimes you'd be working from home. You'd have so much freedom you wouldn't even have to live in this town. You could say goodbye to Fort Sunshine and all its bad memories and chose to live anywhere in the country."

Even New York.

She shook the ridiculous thought away. "Venkat, I appreciate your offer, but honestly, I'm too attached to my work here to leave it and move away."

"Hello?"

Knuckles rapped against the doorframe. Allison stood at the door and Joy felt thankful for the interruption. "Come on in, Allison. Venkat and I were done talking."

Obviously disappointed, Patel mumbled an excuse and left the office.

Allison took a seat at the chair in front of Joy's desk. "I just came to make sure you're okay. I was worried about you after this morning."

Per Hope's insistence, Joy had called Allison the night before and she'd squeezed her in an 8:00 a.m. appointment. Joy hadn't wanted to share the details of why she had broken up with Richard, but at least it had been a good crying and venting session so she was in better condition to work on cheering up her own patients the rest of the day.

"I'm fine, Allison. Thanks for seeing me on such short notice."

Allison kept studying her intently. "Are you sure you don't want to tell me what happened with *you-know-who*?"

"I don't want to talk about it. The important thing is that now you're entitled to tell me 'I told you so.'" She released a powerless sigh and slouched in her chair. The pain and tears she thought she was done with threatened to resurface. "You were right and I shouldn't have let myself get so carried away."

"I'm sorry." Allison extended her hand to hold Joy's and for a moment there was almost tenderness in her stoic stare. "That man doesn't deserve your tears; he deserves punishment."

"No, he doesn't. His role in my life is just over." Joy reached for a Kleenex from the box on her table. "He was a blessing in my life for as long as it lasted, and exactly what my soul needed at the time. It would be greedy for me to want anything more from him."

It was true. Richard had revolutionized her definition of what a man should be and what love should feel like. He'd been a crash course in life enjoyment. He'd awakened her senses and expanded her capacity to feel happiness—and yes, pleasure.

So what if he left her life as suddenly as he'd appeared?

~

Richard stood in front of Josh Levenstein's hospital bed with Samuel and Carl. "Such irony that we finally have what we needed to arrest him, but it's now pointless," Richard commented.

The man was practically a vegetable. His eyes stared at some blank point in the distance. An oxygen cannula clung to his nose.

"He answers no questions?" Carl asked.

"The only response they could get from him was a groan when the doctor rubbed his sternum with his fist—apparently he's still able to feel pain," Richard replied.

Samuel scoffed. "I would rather be dead than in his shoes."

With a grave tone, Carl pointed out, "If karma came to get him, what a way to do it."

Richard felt numb, unable to feel any compassion. For a moment Levenstein's eyes seemed to focus on him and Richard could've almost sworn a spark of contempt shone in them. A chill went down his spine. He must be imagining things; that man could not possibly be so unlucky that the only thing he could do now was feel pain and hate.

Now that *is hell.*

The minute they walked out of the room, a tall, blond man with a distressed expression entered it. Richard recognized Levenstein's bodyguard, probably still hoping for that last paycheck.

As they walked to the elevators, a text message from Ray reached Richard's phone. *"I'm walking there to spare you the carline."* Since Ray's new high school was only a couple of blocks from the hospital, Richard had planned to pick him after school.

He texted back. *"We'll meet you in the hospital lobby."*

As they waited for the slow elevator, Samuel commented, "We've hit a brick wall with the case. Young continues to stick to her story that she had nothing to do with O'Hara's death and I have the feeling she's telling the truth."

"So there must be another LOTU leader you haven't identified yet who's responsible for the death of the other witnesses?" Carl asked.

Richard growled in frustration. "I could've sworn that was Levenstein!"

"But clearly we were wrong, or he wouldn't have been attacked," Samuel pointed out the obvious.

Richard had to be careful about his next step. He couldn't afford to bring up Sanders as a possible suspect to the FBI, at the risk of her revealing what she knew about him. Especially when all he had was a vague hunch. He had to screen her himself. "And no one suspicious has attempted to enter his room?"

"No, but it might have something to do with the fact that his bodyguard is camped outside of the room twenty-four seven." Samuel tossed a thumb in the direction of the room they'd just left.

After they rode the elevator down, Samuel said goodbye and headed for the parking lot while Richard and Carl met Ray at reception. Carl had invited Richard and Ray to join him for dinner out before he headed to speak in Chicago. They crossed the lobby in silence, ignoring the crowd of security guards screening people at the entrance for weapons. Ever since the shooting at the Pulse night club in Orlando, the hospital had implemented insane new security policies.

"So Ray, how do you like your new high school?" Carl asked as they strolled to the valet parking.

"It's okay," Ray replied. "But I'm not staying there for long. Dad already started the process of transferring me to a school in New York City."

"Is that right?" Carl turned to Richard with a flick of the eyebrows.

It felt strange returning to casual talk after witnessing Levenstein's disturbing condition. As Richard handed his ticket to the parking valet, he nodded. "We're using my brother's address in Brooklyn until I find a place."

Carl shot him a curious look, but Richard didn't answer. The boy's future was only one of multiple questions hanging over him.

The back of Richard's mind detected something unusual. Too much light. The awning over the valet station had been removed since he was last there. Probably as part of the constant renovation ongoing in the hospital.

"So you're taking the transfer for sure?" Carl asked.

"It's not like I ever had a—"

Richard sensed more than heard the snap that made him look up. He glimpsed something plummeting from high above them.

Only the combination of his flash reflexes and his training allowed Richard to move fast enough. He pushed Carl and Ray out of the way, bracing them against the hospital wall. A deafening crash sounded behind him and pieces of shattering glass exploded all around them.

CHAPTER 34

RICHARD REMAINED FROZEN, HIS HEART RACING WHILE HIS ears scanned the air until he confirmed nothing else was falling.

"Are you okay?" he asked Ray and Carl, still trapped against the wall by his arms.

They both nodded.

Richard backed away, stepping carefully over the mess of glass spewed across the sidewalk. Judging by the amount of glass and the broken frames on the ground, he guessed the object had once been a large window panel—maybe a pile of them. He studied the scaffolding on the highest floor above them and wondered if they'd fallen from there. No one seemed to be in sight.

In seconds, the valet parking employees, several security guards, and a group of curious people had surrounded them. Apparently, having heard the noise, Samuel was running back from the parking lot.

"What's going on?" Samuel panted.

"This piece of glass fell on us," Richard replied, still trying to understand what had happened.

As he cooled down from the initial impression, terror overpowered him. Had this really been an accident? Was this an attack against him? Or Carl?

Or against his son?

He dragged Carl and Ray back into the hospital with Samuel close behind.

"Sam, I need security to go check that scaffold and make sure this was really an accident."

Samuel gave a single nod and started giving orders to security.

Richard's pulse raced so hard he felt dizzy. Was he paranoid? Was Carl the next target like he'd always feared? Or were they trying to eliminate *him*? How would someone have known he'd be there unless they were intercepting their calls and texts?

Ray's gasp brought Richard back. "Dad, you're bleeding!"

Richard noticed the sudden stings of pain and felt dampness on his neck and back. His reflection in a window showed bloodstains spreading over the back of his shirt and only then noticed that some shards of glass had impaled his back. But he'd been lucky, most had been stopped by his clothing.

"You may need stitches," the security guard commented, pointing at the largest bloodstain on his back. "Let me walk you to the emergency room entrance."

"I'll be fine. They're only scratches," he mumbled in protest.

"No, go," Carl insisted. "I'll keep Ray with me until you get fixed up."

~

Later that day, Joy huffed and rolled her eyes as her sister dragged her out of the car and propelled her to the entrance of Carl's house. It was 7:00 p.m. and she prayed they didn't interrupt Carl mid-dinner—if he was home at all.

Hope rang the bell, then, short of patience, knocked on the door. A few moments later, Carl opened it.

Hope bowed her head. "Good afternoon, sir... doctor... master... Am I supposed to call you Your Holiness or something?"

Carl's confusion was obvious. "Sorry, what?"

"Anyway." Hope yanked Joy's arm and brought her in front of Carl. "There. You take it from here. Since her therapist has proven useless, I'm requesting a second opinion and urgent help."

Smiling, Carl eyed Joy. "What's the problem?"

"Don't ask me, you're the guru and the shrink," Hope answered. "I've had it with this woman. I can't understand why she would want to push away the only man in the world who's really rung her bell. But if I had to guess, I'd say she's scared."

Hope gave her sister a quick hug. "We'll bring the kids back tomorrow after lunch." She nudged Joy toward the door. "Here, sir. See if you have better luck than me talking some sense into her."

Without another word, Hope left.

"Well, you're just in time. I just made tea." Carl signaled Joy to enter and she did reluctantly, dragging her feet.

As Joy followed Carl to his favorite spot on the back porch, he asked, "Your sister seems worried about you. Should she?"

Joy flicked her wrist dismissively. "She's convinced I'm depressed because Richard and I broke up."

"I see." Carl gestured for her to take a chair next to his, facing the river. He served her tea from a white and golden ceramic teapot. "I liked her theory that you're scared. Do you think it makes sense?"

Another time, Joy would've appreciated the gorgeous river view from Carl's backyard. But today everything seemed gray to her. "No. I'm not scared; I'm just disappointed."

Carl tilted his head. "You've done quite a bit of running away from Richard since the first time he showed interest in you. It does look like being afraid from here."

Joy had to admit few people in the world knew her as well as her mentor and her sister.

As he served himself tea, Carl said, "So, let's assume that theory is right and explore it for a moment." He lowered the teapot and extended a plate with biscuits. "Tell me, my dear, what could you possibly be afraid of?"

Always the good student who would never refuse a question, she dug in her psyche for an answer while accepting the treat. "I guess I've been afraid of having to say goodbye when he leaves for New York."

Carl set down the plate. "I see. So you decided to rip off the Band-Aid and break up now?"

If anyone were able to extract unconscious thoughts from her, it would be Carl. Maybe she *had* done a little bit of that.

Sighing, she played with her biscuit. "I used to say I had no attachment to anything in this world besides my commitment to raise my children. I used to say I was spiritually advanced enough not to cling to anything. But now, with him… he's growing roots in my heart."

"And why would you be afraid of getting attached to him?"

Joy tried to understand as she spoke. "Because the only relationship I had before was so bad, I assume."

Carl narrowed his eyes, as if unconvinced. "Was Michael really your only relationship? How about your other loved ones before him, like your parents?"

She shrugged. "They've been gone so long now."

"I see." Carl softened his voice. "I'd forgotten that everyone you ever depended on before left you."

The words lashed her soul, breaking open a Pandora's box of feelings.

That was it. She, the ultimate shrink, had failed to see it. Her mother's premature death, her father's inability to be there for her, the way her high school sweetheart, Michael, had ended up disappointing her… She'd been terrified to depend on Richard.

After so many years, after so much therapy, after swearing she was over it, her original wound resurfaced from the shadows.

Her acquiescence to the theory must've reflected on her face, as Carl slowly nodded. "So that's why you resist opening your heart, isn't it? You're perpetuating your belief, 'I'm here to take care of everybody, but no one can take care of me.' The thought, 'I'm alone in the world, I can't count on anyone.' The fear, 'I'd better not love something too much, or it will be taken away from me.'"

His final words ran through her mind, conscious for the first time in her life. She braced herself and grumbled, "Carl, didn't you say counselors are supposed to step away and let the clients arrive at their own conclusions?"

Carl shrugged. "Counselors have to bend the rules sometimes." He gazed at her with affection. "Is my theory wrong?"

"No." With a groan, she slouched on her chair. "But knowing it is useless. Obviously, this wound will never be cured. I've had countless hours of therapy. I've done all the spiritual work there is. What is left to do?"

Carl patted her hand. "You don't fight it. You embrace it. Like darkness. You shine your light on it and take it one day at a time. Like a chronic illness. Like an annoying fever blister that comes back each time you're sick. You breathe through the exacerbations without beating yourself up over them and live life to the fullest during the remissions."

Joy pondered his words for a long time. "This is a humbling lesson, Carl, and I thank you for bringing this to my awareness." She felt the angst rise again and kept her attention focused on her plate. "But that doesn't change anything with Richard. He's been cheating on me."

"No, he's not! That's ridiculous!" Ray's voice snagged her attention as he walked around the house toward them. In swimming trunks and a T-shirt, he held a surfing board under his arm. His slicked-back brown hair hinted he'd just returned from the beach. Frowning, he set the board on the ground, leaning it against the house wall. "Joy, what are you talking about? Dad's not cheating on you."

Joy didn't understand why Ray was there, but if that meant Richard could arrive any minute to get him, she had to get out of there. "Hello, sweetie. Uh… Sorry." She scrambled up and addressed Carl. "I'd better get going."

Ray closed the remaining distance between himself and Joy. Clicking his tongue, he shook his head. "Joy, I like you. But with all due respect, you can be a little distracted sometimes—that's why you could never beat me at video games. Haven't you noticed how ridiculously hard Dad has been working lately?" He threw his hands in the air. "When do you think he would've had time to cheat on you?"

Joy considered it. *He does have a point.*

Before she could speak, Ray helped himself from the biscuits on the table and casually added, "And that's not even mentioning that he's crazy about you."

"Really?" Carl asked, barely covering his amusement.

"I've never seen him like that in my life!" Ray snorted, then turned to Joy. "You should've seen him after that Friday you crashed on his couch. He spent the whole weekend with a smile plastered over his face, humming old songs and *smelling the pillow you used.*" He looked up to the sky.

Those words should've caused a blast of excitement in Joy, but instead filled her with pain. *He must be making it up; that doesn't sound like Richard at all.* She turned to Carl pleading for help with her eyes. Shouldn't he be the one to tell the boy not to interfere in a conversation between adults? But Carl's suppressed chuckles hinted he was more entertained than upset.

"Anyway." Ready to move on, Ray addressed Carl. "Dad says he got the tickets online and we're flying out the day after tomorrow."

"What?" Joy startled.

Ray replied around a mouthful of biscuit. "Yeah. He decided to speed up the move to New York because he's 'worried about my safety.'" He huffed in exasperation. "You should've heard the reprimand he just gave me over the phone for going surfing."

A vacuum of despair expanded in her chest. "But... did his transfer go through already?"

"His boss Samuel is sending him there to cooperate with the New York office until the paperwork is ready."

Carl sent Joy a sympathetic look and she felt like crying. She'd dreaded that moment of seeing Richard go so badly, and now it had arrived.

Oblivious to her pain, Ray kept talking to Carl. "Hey, Dad also told me to ask you if it's okay for me to spend the night here, because the hospital's going to take longer to discharge him than he thought."

Discharge him? Joy was barely recovering from the last news and now this. "The hospital?"

Apprehension flashed on Carl's face. Before he could intervene Ray said, "Oh, Carl didn't tell you?"

"Tell me what?" Joy's heartbeat sped up.

"The three of us almost got killed earlier. Dad's in the ER right now, getting stitches."

CHAPTER 35

O
N HIS WAY HOME FROM THE ER, RICHARD CALLED SAMUEL for an update.

"It's okay. We're pretty sure it was just a construction accident." Samuel tried to reassure him.

"That pile of glass could've fallen on Ray's head. It could've killed him. And Carl too."

"But it didn't. Relax. This is not the LOTU modus operandi."

"But it doesn't have to be. You've heard Carl. These people are unstable. And as they find themselves corralled, their methods are likely to become more drastic."

From force of habit, Richard parked in his driveway. Over the past weeks he'd gotten used to leaving the garage free for Joy.

"How was the ER?" Samuel asked.

"A pain in the neck," Richard replied, turning off the engine. "They made me surrender my gun even after showing my badge! They claimed that I was there as a patient, not as a law enforcer."

"Yes, the hospital reinforced their weapons control policies recently."

"Bullshit. It's a premeditated humiliation to break people's wills." He exited the car and slammed the door shut. "The ER doc tried to make me stay overnight—something about a temperature and making sure I didn't have an infection."

"You refused medical advice?"

"They were talking nonsense; I feel fine. They drew like a gallon of blood and ordered me to see my doctor to follow up on the results."

Samuel cleared his throat. "Anyway, I have some news. While you were in the ER, that kitchen worker from the jail identified Levenstein's bodyguard as the person who brought her the pills to add to Hayes' food."

Richard stopped walking to his house. "His bodyguard? The same one visiting him in his hospital room?"

"I alerted security to search for him at the hospital, but he was already gone. Our team is working on researching him right now."

Could the bodyguard also be working for the other LOTU leaders? Had he been visiting Levenstein's room to verify he was no longer dangerous and potentially eliminate him if he woke up?

Could he have been involved in the falling glass incident?

"Anyway. You've had a long day. Go rest," Samuel said. "I'll see you tomorrow to start wrapping up before you leave." Samuel disconnected the call and Richard slowly made his way into his house.

Richard entered the living room and collapsed on the couch. The wounds he'd just received stitches for were starting to hurt as the anesthesia wore off. But that was the least of his pain. His whole body ached from the brutal exercise and the tension of the past days. Now as he sank into the sofa, he wondered if he'd been too quick to reject the doctor's recommendation to stay admitted.

As he cooled down, terror descended over him. He felt powerless, shaken, and exhausted. He wouldn't have peace of mind until he saw Carl and Ray safe, far away from here.

He was so overwhelmed it took him a while to notice another presence in the room, inching toward him. He normally would've sprung up and attacked the uninvited visitor, but his soul immediately recognized Joy's energy.

Joy eased around the recliner. "Hello. Sorry for showing up without calling."

Filled with emotion, he rose from the couch and surveyed her face eagerly, trying to read her. Had she forgiven him for how harsh he'd been the last time they'd been together? "Hi." It was all he could think to say.

"I was so worried when I heard you'd gone to the emergency room." She took a tentative step toward him. He could sense her struggle in her cautious posture.

"I'm so glad you're here." He wanted to take her in his arms but didn't dare. Instead, he extended his hand and was relieved when she took it.

"You okay?" she asked softly, taking a seat on the couch.

He sat next to her and clutched her hand. "I'm fine."

She seemed as torn as he was about the distance separating them. "Ray also told me you're going to New York and I didn't want your last memory of us to be that fight we had."

He didn't feel like asking where she'd seen Ray. "I'm sorry." It was all he could say. He was sorry for having to say goodbye, let alone this quickly. He was sorry because even now, when it might be the last time he saw her in his life, he was unable to tell her how much he loved her. "I'm sorry for my harshness that night."

She forced a joke. "Buddy, you owe me a million childhood stories."

They chuckled together, then her sweet face became serious. "No, *I* am sorry. I was hysterical, out of my mind."

"You were not." He tightened the grip on her hand and forced a smile. "Angel, even on your worst day you're more reasonable than my average ex on her best day."

Her eyes sent a thank you and she slid closer to him. "I came to apologize for not believing you that night. You were right all along. I was pushing you away because of my own unfinished business."

"I'm the one who has to apologize." He held her hand against his face and then kissed it. "And I wish I could explain why I was with that woman—but I can't."

"It's okay. You don't owe me any explanations." She added her second hand to his. "I'm the one indebted to you. You saved my life; you showed me what love could really be; you taught me to smile again… If I have any chance of being happy ever again, it's thanks to you."

A stab a thousand times more painful than the wound in his back pierced his soul. "The only thing that hurts me more than imagining you unhappy is imagining you happy with someone else."

He tugged on her hands and pulled her gently into his arms. The second they embraced, the pain eased and peace trickled into his soul. They embraced for a long time; her soothing energy filling him.

"I'm sorry," he repeated, kissing her face.

"Don't be." Her touch on his back felt so delicious he didn't mind the stinging in his wounds. "That's all I came to say. I don't want us to end on a sour note."

"I don't want us to end—period." He held her tighter, to prevent her from leaving his arms.

"But we have to end." She moved her head from the groove between his neck and slowly came out of his arms. "Sweetie, I've accepted it already. You belong in New York."

He sighed, feeling completely powerless.

"You have a mission," she said softly, caressing his hair. "Maybe I was sent into your life as an instrument to help you in it, and now my role is done. No one can solve this case better than you. And if New York is where you need to be... so be it."

He wished he could promise her he'd figure out a way to keep in touch. But in the midst of his exhaustion and overwhelm, he couldn't see a way out. He denied with a headshake. "I wish I could explain why I haven't been able to come clear to the FBI about us... but I can't."

She placed two fingers on his lips. "It's okay. I just want you to know that I'll be fine. I'm stronger than I seem."

"I know." He felt a knot in his throat. "Maybe I am the one who's weak." He took her in his arms again and held on to her like a lifeline. Losing the battle with the tears, his chest shook in a controlled sob and his voice broke. "I don't want to lose you."

She sobbed too, but kept herself together better than him. "You're not going to lose me and I'm never going to lose you," she mumbled, against his hair. "Don't forget that this is a world of illusions, and the biggest of all is the illusion of separation. Like cells in the same body, you and I will always be connected, no matter where we are."

She pushed away from him to look in his eyes. "I always tell my patients' loved ones, when someone dies or goes away, they leave behind a legacy for us, and we get to inherit their best qualities. From now on, everywhere I go, I'll carry a little bit of those traits I always envied in you. I'll carry your strength and your determination. I'll carry your ability to notice detail, feel pleasure, and enjoy life."

He nodded, while drying his eyes with his palm. "And from now on I will always carry in me a little bit of your compassion, your kindness, and your empathy."

They sealed the promise with one long last kiss, a kiss that tasted of sweet memories, bittersweet nostalgia, and a sour anticipation for a cold future.

She rose from the couch and pulled him by the hand. "Come to bed, you need to rest."

He resisted it. "I still have work to do."

"Come on," she insisted. "Let me take care of you one last time. Not because I have to, but because I want to."

She walked him to the bedroom. Gently, she helped him out of his shirt, pants, and shoes, and made him lie on his side in bed. Staying away from the cuts in his back, her hands skillfully massaged his aching shoulders and chest, giving him one last taste of heaven.

～

Richard was starting to doze off and Joy kept running her hands over his body, absorbing his image for the last time. Her eyes and fingers committed to memory every bulge of his muscles, the tattoo on his right arm, the hard ridges of his shoulders, the left one lower than the right since that injury.

She had no doubt she'd crash later, but in that moment she

surprised herself with how peaceful she felt. She'd meant every word she'd said to him. And the only words she'd left out were the words, "I love you." Not pronouncing them was her last gift of love to him, to spare him the obligation and stress of saying it back.

By his deep, regular breathing she guessed he was asleep. She leaned over and brushed her lips against his one last time, and his hand caught her arm before she could pull away.

"Please, stay with me," he whispered.

She tensed up. "You need to rest."

"No," he argued. "I need *you*."

His tired hazel eyes seemed to beg her, but she hesitated. She had to leave now, while she still had the determination. She couldn't possibly prolong this suffering. But his silent plea wore her conviction down. Kicking off her shoes, she joined him under the blankets.

His lips immediately fused with hers and his arms sought to erase the distance between their bodies. Her fingers caressed him first with caution—following the guidance of his winces of pain and groans of pleasure—then freely, as if they'd memorized his body or shared a nervous system with it.

He kissed her like he'd never kissed her before, with a new level of surrender and powerlessness. She kissed him back with a passion that should've scared her, but instead exhilarated her. Every touch of their hands carried the sweet agony of knowing this was their last time. Every piece of clothing shed was a cry, and an unshed tear. But every moan and ragged breath was a prayer of gratitude for the love they'd shared while it lasted. If past, present, and future were just another illusion, their love could make this moment endure forever.

CHAPTER 36

T HE NEXT MORNING RICHARD WOKE LATE TO AN EMPTY BED. He'd fallen asleep so deeply in Joy's arms he didn't even notice her leaving. He closed his eyes for a moment, torturing himself by reliving their night. The lingering bliss of her presence mingled with the pain of saying goodbye.

He dragged himself out of bed, his body aching and his back screaming in protest, and tried to put away his gloom to get ready for work.

He was an hour late when he arrived at the office. The moment he walked in, Samuel skipped the greetings and launched into the newest update. "Breaking news! Our facial recognition software matched Levenstein's bodyguard to a Russian hacker, Boris Ivanov."

Richard shook himself from his melancholy to try to catch up. "So he could've been the person who helped Levenstein hack into the medical records."

"Exactly."

Richard processed the information.

"Now we're pending a positive ID from Dr. Young, if she can confirm he was in the meetings. Could he be the LOTU leader we're missing?"

Richard frowned. "I doubt it. I remember how Levenstein treated him. They behaved more like master and slave than equal partners."

Samuel clapped once. "But at least we finally have a potential informant we can chase! One who's *alive*! Man, I needed that. I've been so bummed about you leaving."

Leaving. Richard could no longer bottle up his despair. His plane to New York would leave tomorrow morning.

"I'm really going to miss you, my friend." Samuel placed a hand on Richard's shoulder. "But I have to remind myself that you'll advance the case more from there. The resources we have here don't compare to those in the New York field office."

Richard could hardly hear him. Today he had Joy's memory stuck to his soul like a leech, his longing giving him a taste of what life in New York was destined to be.

His sorrow must've reflected on his face as Samuel's expression filled with worry. "Man, are you okay?"

"Yeah, I'm fine." Richard avoided his friend's eyes.

Samuel drilled him with the inquisitive gaze of someone who knew him more than he knew himself. "Bro, are you doing okay? Seriously?" he repeated, then he glanced at the closed office door and lowered his voice to a whisper. "You're down about leaving *her*?"

Judging by the worry in Samuel's eyes, something in Richard's countenance must've answered affirmatively before he gathered himself to cover it. He shrugged. "It doesn't matter now."

With slow, tired movements, he got up and shuffled away. He was about to open the door when Samuel's voice stopped him.

"Okay, you were right!"

Richard pivoted slowly. "Right about what?"

His voice down to a whisper, Samuel squirmed in his seat. "You were right. If you confess your involvement with Clayton before they find out, you may get away with not being fired."

That was so unexpected Richard had to take a step back to regain balance. "Sam, what are you talking about?"

Samuel shrunk into his chair, as if giving up out of pure exhaustion. "I... I curb-sided a friend who owes me a favor. He works in the disciplinary action committee."

"Sam! You didn't tell on me, did you?" Richard asked, tense.

Samuel shook his head. "I didn't give your name. And I trust this man's discretion completely. I gave him a vague recount of your situation, I told him 'this agent' had come to me debating between confessing and resigning and I had stopped him, first wanting to find out his options."

Richard returned to his chair, holding his breath. "What did he say?"

Samuel puffed. "Pretty much what you'd already guessed. If you come clean, and if you argue that you only pursued this woman *after* she was already exonerated, they'll probably go for just a suspension without pay."

Richard's pulse quickened. Of course, a month without pay would be difficult. But it was doable, and much better than being fired. "What about revealing my identity to her? And admitting to her there was an ongoing murder investigation? Can they consider that breaking confidentiality of the case?"

Samuel tilted his head. "There are gray zones. If you could claim that you had to blow the cover because it was necessary for someone's safety or to advance the case, they're likely to let it go."

For the first time in days, hope began to glow inside of Richard, like a match that had just been struck. Yes, he could claim that. The information he'd gotten from Joy the night he'd revealed his identity led him to solving the case later.

Samuel continued, "He hinted that you may have an even better chance if you're able to show this wasn't an irresponsible, impulsive act, but you have serious intentions with this woman. We're talking, future wedding bells."

Reflexive panic filled Richard. Few things in the world scared him more than the thought of marriage again.

Yet for the first time, the idea wasn't unthinkable. He surprised himself with the thought that, if there was one person he'd be willing to take that jump with, it was Joy.

And then, immediately, his hopes deflated. Samuel didn't know about his most important fear—that a close dissection of the case could uncover his lie under oath, especially if Sanders decided to talk.

"Why didn't you tell me before?" Richard's trained eyes couldn't help noticing that Samuel's expression wasn't cheerful.

"There's one drawback." Samuel paused. "If you come clean, they'll have to remove you from the case."

Richard couldn't believe he'd overlooked that obvious detail. He tapped his own forehead. "You're right! Personal involvement."

Samuel's shrug indicated that the answer was obvious. "You can't work on a case that directly affects your significant other."

No point in mentioning she was also an informal consultant for the case. "But… this case has been the biggest breakthrough of my career. If I get removed from it, I'm nobody. I can't even go back and work undercover anymore."

"That's the reason I hesitated to bring it up," Samuel confessed. "If you take this route, you may be able to come out of hiding with her. But we're losing you on the case anyway."

Richard ran a hand through his hair, trying to assimilate it all.

But at least he had a sliver of hope now. He had to talk to Sanders and get the evidence she had against him.

"Whatever you decide to do, bro, just remember," Samuel said, "all this is assuming that you come clean. That you tell them *before* they find out some other way."

He nodded, and swallowed hard, adding one more thing to his to-do list.

He also had to make sure Allison Connors didn't carry out her threat to denounce him.

~

Richard had eliminated Connors as a suspect long ago. As a psychologist, she didn't have the medical training necessary to plot the murders. But he still hadn't ruled out that she might've been involved in the harassing messages Joy had received, maybe in an attempt to push her to move away from him.

But today he had an even bigger priority; he had to persuade her from denouncing him to the FBI for his involvement with Joy.

They met at the Masden Center parking garage during her lunch break and he went through the routine of searching her for wires and turning off her phone. Then, they sat in his SUV, the engine running.

Richard studied the woman, her spine erect, not touching the back of the passenger seat. The contempt radiating from her glare made it difficult for him to choose his words.

"I don't have all day, Fields. Speak," she said in her monotone voice.

He drew in a lungful, recalling his own words to Joy the night before. *And from now on I will always carry in me a little bit of your compassion, your kindness, and your empathy.*

Evoking Joy's essence, he remembered something he'd read in the bio of one of Connors' self-help books, that she was a survivor of childhood abuse. Talk about something he could relate to. Compassion filled his heart as he tried to imagine how much unhealed pain she tried to cover behind her cold attitude.

"I'm here to appeal to your common sense and professional ethics," he finally said. "I think you know that if you ever out me to the FBI, you'll be hurting Joy as much as you would be hurting me."

Maybe there was some truth about "putting out vibes," or maybe something in his facial expression or his voice had changed subtly along with his attitude, but Connors seemed to sense his change and relaxed a notch. "It might make her suffer at first, but it would be for her own good in the long term," she replied, but an ounce of defiance had gone from her voice.

He shook his head softly. "Joy would be dragged into a scandal. Reporters would chase her even more than now. She would never have peace."

Connors remained silent for a while then cleared her throat. "You have a point."

Her answer gave him hope, but he held on to caution. "If there is one thing you and I have in common, it's that we care for Joy. I'm appealing to that to request your discretion."

Connors' tension continued to relax until her squared shoulders dropped. Slowly, she eased back into the seat. After a long pause, she said, "I need to apologize for being so rude the last time we talked."

Wow. That worked out way too well. "Do you?"

She avoided his eyes. "I'm an intelligent enough woman to know not to verbally harass a federal agent. I think you'd easily infer that if I did, it was out of a knee-jerk reflex to protect someone I love."

"I'm aware that you've helped Joy in the most difficult times of her life. I appreciate that."

She bowed her head once. "In her usual generous nature, she hardly remembers now; but back then in college, Joy's kindness toward me made a huge difference in a difficult time of *my* life. I used to consider her a friend—even if I can't claim friendship with her now because I'm her therapist."

Maybe the woman did care for Joy. Moved by her confession, Richard doubted she could be involved in the harassing messages.

"I'm not allowed to reveal to you how much I know about her years with O'Hara," she continued. "But I'll tell you that it tore me apart to witness her suffering from a distance. For the first time in two years, she was finally recovering her peace; it broke me up to see you'd entered the scene and taken that peace away." She cleared her throat and shot him a warning glare. "But I scorn sentimentalism. So I'd really appreciate if you never repeat any of this to her."

"You have my word." He suppressed his amusement. "Can I count on your discretion then?"

She scrutinized him for a while in silence, then blurted, "How serious are your intentions with her? Are you ever planning to offer her marriage?"

It was the second time in a matter of hours someone confronted him with that question, and the fact that he hadn't immediately rejected the possibility stunned him. "I wish I could tell you I had a clear plan. But I'm afraid right now I have no control over our future; I'm leaving for New York tomorrow."

"I interpret that as a no," Allison said, her expression closing up again. "If you know it's a matter of time until you have to break her heart, why bother to even contact her again when you get to New York? She's already starting to make peace with the idea that your affair is over. Do something generous for the first time in your life and let her be."

"You didn't answer my question."

She opened the door to exit the car. "I will not be the one to report you."

"Thank you—"

"Don't." She stood next to the car, holding the door open and drilling him with her blue gaze. "I'm not doing this for you, but for her. Be aware that I'm ready to go to any extremes to defend her if you ever try to steal her peace again."

She shot him one last icy glare then, without another word, she shut the car door and walked away.

Well. He'd count that as a victory.

～

At the end of the workday, Joy returned to the Hospice House to pick up the purse she'd forgotten. She'd spent the last hour on the phone with a newly widowed patient and felt exhausted. Sometimes, after sessions like this, she felt as if she'd given the patient a transfusion from her own blood.

For the first time in the whole workday she had a moment of quiet with her thoughts, and the sadness she'd been trying to suppress made its way back full force.

Her visit to Richard last night had a different outcome than she expected. She'd hoped to walk out of there feeling peace and resignation, but now she hurt more than ever. As wonderful as spending one last night in his arms had been, it had only sharpened the pain of knowing he was leaving tomorrow.

I have to stop being selfish. I have to let him go for his own good and the good of his investigation, she repeated in her head like a mantra.

When she opened her office door, she was surprised to find the lights turned off. She hit the switch, but nothing happened. Could all the light bulbs have burned out at the same time? Had the breakers tripped? Absorbed in her thoughts, she barely registered something else that didn't make sense. The room was nearly pitch dark and that wasn't normal for 6:00 p.m. Someone must've closed the window blinds and curtains. The cleaning ladies?

She made a mental note to call maintenance about the malfunctioning lights. As she entered, her foot kicked something away and she guessed it was Arthur's toy baseball bat. Her office floor was still cluttered with toys from the kids' last visit. Careful not to trip over them, she used the flashlight feature on her phone to guide herself to her desk.

And that was when she heard the voice, feet away from her. "Joy, come here."

She would've fainted if it hadn't been for the adrenaline discharge that rushed through her body, raising her blood pressure and sending her heart to a sprint. She knew that sound, and it was her worst nightmare come true.

It was Michael's voice.

CHAPTER 37

R ICHARD AND PITBULL HAD REVISED THE PLAN A DOZEN times. Richard would make one last attempt to get the phone from Sanders. Meanwhile, four of Pitbull's men would sit in a truck outside the bar, waiting for instructions. If Richard was unable to get the phone from her, the men would ambush her and demand it as soon as she exited.

He'd soothed his own scruples by repeating to himself it was for a good cause. He was doing it to protect Pitbull. And he was also doing it for the woman he loved. Only when he held that proof in his hands, could he take the risk of coming clean to the FBI about Joy.

The first part of the plan was ongoing. He'd begged, threatened, and tried to blackmail Sanders back, by putting on the table any secret the FBI knew about her past—all the while offering alcohol, trying to get her drunk. Nothing seemed to work so far. "Blair, any satisfaction you can get from having me under your control can't be worth the anxiety of knowing I won't rest until I get that phone from you. You should give it to me, for your own peace of mind."

He sent her his most menacing glare, but her satisfied smirk hinted she enjoyed his veiled threat. "You're not going to hurt me. I know."

"Not me, but other people might."

"You mean those friends of yours who keep trashing my home every time you and I meet?" she winked at him.

Damn it. That woman was impossible to scare. "Well, the man who saved my life is desperate."

"I'm not interested in hurting him or turning him into my enemy. You can send the message that if it ever becomes necessary to bring this to the light, I'll make sure to conceal his face in the video." She took a sip from her happy hour vodka. "My interest is solely in you."

That was good news for Pitbull, but it didn't help him. He decided to change strategies. "Give me back the phone, Blair," he said. "Do it for your own good karma."

She snorted. "Karma is bullshit." She tipped back her vodka shot, finishing it in one gulp.

He studied her intently. "Do you think so?"

She gestured to the waiter to bring her another round. "I don't believe in karma. I don't believe in reincarnation… The only heaven I believe in is the pleasure we can grab right now." She drew circles on his arm with her finger. "Although *I* can make any man's life heaven— or hell."

I believe you. Richard had the strong feeling that her spontaneous comments disregarding reincarnation and divine justice were genuine. A LOTU member would never say the things she had.

"Blair, answer a question," he asked as she accepted the next drink. "The clues you gave me about Patel and Young… were they true? Or were you trying to throw me off track?"

"Of course, they were true. I got the information directly from Maureen O'Hara, when my client and I were working with her."

"*Were?*" he asked, interested. "As in, not anymore?"

She straightened his shirt collar. "She ended up firing my client because he didn't feel comfortable doing what she asked."

"What do you mean?"

"Besides wanting him to investigate the death of O'Hara, the woman wanted his help stalking and harassing her daughter-in-law."

A chill slithered down Richard's spine. "O'Hara's widow? Why?"

"Maureen O'Hara wants her out of this town to stop fueling the ongoing scandal." She took a large sip. "But apparently she has someone else working for her now."

Someone else?

"Why would you believe I'd want to throw you off track?" she asked, scrutinizing him.

"I never understood why you would want to help me."

She seemed to disrobe him with her eyes. "I told you. I wanted to show you what a great team we could be together. I still haven't given up on that."

Pitbull's text message reached his burner phone. *"Any luck? Or should we launch Plan B?"*

Richard stared at the message, haunted by second thoughts. *What am I doing? What would Carl say if he knew I'm about to resort to violence?*

What would Joy think of me?

He quickly texted back, *"Cancel Plan B."*

Unaware of the danger she'd just escaped, Sanders rose from her chair and got closer. "That's why I can't give you that phone back. If I do, I'd lose any excuse to see you again." Her fingers traced the contours of his jaw. "You might claim that you're only here to get that proof back from me. But I prefer to believe that deep inside you want me as much as I want you."

Damn it, this woman is relentless. The memory of how Blair's lack of boundaries had cost him Joy filled him with rage and he had to make an effort not to shove Blair away. Instead, he slowly rose from the chair, preventing her from kissing him. Before he could escape, she clasped his arms.

With her face lifted toward his, she clung to his shirt collar, pleading, "Richard, all I want is a chance to pick up where we left off. Give me one night, to remind you why I think we'd be so perfect for each other." She caressed circles on his chest with her hand. "Just one night. And then if you don't change your mind about me, I'll give you back the phone."

His pulse sped up. He knew he couldn't trust her. Yet the old Richard would've known what to do. He'd say yes. He'd humor her with a night of passion—or at the least would make her believe he would—then, he'd slip something into her drink. He'd use the opportunity to extract information from her, search her purse and clothes, search her house himself—much better than Pitbull and his men could ever do.

"You're my obsession, and I won't be able to be rational until I get you out of my system," she continued. "Come home with me tonight. Take my offer, and after that I'll set you free."

His heart raced. *Take the offer, you idiot*, his old self kept telling him. *It's your only chance; you and Joy are on a break, and you know you're doing it for her.*

But the new Richard couldn't.

Thank you, Carl Andrews. Thank you, Joy Clayton. Now I'm cursed with a freaking conscience.

"I can't, Blair. I'm… I'm with someone else."

She frowned and loosened her grip. "That didn't stop you before."

The answer came to his lips at the same time it formed in his brain, surprising him. "This time is different. This woman… She's the woman I want to spend the rest of my life with. I love her."

There. It was out now. What he'd been struggling to admit to himself and had been unable to tell Joy had been shared with no one less than the woman blackmailing him.

He braced himself internally for Blair's explosion. To his surprise, she dipped her chin and eased back. "I see."

She grabbed her drink from the table and finished it in one gulp. Her calmness infused him with hope.

But the brief hope was soon shattered by the waves of grief and rage alternating on her face when she glared back up at him.

Shit.

She grasped his arm so tightly her nails pierced his skin. "Think hard before rejecting me, Fields. By doing that, you're digging your own grave." Despite her contorted features, her voice was icy. "Do you understand the dangerous enemy I can be?"

Her glassy eyes spoke of fearsome insanity hiding behind her put-together appearance. He could almost see the slow-boiling rage building inside her. He may not remember Blair, but if she was anything like his old type of woman, hell was about to break loose.

He debated whether to use force to free his arm, but instead, he took a deep breath and invoked Joy's essence. *What would Joy do?* She'd say to see Sanders not as an enemy, but as a fellow suffering human being.

He tried to look at her with different eyes. Sanders must've had a very lonely, loveless life if she clung to a man who cared so little about her he didn't even remember her. Instead of trying to break the grasp of her fingers, he patted her hand gently. "Blair, have you ever thought you don't really need to blackmail me? That the gratitude you'll inspire in me by giving me the phone voluntarily will get you more in the long run?"

Her head jerked back in surprise and she released him.

"If you hold on to that phone, you may have the false promise of one potential gain in the future," he went on. "But if you surrender it now, you'll have made a new friend who owes you a favor and will be ready to help you anytime, in any way you need it, for the rest of our lives."

For a moment her eyes softened and she seemed hesitant—but it was brief. "But I don't want you to be my friend. I want you to be mine."

Without looking away, he slowly shook his head. "But that's the only thing I can't give you."

They locked gazes for the longest time. He felt like they were in a tug-of-war, with her pulling toward war and him pulling toward peace.

"Your loss." She broke the eye contact first and picked up her purse. "Lucky for you, I'm too drunk right now and can hardly think straight. We'll have to resume talking later."

A flash of pain crossed her face as she touched his arm one last time. "I'll let you be—for now. But this won't be the last time you see me."

Richard watched her walk out of the bar swinging her hips, her head up, without looking back. He had the strong feeling it was true, that would not be the last time he'd see Blair Sanders.

He searched for cash in his wallet to cover the check, debating who to call first. He had to call Pitbull and convey her message that he was relatively safe, hoping he'd drop it and not try to hurt her. But he also had to call Samuel and share his suspicion that Maureen O'Hara was behind the harassing notes Joy had been receiving.

Before he could make up his mind, his phone rang with a number he didn't recognize at first glance. His memory told him it was one of the extensions from Holloway Hospital.

"Hello?"

"Hello, may I speak to Mr. Richard Fields?" a confident masculine voice asked on the other side of the line.

"Speaking."

"This is Dr. Hunton, from the emergency room at Holloway. We need you to come back to the ER immediately. Your blood cultures are growing dangerous bacteria."

~

"Joy. Joy, come here."

Joy shook, terrified. Michael's voice invoked her from somewhere inside the office. She should've screamed and run away crying for help. But something stopped her.

No. I'm not falling for this. She felt as if Richard's spirit possessed her, infusing her with strength. *I know Michael's dead. And I'm done running away.*

Trembling, she pushed through the waves of nausea from the flashbacks and inched her way, lighting her path with her cell's light. The voice became louder as she approached.

The sound came from her computer, where a short video clip replayed over and over again. It was a fragment of one of Michael's speeches, where he asked her to join him at the podium.

"Joy. Joy, come here."

She pressed a hand against her chest, feeling as if life returned to her body.

She moved to turn it off, but then stopped herself.

Don't mess up the fingerprints.

It was as if Richard was speaking in her head. She grabbed her cell and searched in her recent calls until she found Agent Elliott's cell number.

"Hello, Dr. Clayton?" he picked up on the first ring.

"Agent Elliott, I think someone was in my office." She walked toward the windows to open the blinds.

"Did they leave another hoax message?" he asked.

She pulled on the different cords, trying to find the right ones to raise the blinds. "They left a video clip of Michael playing on my computer. I think—"

Her next words died on her lips. The blinds finally pulled up allowing some light into her office. Michael stood on the wall next to the windowpane.

She dropped the phone with a scream and curled in a corner of the office, shivering and covering her head with her arms.

"Dr. Clayton? Are you there?" She could faintly hear Agent Elliot's voice coming from her phone. But a stronger voice spoke, and it came from inside.

"Don't be scared. Michael is gone. He's not really here." Richard's voice in her mind coaxed her.

Her cold fingers slipped from her cheeks. Michael's blue glare pierced her and her skin filled with goose bumps, but she rose from the floor and stepped toward him anyway. Relief hit her when she realized it was the same portrait that had been delivered to her house.

She leaned on her desk, catching her breath and gathering herself.

"Dr. Clayton, are you there?" Agent Elliott's voice sounded in the distance.

She retrieved her phone from the floor. "I'm here; I'm fine. But I need you to please send someone to investigate what happened. Whoever broke into my office might still be in the building."

"I'm on my way."

She disconnected the call and studied the portrait, still keeping her distance. Someone had either picked up the portrait from the curb at her house or delivered an identical copy of it. Regardless, someone was trying to mess with her mind.

As she exited her office, she recalled a sudden memory of the day Richard showed her the sea turtle tracks on the sand. Her eyes fixed on the floor, confirming there was scuffing on the linoleum floor. Someone had dragged the heavy portrait through the door instead of lifting it.

She followed the faint intermittent tracks to their source. Whoever was responsible for this had to be someone with access to her office. Someone who knew her routines. Someone who was familiar enough with the place to know how to avoid the security cameras.

And the markings on the floor clearly indicated who that person was.

She strode the remainder of the distance to the office at the end of the hallway and slammed the door open.

At his desk, Patel startled at the sound. "Oh, Joy, you scared me!" He pressed a hand to his chest. "I got lost in my paperwork and hadn't realized it was this late. Everything okay?"

She glared at him. "I know it was you who brought that portrait to my office and left that video playing. You're the only other person with a key to my office."

Shock flashed across his face, but it was also mingled with guilt. His voice trembled. "I… I don't know what you're talking about."

"I should've known," she continued, strolling toward him. "The condolence cards without mail stamps... You were covering for me every time I took off, so you're the only person who could've known my ins and outs enough to leave them without being caught."

"I... I swear I had nothing to do with..." His voice weakened at her conviction. The mixture of emotions in his countenance turned into pure shame and guilt. His voice was almost a whisper. "I'm sorry."

Joy was taken aback. Despite her act of confidence, she wasn't prepared to confirm her suspicion. "How could you do this to me? I thought you were my friend."

"I'm sorry," he repeated. "I desperately need the money."

"So, you did all this to scare me and push me to the edge," she said with a weak voice. "You wanted me to run away from this town and join in your projects."

"It was not only that. Someone paid me to do this." He avoided her gaze, reluctant, but finally met it again and confessed, "I've been working for Maureen O'Hara."

～

"I'm going to kill him!" Sitting on the narrow ER bed, Richard clenched the room's phone receiver while talking to Samuel—that area of the hospital had horrible signal and his two cells were worthless. "I always knew that Patel was hiding something! But why would you let him go?"

"Some lawyer showed up, apparently sent by Maureen O'Hara, and refused to let him come with us unless we produced a warrant. And it's not like I had a huge charge to press against him that I could get an emergency one after hours."

"Yes, you did, harassment!" Richard rose from the bed and strode to the door, but the corded phone pulled back and he had to stop. "The pranks he played against... Dr. Clayton bordered on psychological torture. You could've made a discretionary decision to arrest him until we verify he's not connected to the plot to kill O'Hara."

"That would've been a stretch, when the guy openly confessed he'd been following orders from O'Hara's mother."

Richard paced, but the room was so ridiculously small it only allowed for a few steps in each direction. He cursed the powerlessness of being stuck in the ER.

Richard dreaded being back in the hospital, where they seemed to derive pleasure in rendering people helpless. He'd been forbidden to bring his gun inside again. He had to wait for hours to be triaged, and then no one seemed to have any freaking idea of why he was there or who had called him.

The triage nurses had finally tracked down the doctor who'd contacted Richard and brought him in. Then someone had explained that they needed to get some more tests to decide if his blood culture results were real or a fluke. He'd hoped this would be a quick trip, in and out. But now near midnight he was afraid he wouldn't get any sleep before his flight to New York in the morning.

"So that would explain how the harasser had access to O'Hara's email password! But why would Patel make a deal with Maureen O'Hara?" he asked Samuel.

"Remember what Young said about O'Hara's mother wanting to force Clayton to move with her to Connecticut? Don't ask me how they met, but somehow Patel convinced Maureen O'Hara that the best way to achieve that was if Dr. Clayton joined him in his plans to turn them both into holistic medicine personalities. In that way, Clayton could work from anywhere in the country, and would need her mother-in-law's help with the children whenever she traveled. But there was something in their way."

"The Hospice House," Richard reflected. "That bastard Patel knew that the only thing stronger than Joy's commitment to that place was her PTSD about her husband's death."

"Exactly."

Furious, Richard hit the edge of his fist against the wall. "Maureen O'Hara should consider herself lucky that I'm unable to hurt a woman. But I wish I could get my hands on that Patel and strangle him myself."

"Let's see what happens with the judicial procedures. Maureen O'Hara is a powerful woman and I wouldn't be surprised if she and her dozen lawyers find a way out of this."

"In the meantime, I want Patel locked up ASAP," he insisted. "I don't want him near... Dr. Clayton ever again."

They ended the phone call and Richard pondered. Patel denied having had anything to do with the LOTU or Michael O'Hara's death, but of course, a guilty person would. Was this really just an unrelated thread, distracting them? Or could Patel still be linked to the LOTU?

"Good evening, Mr. Fields." A scrubs-clad ER physician entered the room, dragging a laptop on a wheeled stand.

"Thank God you're here, doctor!" Richard approached him. "I really need to get out of here."

"Well, your labs are back and I'm afraid the news isn't good." The man pointed at the computer screen. "You have an extremely high white blood cell count. We have to assume the result of your blood cultures is real and not a contaminant."

Richard snorted in disbelief. "But I feel perfectly fine!"

"Still, this could be something serious. We're going to need more cultures, some x-rays... and in the meantime, until we find the source of the infection, we need to start you on intravenous antibiotics."

"Intravenous? But I have a plane to catch in a few hours." Richard cussed internally wondering if he'd even make his flight. "What does that entail?"

"I hope you purchased insurance for that flight." The doctor grimaced an apology. "We're going to need to admit you."

CHAPTER 38

THERE WAS NO DANCING THAT MORNING; JOY'S FEET WERE dragging when she arrived at the Hospice House's courtyard. She barely had the energy to wave at the elderly residents and staff as she headed to her office.

The past hours had been among the most surreal in Joy's life. Still processing the news that she'd lost her most supportive business partner, she'd spent the evening dealing with police reports and the night on the phone with Maureen's lawyers, who were trying to convince Joy not to press charges. All she wanted was to disconnect from anything that reminded her of Michael. She was seriously considering agreeing to withdraw the charges in exchange for some contract that got Maureen O'Hara out of her life forever.

And—by the way—right at this moment, Richard's plane must be taking off, heading to New York.

The hectic night hadn't allowed her to dwell much on this. But the rawness in her soul was becoming harder and harder to ignore. While she'd been stuck in the sadness, today she woke up filled with regrets. She kept wondering again and again why she hadn't left Michael when she first considered it, years before his death. Maybe if she had, she and Richard would've crossed paths in a way that didn't make their relationship forbidden.

She opened her office door and, lost in her dark thoughts, she jolted violently when she found Michael's portrait still there.

She covered her mouth to conceal a gasp. *Darn it.* She needed to arrange for someone to come pick up that thing and take it to the dumpster.

Joy's hands trembled. Yesterday, the adrenaline had protected her from the PTSD flare, but today the piercing blue eyes of the man in the portrait terrified her. Patel's plan had almost succeeded. Even now she wondered if she'd ever be able to set foot in that office without thinking about Michael.

She grabbed the pink and golden throw lying on top of the maroon recliner and tented it over the portrait to cover it from sight. As she finished, a knock on the open door got her attention. "Good morning. Sorry to show up unannounced."

To Joy's delight, Carl leaned against the doorjamb. But to her surprise he wasn't alone. Ray stood behind him.

"Guys! It's so good to see you!" She rushed to hug them both, forgetting for a moment about Ray's reluctance for public affectionate gestures. "But… what are you doing here?" she asked Ray. "I thought your plane had left already."

"Richard and Ray had to cancel their trip," Carl answered for Ray, then worry filled his features. "Because… Richard was admitted to the hospital."

Joy's stomach dropped. Had he been shot? Had he been stabbed again? Had he been hit with a car? Was this a real health crisis or could it be a plot from the LOTU to kill him?

She could barely recognize her breathless voice. "What happened?"

"We don't really know," Ray shrugged. "They gave us a bunch of medical jargon that means nothing to me."

Joy would've done anything to call the ER and find out what was going on, but of course, she couldn't. Officially, she was neither his doctor nor his family.

"So, right now we don't know when we'll be leaving," Ray concluded. "I guess after he gets out of the hospital. Anyway. When we went to see him, he asked us to stop by and fill you in, since he has no cell reception in the ER. He says he knows you can't go see him and just wanted us to tell you not to worry."

Ray was right, and that was the worst part; she couldn't even run to Richard's side and make sure he was okay like another loved one would.

As if noticing her sadness, Ray shyly touched her shoulder and chuckled. "He *really* wanted me to tell you not to worry. Gee, I told you that guy is crazy about you."

In the midst of her blues, that made Joy smile. "Did you really mean what you said that day? About him smelling my pillow?" She reached for her purse on the table, hoping to find a Kleenex to dry her upcoming tears.

"I know it sounds like I'm making stuff up," Ray replied, then rolled his eyes. "This is the guy who can't say 'I love you' to save his life. I've heard him say it like twice in fourteen years."

Tell me about it.

"But," Ray added, "his 'thing' isn't words. With him you need to read the love between the lines."

In her purse, Joy's hand felt something irregular. She took it out and found the Ziploc bag full of seashells Richard had mailed her.

Her heart tightened into a knot. She'd never before met someone who made her feel more seen and heard than Richard.

Ray excused himself to answer a call and when he stepped out of the office, Carl addressed Joy. "Are you okay, dear?"

Joy stayed frozen, staring at the bag in her hand. "Ray is right; I failed to see Richard's love. By pushing him away with my senseless jealousy, I ruined what could've been our last peaceful days together."

"Stop it." Carl reached for her free hand. "You're beating yourself up again. Self-flagellation won't get you anywhere."

"But I have so many regrets." She shook her head. "I regret that Richard and I wasted so much time we could've spent together, all because I kept running away from him, unable to get over my trauma with Michael."

"Enough sadness, enough regrets, and enough fear," Carl pointed out softly. "My dear, you're stuck in those feelings because there are others hidden in the shadows. Other feelings that you've never allowed to surface."

Ray poked his head into the office. "Hey, Dr. Carl, do you mind if we go? You promised me breakfast, and I'm starving."

Carl bowed his head, then hugged Joy goodbye before following Ray.

There are other feelings hidden in the shadows.

Joy locked the door, walked back to Michael's picture and uncovered it. Facing those blue eyes again, flashbacks of the years living in terror rushed through her mind: The sleepless nights during the "bad days," walking on eggshells, and fearing he could hurt her or one of her boys. The nerve-wracking "good days" waiting for the other shoe to drop any minute. The bottom-of-the-pit depressive days, afraid he might make an attempt on his life; the equally terrifying high days, trying to protect him from manic self-endangerment. And those rare days on the way up and down, when he would behave almost normally, hurting her with a glimpse at what life could've been if he weren't ill.

"I wish so much he wasn't dead so I could kill him," Richard's voice repeated in her mind. *"But that wouldn't do. The one who needs to kill him is* you."

Joy grabbed the first blunt object she found, the toy baseball bat lying on the floor. Trembling, she stood in front of the picture and took a tentative swing at it. The impact of her weak effort barely made a sound, yet the huge wave of emotion that rose in her chest shocked her. She hit it again and the wave multiplied. Then an inexplicable rage seized her and she was out of her mind, swinging the bat, hitting the picture, grunting, crying, sobbing.

With every hit to the portrait a new memory of Michael flashed in her mind. *Hit.* The way he ruined her graduation party with his jealousy. *Slam.* The awful way he treated her on their wedding night. *Thump.* The way he yelled at her when her first baby wouldn't stop crying.

Tears running down her cheeks, she threw the bat on the ground and punched the picture with her fists. The intensity of her rage scared her. She cried and punched and yelled until all the strength was drained from her arms and her legs and she could do nothing but collapse on the floor.

Sobbing, she evoked the memory of Richard's soothing arms embracing her. The image of Michael's face surfaced in her mind one more time, and it held an expression she'd never seen before. On it, she saw shame, and regret, but also relief. She felt as if he were asking for forgiveness and thanking her.

And then he was gone.

Panting, Joy dried her tears with the sleeve of her dress and stood up. She felt tired, but strangely at peace. She studied the portrait again and was surprised to realize there was little feeling attached to it. She felt freer than she'd felt in her life.

She felt exhilarated. Richard would be so proud of her!

Richard! He was still at the hospital. How could she have any peace of mind until she saw him and confirmed he was okay? Suddenly, she felt like an invisible force holding her back had vanished.

"Hello? Everything okay?"

Only then did Joy realize someone had been knocking at her office door. She dried the last of her tears before opening.

Probably alerted by the sound of her screaming, a small crowd stood outside the door. A worried Allison led the group. Behind her peeked Ava, the office manager and Malcolm, the elderly resident who was Joy's dancing partner. A few other concerned staff members gathered around them.

"Are you okay?" Allison asked. "I heard about what happened last night and came to check on you. And then we heard someone screaming."

Joy took a deep breath. "I'm okay." She turned to Malcolm. "Would you help me arrange for someone to throw this picture into the garbage bin?" She turned to Ava. "And would you please tell Dr. Harris she was right; I shouldn't have come to work today, and I appreciate her offer to take over."

The office manager nodded and the group dispersed, except for Allison, who entered the office, still visibly disturbed despite her expressionless face. "Are you sure you're okay?"

Joy's eyes returned to the bag of seashells on her desk and she stood motionless, her eyes lost on it. Maybe the high of the moment was impairing her thinking, but suddenly nothing made sense to her. Why couldn't she be by the side of the man she loved when he was in the hospital? Why did she have to sacrifice herself again, without fighting for what she wanted?

Allison repeated, "Joy, is everything all right?"

After a long silence, she said, "I'm sorry. I need to cancel all my appointments with you. I may not return to see you anymore, because—" She stopped, amazed by what she was about to say. "Because there's a chance I'm moving to New York."

Not even the Botox could conceal Allison's astonishment. She gaped as Joy picked up her purse and the bag of seashells and dashed out of the place.

Joy ran as fast as she could back to her car. She needed to talk to Richard and make sure he was fine. She had to tell him she was willing to follow him. It might not be immediately; she still had tons of things to figure out. But he needed to know that she loved him and was willing to wait for him.

"*I need to see you!*" She texted him. But the message soon returned as undeliverable and she remembered Ray had mentioned Richard had no signal.

She arrived at her car and, from the app on her phone, she logged into the hospital medical records system. She couldn't leave a trail by accessing his records directly. Instead, she reviewed the census list for each one of the hospital floors and units until she found his name.

She was about to head to his hospital room, but stopped herself.

She couldn't show up unannounced and risk generating suspicion about their relationship. She needed to call him first.

"Never call me from a phone traceable to you. Better to find a random landline, unlikely to be bugged, like a pay phone."

Pay phone? Did those even exist anymore?

Yes. She remembered seeing some at the airport. And the airport was close enough to the hospital she could be in his room within minutes if he gave her the green light.

She turned on the car and took off.

CHAPTER 39

"**W**OULD YOU LEAVE ME ALONE? NO. I DO NOT WANT A sleeping pill!" Richard knew he was being harsher than necessary to the young nurse standing next to his hospital bed. But he'd had a lousy night and felt crankier than ever.

He'd had zero sleep last night in between bumpy stretcher rides to different tests and endless phone calls, trying to figure out what to do with Ray and their canceled trip. It took forever for a room to become available because he needed to be in isolation—reportedly his infection was a potential danger to other patients. Every staff member who came into contact with him wore gowns and gloves—and some of them even wore masks. *What a thrill.* He felt powerless enough without his gun, so he refused the added humiliation of nudity and wore the hospital gown on top of his pants and button-down shirt.

Not to mention his apprehension about being in the hospital—the most dangerous place to be for someone the LOTU disliked.

And after that nightmarish evening he had to face this nurse who looked barely older than Ray, trying to twist his arm all night about accepting a sleeping aid. "Listen to me, drug-pusher," he said, glowering at the gowned young woman. "I'm aware that your job gets easier if your patients are knocked out so they don't bother you. But when I said, 'I don't want a sleeping pill,' I meant, 'I don't want a freaking sleeping pill.' Now go torture someone else with your poking, your probing, and your unnecessary three a.m. vital signs. Understood?"

Unaffected by his infamous killing glare, the young woman walked away, mumbling something about difficult patients. Richard knew from experience that nurses were harder to scare off than drug cartel gangsters.

His mind settling down for the first time after that hectic night, he realized he had to call Samuel and inform him of what was going on. Being in the hospital meant he was at his most vulnerable; and he was unarmed.

Neither of his two phones had signal, so he searched for Samuel's number and reached for the corded phone in the room. The moment he touched the receiver, the phone rang.

"Hello?" he asked.

"This is Angel."

He immediately recognized Joy's voice and his heart jumped. "This is Guardian."

"I'm calling from a payphone at the airport," she said. "Everything looks clear here."

Knowing it was unlikely someone had had a chance to bug the room line, he answered, "Everything looks clear here too."

Her voice shook on the other side of the call. "First things first. If something bad happened to you, I'd never forgive myself. We've wasted so much time apart instead of together and it's my fault. I'm so sorry."

Bitter sweetness spread through his veins. There she was, compulsively apologizing again.

She continued, "I changed my mind; I *do* want to be selfish. I don't want to lose you. Ever."

A bolt of joy swept through him, but before he could react, she added, "I'm willing to try to make this work, no matter how impossible it seems." She hesitated before finally saying, "I love you. I love you more than you can imagine."

Emotion overwhelmed him. "You know I have trouble with those words. But I hope you also know that I feel the same way." He struggled with the words one more time and when they came out, his voice was almost a whisper. "I love you too."

She sobbed on the other side of the line. "I thought I'd never hear that again."

He wished he could reach through the phone and take her in his arms. Suddenly, nothing mattered. He didn't even feel angry anymore about the annoying nurse reentering the room.

The young nurse showed him a bag and mouthed, "Your antibiotic." He waved her off and mouthed her to leave, but she ignored him and busied herself with his IV pump.

Joy had finally recovered her voice. "I was so worried when I got your message. Are you okay?"

"I'm fine, Angel. Just cranky after the most ridiculous few hours." He threw the nurse a killer look. She shot him the stink eye and left the room.

"What do they say?" she asked.

"They have me in an isolation room. They say my blood cultures are growing antibiotic resistant MRSA and pseudomonas and that I had a fever and need IV antibiotics."

Joy went suddenly quiet.

"Angel?"

"I don't like this. What if this is a trap? What if they brought you to the hospital to kill you too?"

He stiffened. "Actually, I was about to call Samuel to ask him to send some vigilance. It doesn't sound like what the other victims went through. But what should I be on the watch for?"

"Don't let them offer you any sleeping pill or sedative. That could mean they're trying to incapacitate you so you don't feel the burning of the potassium chloride. And whatever you do don't let them give you any IV bag."

He turned sharply toward the small IV bag of "antibiotics" running wide open. He rushed to turn it off, but his hands suddenly felt clumsy. A cloud of drowsiness crept over him.

While pressing random buttons on the pump attached to the IV pole, trying to turn it off, he said, "Joy, they just started an IV bag and I'm getting sleepy." His words sounded slurred. "Would that be a symptom from receiving potassium chloride?"

"No. That would kill you so fast you wouldn't even see it coming." She stopped. "Unless they're trying to sedate you to come give you the injection later. That must be a sedative! Stop that IV!"

His clumsy fingers gave up on the IV pump and tried to peel back the tape securing the IV catheter in his arm to take if off. Even that was too much for his slow brain to manage. He was falling asleep fast. Using all his strength to try to stay awake, he pulled the IV tubing and ripped it off his arms, undoing the tape at the same time. A small stream of blood trickled down his arm. "Joy—please call Samuel—and—"

And then everything went dark.

～

"Richard? Hello? Richard?" Terror clawed at Joy's stomach and her heart raced faster than it ever had. Shaking uncontrollably, she hung up the payphone, took her cell and called 911 while heading for the exit.

"Miss! This is an emergency! I need you to send the police to Holloway Medical Center, room 312." As she said the words, she realized this would take much longer than she could allow. The operator sounded confused and wanted explanations. She had to call Agent Elliot.

Still talking with the EMS operator, she sprinted to her car in the airport's parking lot. She was close enough she'd make it to the hospital sooner than any patrol could.

But could she get there in time?

～

Richard must've fallen asleep for a moment, but he jerked up, forcing himself to stay awake. He'd been trained how to stay alert even if someone drugged him; he had to remain in motion. He had to get up from the bed and walk around. He had to cause himself pain. Hell, he had to get out of the room and get where other people could see him, so no one could touch him. He sat on the bed, but felt dizzy and fell back right away.

They gave me Valium or Versed.

He'd read everything about the symptoms. The dizziness, the sleepiness, the feeling of detachment. He fought again, struggling to sit on the bed and pinching his own arm to force himself to awaken. He'd only gotten a fraction of the intended dose and hoped he could overcome it.

The door opened, and a blurry figure wearing a gown and a surgical hat and mask entered holding a large syringe. Richard tried to cry for help, but he was losing the battle with sleep.

The person headed straight to the IV pump tubing, ready to inject something, then noticed the catheter was off his arm. "What the hell?"

It was a male voice. A familiar voice.

Using all this strength to stay awake, Richard swung his arm and ripped the surgical mask off the man. An enraged face glowered back at him, confirming his suspicion.

It was Levenstein.

CHAPTER 40

RICHARD WONDERED IF HE WAS HALLUCINATING. "You? That's not possible."

Levenstein ignored him, while searching the room for something and mumbling cuss words. "Why did you have to rip out your damn IV! Now I'll have to find a vein by myself!"

Seeing the man he thought near death discharged adrenaline through Richard that helped wake him up a little more. "You faked it all? The GI bleeding? The vegetative state?"

Levenstein grabbed a small package lying on the nightstand and a glove from the box on the wall. "It wasn't hard to aggravate my old ulcer, and it doesn't take much blood to look dramatic lying on the floor." He tied the glove around Richard's arm, using it as a tourniquet.

Richard pulled his arm, trying to free it, but Levenstein immobilized him by pinning his forearm with a knee while continuing to look for a vein.

The peaking sedative effects robbed Richard of his ability to feel panic or any motivation to fight, but his analytical brain still struggled to make sense of what was going on. "But you almost bled to death. You were intubated for days."

Levenstein grunted. "That part wasn't planned—and it sucked. I guess I did a little too good of a job." He tapped on Richard's arm. "But it was worth it to make it all look even more legit. After that it wasn't difficult to trick the stupid hospital neurologist about my brain damage. Everybody knows Dr. Paterson is inept." He opened the package producing a butterfly needle, which he connected directly into the large syringe.

The needle bored into Richard's arm and the pain gave him the nudge he needed to react, pulling his arm from under Levenstein's knee. Taken by surprise, the man lost his balance and dropped to his hands and knees.

Richard removed the tourniquet and tried to get up, but the room spun and his body felt numb.

Cussing under his breath, Levenstein staggered back to his feet. "You bastard. You're going to regret this."

Stretching his arm toward the bed rail, Richard tried to reach for the nurse call button, but Levenstein clasped his wrist. With his free hand, he picked up the syringe from the floor. Immobilizing Richard's legs by sitting on them and holding his free arm with his elbow, he searched for a vein on Richard's neck.

~

Joy had used the hands-free in her car to call Agent Elliott, who was caught in some meeting across town. She sped the short distance from the airport to the hospital, left her car poorly parked in the drop-off area and bolted inside.

The security line stretched to infinity and back. Not wanting to waste any time, Joy flashed her hospital ID and raced to the staff elevator. But the elevator wouldn't come fast enough, so she rushed up the stairs to the third floor.

Joy prayed harder than she'd ever prayed. She had to make it there before whoever had tried to sedate Richard got to him. If they gave him the potassium, he'd be dead instantly.

She gasped for breath when she arrived at the third floor, but didn't stop. Ignoring the protests of the nurse warning not to enter an isolation room without protective gear, Joy dashed in, finding herself in a small antechamber typical of isolation rooms. She slammed open the door of the second room and entered.

She froze in surprise. A man pinned Richard down on the bed with a syringe poised over his neck.

Something she'd never felt before descended upon her. It was similar to the courage she'd felt earlier, when she swung the bat at Michael's portrait. But this time it was much stronger. She grabbed the IV pole standing next to the bed and hit the man on the head with all her strength.

Taken by surprise, he lost hold of the syringe and dropped it. He then released Richard in order to brace himself against the blows, ducking. Joy kept swinging the IV pole again and again, hitting the man with it wherever she could. She'd once sworn she would never use violence against anyone, but this was different. She wasn't only standing up for herself; she was fighting for the man she loved.

"Help! Please, someone help us!" she yelled, even if she knew the double doors on the isolation room made it unlikely that anyone could hear her. She expected the nurses who'd tried to stop her would come in any second.

The man had been stunned at first. But now recovering from the surprise, he got hold of the pole and swung it away, propelling Joy across the room. She crashed against the wall and right before she fell to the floor, caught her first glance of the man's face.

She couldn't believe her eyes when she recognized Josh Levenstein.

He extracted a phone from the pocket in his scrubs pants and dialed someone. "Emergency plan in motion, Boris. Rooftop. *Now.*"

~

In his mental fog, the image of Joy crashing to the floor awakened a surge of rage in Richard, helping clear his mind. He stumbled out of bed and charged Levenstein, tackling him.

Pinning him on the floor, Richard hit Levenstein with his hands, elbows, and knees, giving it all he had; but his strikes were poorly aimed and his punches inferior. Yet he welcomed every blow he received back, as every bit of pain woke him a little more. With the advantage of a clear mind, Levenstein reversed their positions, then elbowed Richard in the neck, nearly making him pass out.

"Help!" Joy yelled again, while leaning on the wall as she rose from the floor.

Two nurses entered the room, clad in protective gear from head to toe—gowns, gloves, and masks. No wonder it had taken forever for them to come. But they seemed paralyzed with shock, just standing near the door.

Noticing the nurses' arrival, Levenstein crawled across the floor, picked up the syringe and took hold of Joy's leg. She elbowed him in the head, but before she could shake him he rose and immobilized her arms in the back with one hand while using the other to point the syringe at her neck. "Nobody move or I'll kill her."

Joy, who'd been trying to wiggle herself free, stopped cold at the prospect of the needle so close to her skin.

Terror shook Richard, jolting him awake. He scrambled to his feet, determined to conquer the mental fog. "Let her go. *Now.*"

"The police are on their way, Josh," Joy whispered. "Don't make things harder on yourself. Surrender now."

Ignoring her, he kept pointing the syringe at her neck while walking backward and addressing Richard. "Unless you want to see her dead you will make sure nobody follows me, understood?"

Richard's heart pounded. "It's me who you came to kill. Take *me* as a hostage. Let her go." He took one step forward.

"Richard, no," Joy begged.

"You! Move away! And you, open the doors for me!" Levenstein barked at the nurses while towing Joy.

As the nurses obeyed, Richard shed the hospital gown he still wore over his clothes and darted after them. If he could stall the man long enough, the police might arrive. "I'm worth more to the FBI than her and will get you more negotiation power," he yelled as Levenstein strode down the hallway. "Let her go and take me!"

"I said do not follow me!" Levenstein elbowed the button on the wall to open the automatic doors and leave the unit.

As Levenstein lurched toward the nearest elevator with Joy, Richard jogged behind them. He hoped that the elevator got delayed so he could win more time. Unfortunately, it opened the moment Levenstein pressed the button, and it was empty. The man entered, hauling Joy with him. He maintained eye contact with Richard while holding the needle right at her neck, wordlessly warning him not to attempt anything as the painfully slow door closed.

~

Joy's heart sprinted as the hospital's old-fashioned elevator inched its way up, the rumble of its machinery obscured by Levenstein's agitated breathing. His hands were freezing and his grip hurt as he clasped her arms behind her back. He held the needle millimeters away from her neck.

The shock over Levenstein's presence paled compared to the terror she felt at that moment. It would only take a nervous jerk of his hand for the needle to pierce her jugular and inject the lethal substance into her bloodstream. But the worst part was knowing he'd probably kill her anyway once he'd escaped.

"Why are you doing this, Josh?" She tried to keep her voice calm. "Surrender to the police. They may reduce the charges if you cooperate—"

"Nonsense!" he yelled. "You don't understand. *They* are going to kill me. Being in jail is not going to stop them. They'll kill me just like they killed Rachel."

Blood froze in her veins. "Wait… I thought *you* killed her. And the other two."

"Yes, but I wasn't alone. And the others won't hesitate to silence me too. That's why I had to find a way to make it seem like I was no longer a threat. I was getting ready to fake my death once I got to the nursing home." He growled. "But of all the imbecile FBI agents in this stupid town, the only one with half a brain is Fields. And I knew he wouldn't let it go. That's why I had to kill him before going away."

The elevator door opened and he dragged her out. The sound of police sirens infused Joy with hope, but it was brief. The blast of wind that hit her announced they'd never make it in time. Josh was taking her to the helipad, where a helicopter dipped toward them.

∼

The burning pain in his left leg punished Richard as he climbed the six flights of stairs to the hospital rooftop as fast as he could. He wondered for a moment if he'd been reckless to attempt that climb, especially when he was still unsteady from the residual influence of the sedative. But he couldn't afford to wait for the sluggish hospital elevators.

He was breathless and sweating when he made it to the top and pushed the old metal door, stepping out to the rooftop. His gut wrenched when he saw Levenstein heading to a helicopter, still holding Joy.

He ran behind them yelling, "Stop!"

Levenstein ignored him and kept moving toward the helicopter.

Damn moment not to be carrying a gun! "Stop!" Richard's photographic memory identified the black and red helicopter as belonging to a local sightseeing company and recognized Boris, Levenstein's bodyguard, sitting next to the pilot. Holding onto the last hope that the pilot was someone who respected law enforcement, he pulled his badge out of his pocket and waved it while yelling, "FBI! Stop!"

Boris was obviously startled to see him. He locked eyes with Richard for an instant before his focus darted to his approaching boss and then back to Richard's badge. He seemed torn for a second, as if weighing duty against self-preservation. Then, he tapped on the cabin door and yelled instructions to the pilot. Soon the rotation of the blades sped up again and the helicopter lifted away.

Without Levenstein.

The stupefaction on Levenstein's face, as he turned around watching the helicopter fly away without him, was something Richard would remember forever. The man's karma had come back to get him in the most practical of ways. After years of treating his employees like garbage, Levenstein had no loyalty from them.

Recovering from his shock, Levenstein used Joy to shield himself and pointed the needle back at her neck, speaking to Richard. "Stay away from me or I'll kill her."

Richard felt hatred grow inside. *I swear, if you hurt her I'm going to kill you with my own hands.* He didn't give a damn about losing another informant for the case.

He'd heard the police sirens arrive not long ago and he hoped someone at the nurse's station would direct them to the rooftop. If he could only stall Levenstein long enough. "You won't do that," he answered with a calm but loud voice. "If you push that IV, you'll lose all the leverage you have."

"I'm surrounded anyway. I have nothing to lose," he answered. "I may kill her just to hurt you and then jump to my death."

Just to hurt me? So he does know about us?

Levenstein dragged Joy to the edge of the rooftop and Richard's heart clenched.

Desperate, Richard scoured his brain for any bit of training about how to handle a hostage situation. *Active listening. Empathy. Rapport.*

Bullshit! He was too desperate for any of that. They were not kidding when they said no one should work on a case involving someone they cared about.

"No. You're not going to kill me." Joy's voice sounded incredibly calm, yet radiated an authority that made Levenstein stop and look at the back of her head.

She continued, looking over her shoulder to make eye contact. "You're not going to hurt me. And it's not because you're afraid of the police, or of Richard. You're not going to do it because you care about me."

Levenstein stumbled in surprise and must've loosened his grip, as Joy slowly freed one of her arms. Holding his gaze, she rotated to face him.

Richard realized Joy was keeping Levenstein distracted to give him a chance to formulate a plan. The man was still clasping one of her arms and kept pointing the syringe at her neck, but she kept looking straight in his eyes, speaking in a soft, hypnotic voice. "I do believe you are capable of love. Even if you don't know how to express it. I know you love your daughters."

Something softened in the man's eyes. Joy's free hand subtly shifted closer. "I know you've loved many of your patients, even if you'd never admit it. I know you loved your dog, Brownie"—Levenstein's features contorted at the mention of his dog—"And I know that, in your way, you love me."

Alternate waves of anger and sadness crossed his expression, then he took another step toward the edge of the rooftop, tugging on Joy.

Fright made Richard's pulse skyrocket. Mentioning the deceased dog may've been a mistake that would encourage the man to jump. His training might be failing him, but Carl and Joy's influence came to the rescue. He had to find compassion in his heart to connect with the man. He had to find the common ground between them. "She's right. You *love* her, and boy I know exactly how you feel, because I do too." He took one slow step toward them.

"Stay away from me, Fields!" Levenstein said, but his voice sounded a notch less threatening than before.

"You were so right that day; Joy is a different species than you and I are. She's an angel, a new gold standard in love and compassion. And you feel like scum compared to her, so it's difficult to find the words to express that love she inspires."

Still clutching Joy's arm, Levenstein stood at the very edge of the rooftop, but he seemed undecided.

Richard took another step, but they were still out of his reach. "I get it. You and I have more in common than you imagine. I don't blame you for cooperating with killing O'Hara; I sometimes wish I could've killed him myself for how miserable he made Joy. That's why I want to help you."

"No one can help me!" Levenstein's hand with the syringe trembled and moved an inch closer to Joy's neck. "I have no family. No friends. No one who will grieve for me when I die. Even my daughters and my ex think I'm worth more dead than alive."

The needle threatened to scratch Joy's skin, as Levenstein's fingers continued to shake. Afraid of startling him, Richard stopped walking.

Joy took over. "I know there's good inside you, Josh." She caught the man's attention and held it, preventing him from looking at Richard, so he resumed his slow advance. Joy's hand slowly moved toward the syringe. "I know that when you started your journey as a doctor you did think you could make a difference."

The man's lower lip quivered. "And now nothing matters."

Richard kept inching toward them. His keen ear could hear the elevator approaching and a second later, people running up the stairs.

"It's over, Josh. You want it to be over." As Joy's fingers reached the syringe and took it away, relief flashed on the man's face and his arm went limp.

Richard took one more step and immobilized Levenstein's arms, pulling them away from the rooftop edge.

A second later, the elevator doors opened and the police arrived.

～

After the explosion of relief, the rest of that day was forever a blur in Joy's memory. She applauded herself for holding it together, and also for not throwing herself into Richard's arms in front of a dozen witnesses, including police and FBI agents.

Under her protests, officers escorted her to the emergency room to be examined. When the doctors declared her unharmed, the police held her in one of the hospital meeting rooms and she answered questions from agents and officers for what felt like hours. Luckily, so far she hadn't needed to reveal anything compromising about Richard. Since she was a physician, somehow the interviewers assumed she'd been in the nurse's station by coincidence.

She was answering questions from the tenth person that evening, when Richard walked in with another agent and her soul lit up. How long had she been there? Richard had showered, shaven, and changed into his work clothes and appeared as refreshed as if he'd just come back from a vacation.

Wearing the usual mask of indifference he kept around her in public, he bowed his head in greeting while extending his hand. "Dr. Clayton."

"Agent Fields." She imitated his formal gesture and accepted his brief handshake. Only the presence of the two other people in the room prevented her from coming apart with relief that he was doing fine.

"I wanted to thank you in person for your intervention today and make sure you were okay," he said with the perfect mixture of polite concern and detachment. "This must've been an exhausting day for you. Should we stop and resume the interviews later?"

Not as good as an actor as he was, she sent him a deep thank you message with her eyes. "I'd really appreciate if I could go home now and relieve the babysitter."

"Sure. Come on, I'll walk you to the exit."

He held her arm and escorted her out of the room. Her skin shivered at the casual contact.

They entered the elevator and the door closed. The moment it started moving, he pressed the stop button.

Joy had barely recovered from the jarring motion of the sudden halt, when she found herself pushed against the elevator wall, surrounded by his arms.

He kissed her with desperation, and she responded frantically. Into that kiss, she poured all the terror from the past few hours. She could feel him doing the same.

Releasing her lips, he showered her face with small kisses, while trembling. "I'm so relieved you're fine. If anything would've happened to you…" He stopped and kissed her again.

The tears of fear and relief she'd been holding made an appearance as she feasted on his mouth, delighting in his touch. But to her surprise, she felt much stronger than she expected and didn't notice the usual symptoms of PTSD. Something had shifted in her since that morning, when she embraced her anger against Michael and allowed herself to channel that anger to defend the man she loved. Somehow she no longer felt like a victim.

Her head spun when he let go of her mouth and she felt grateful for his arms stabilizing her. Breathless, she asked, "Weren't you supposed to stay in the hospital?"

"I signed myself out against medical advice—again. I know I'm fine."

"Are you sure?" She scrutinized him looking for signs of illness.

He caressed her cheek. "A lot has happened in the past few hours. I gave Samuel the description of the helicopter and the police intercepted it at a local sightseeing tours heliport. Levenstein's bodyguard surrendered and confessed immediately. He'd hacked the hospital medical records to fake the fever in my vital signs and my lab results. One nurse in the ER and one on the medical floor helped, and also helped him the day he dropped the glass panels on me—all following Levenstein's instructions. He also hacked the security camera we had in Levenstein's hospital room to allow him to sneak out without alerting us to go give me the injection."

Remembering the medical plots they'd brainstormed together,

she assented. "So the glass accident was the excuse to get you admitted so they could kill you later."

He nodded. "I delayed their plans when I refused admission that day."

Joy couldn't believe that her wild murder theories had proven true.

"Normally, I wouldn't share this much, but as an unofficial part of the investigation team, I thought you deserve to know." His lips slid to her neck. "We could never have solved this case without my favorite anonymous consultant."

She caught his face to stop him from kissing her and made him look at her. "Sweetie, it's not over. Josh mentioned he was afraid for his life because there are other LOTU members willing to kill him like they did Hayes."

Richard froze and his features clouded with worry.

"Is he talking about another branch of the LOTU in New York?" she asked. "Like Blair Sanders said in her article?"

His FBI agent mask descended upon him. "I'm sorry. I'm not allowed to confirm or deny that statement."

Well, he'd just confirmed it.

"That's why it's so important that you go to New York, right?"

He seemed like a kid who'd dropped his slice of birthday cake on the floor. "How about we worry about that later?"

Resigned, she nodded. "I agree."

They kissed again and she was glad that in that hospital everyone had learned not to wait for the elevators.

EPILOGUE

T HANK GOD FOR LOYAL FRIENDS WILLING TO BABYSIT JOY'S kids. And thank God for Richard's favorite hiding spot, the beach house in Pineapple Beach. He'd really needed the past two days to recover from recent events.

This time, the sunsets, ocean sunrises, and delightful routines felt surprisingly familiar. He felt like they'd never left the place, and every event since their previous trip had been a dream. Today, they'd dared to grab brunch at the local diner, him wearing his cap and glasses, her wearing her blond wig, posing as a couple on their honeymoon. Continuing the game, he'd insisted on carrying her in his arms across the threshold, while she giggled uncontrollably.

He dropped her on the bed before diving after her.

Her laughter winding down, she removed her wig, wiggled in bed to face him, and encircled his neck with her arms. "I don't want this weekend to be over."

"Shh! Stop it! We still have half a day, let's enjoy it!" He nuzzled her neck, savoring her smell. "And I already planned our next trip, the weekend after next. A friend is lending me a cute riverside cottage not far from here. We'll have the river sunsets right in the backyard."

She nodded in silence. They'd made the wordless agreement to enjoy the next weeks to the max since he'd decided to stay in Fort Sunshine until his transfer came through. For the first time, he blessed the slow bureaucracy that made non-urgent paperwork in the FBI take forever.

"Can you get your friend Fe to watch the kids again?" He hoped he wasn't stretching Joy too thin. Now that she'd cut all communication with Maureen O'Hara, her childcare options had diminished.

It was ironic that Joy's attempt at compassion—withdrawing the charges against Maureen—had also served as the worst punishment for the woman—removing her contact with her grandchildren as she agreed to settle in Connecticut.

"Hope is always willing to help so we can meet," she replied. "It would just be a little easier if we didn't have to hide." Her eyes slid to the blond wig on the bedside.

"I know." he moved a strand of dark hair off her face. "Samuel is working with a friend at the disciplinary action committee. We just have to plan the best strategy before I talk to my bosses about us. It's just a matter of time." His heart beat a tad faster when saying the words. Blair Sanders seemed to have vanished lately, reportedly shooting her sensationalist TV show somewhere out of state. He hoped to keep his disciplinary action process as quiet as possible, to avoid tempting her to come back.

They kissed again. Only recently could he kiss Joy without feeling desperate. Finally, he was no longer afraid she'd run away from him any minute.

As if reading his thoughts, she broke the kiss to ask, "After everything we've gone through you're not going to end up dumping *me*, are you?"

"What? Goddess, I'll never 'dump you.'" Snickering, he slid a finger over her lips. "If I wanted to get rid of you, I'd just stop watching you when you cross the street."

She hit him with the pillow and they laughed together, then he silenced her with another long kiss.

When the kiss ended, she ran her fingers through his hair. "Now seriously. This is scarily good, isn't it? Somehow I'm afraid we're going to ruin it."

"No way, " he countered. "We'll find a way to make it work across the distance until I'm free to travel and see you openly."

"I'm not talking about the geographical distance." Her face turned serious. "I'm talking about the labyrinths inside our minds."

He asked the question with his eyes and she clarified. "I'm afraid we're not done running away from happiness. That one of us is going to freak out again and push the other one away. I did for months, and I'm worried next time it might be your turn."

He chuckled at her ridiculous worry. Maybe some day he'd get over his block against loving words and would be able to explain how hopelessly he belonged to her.

His phone ringing interrupted his thoughts. He cussed under his breath and shot her an apologetic look.

She appeared as frustrated as he felt, but sighed, resigned. "Go ahead."

He grabbed the phone from the nightstand, and, noticing it was a call from work, walked out of the bedroom.

"Sam, you know I took the weekend off and I warned you—"

"Josh Levenstein is dead!"

Richard slapped his own forehead. "That's impossible! We had him in custody! We had him…" He stopped and took a deep breath. "What happened? Blood pressure drop? Blood sugar drop?"

"Nope." Samuel's agitation showed through his fast talk. "A sniper with a long-range weapon shot him in the head as we were transferring him to the county jail."

Shocked, Richard had to take a seat in the nearest wicker chair. "What?"

"Just what I said. Obviously, your friend Andrews was right. It was a matter of time before the LOTU members snapped into more aggressive measures when they found themselves against the wall."

Frustrated, Richard raked a hand through his hair. If the LOTU had switched to such blatant methods, it was hard to imagine how they could fight them.

"But that's not all I called you about."

"We just lost our best potential informant. Can there be more?"

"Remember the episode of the glass panels falling on you?"

"Yes?" Richard tensed up.

"Levenstein's bodyguard maintains he was just an employee and doesn't know much about the LOTU. But he confirmed that they were planning to kill you. Apparently, Levenstein and the LOTU have been tracking you by intercepting your phones."

Richard's stomach dropped. *Phones? In plural?* Had someone also intercepted the texts he'd been sending Joy from his burner cell? Was that why Levenstein seemed to know about Joy and him?

"Thanks for filling me in, Sam. I'll be there early tomorrow." He disconnected the call and rose from the chair, assimilating everything he'd heard.

Joy had come out of the room and noticed his worried expression. "Sweetie, is anything wrong? Do you need to go back to work?"

Still shocked, he shook his head in silence.

"How about that phone call?" she insisted, studying his face.

"We'll worry about all that tomorrow." He inhaled deeply. "Right now, all I want to do is love my woman."

Smiling, she wrapped her arms around his neck. "That sounds like a good plan."

Her succulent lips reached for his and he delighted in them. The tip of her tongue playfully enticed his mouth, flipping the switch in his brain and taking over his consciousness. The next day he'd have to pick up his gun and confront the darkness in the world. But for the next few blissful hours, he'd allow himself to feel full happiness and relish the light.

Get The Next Book For Free!

Would you like to see Richard and Joy overcome the obstacles between them and get their happily ever after? Don't miss this book's sequel *Just for Joy: Beyond Achievement* (Available Now). Get it for free by signing up for my Newsletter Here.
mailchi.mp/dd04a115f901/beyond-romance-free-book

Or take a step back in time and dive into the prequel, *Beyond Physical: A Mystery Romance*. This is a standalone with no cliffhangers and happy-for-now ending, relating the story of when Richard and Joy met and fell in love during the O'Hara case.
www.amazon.com/gp/product/B083HM2XKN

All books can be read after this book without major spoilers.

NOTE FROM THE AUTHOR

Dear Reader:

It is an honor to me that you took the time to read this story. I hope you've enjoyed it.

My goal is to write romance and mystery stories which are not only entertaining, but also enriching for the soul. Striking a balance between those two objectives is sometimes difficult, as it is to decide the right amount of sexy-spice to add into the mix.

I'd love to hear from you. What did you like in the story? What did you not like? What would you like to see more in future books? I would really appreciate if you could take the time and leave a review at Amazon, Goodreads, your blog or any other venue of your preference.

Please visit my website and sign for my email list for free short stories and sneak-peeks in future releases at www.pichardo-johansson-md.com

Please also feel free to email me at pichardojohanssonmd@gmail.com—I'm a busy lady, but I'll do my best to answer all emails.

Thank you again for reading me.
Love,
Diely

OTHER BOOKS BY THIS AUTHOR

Sunshine State Series
Book 1: *Hope for Harmony: Baby Makers vs. Peter Pans*
(Hope and Tom's story)

Book 2: *Just for Joy: Beyond Achievement*
(It intersects with the Beyond Romance series)

Book 3: *Faith is Fearless: Normal is Overrated*

Book 4: *Grasping for Grace: Never Grow Up*

Book 5: *Longing for Love: A Funny, Sweet and Sexy Romance with a Medical Twist*

Check my website at www.pichardo-johansson-md.com/books/ for more details.

And don't forget to join my e-mail list for further information about these two and other upcoming books.

Love,
Diely

ABOUT THE AUTHOR

Dr. Pichardo-Johansson is a Board Certified oncologist practicing in Florida. Her Romance specialty is "Connection of the minds and the souls, more than only the bodies." Her Mystery specialty is "How to murder someone and ensure a negative autopsy."

Also a cancer survivor, she's a firm believer in the body-mind-spirit link and the healing power of laughter. Her motto is that "The Best Health Booster Is Wanting to be Alive." For that reason, she only writes positive stories, uplifting for the heart.

She is a mother of four children, including twins and a child with special needs. She lives in Melbourne Beach, Florida with them and her Soulmate Husband, a reformed eternal bachelor turned into happy stepfather.

Made in United States
Orlando, FL
05 March 2022